Praise

MW00817756

"*Forged in Grace* is a beautiful, raw and affecting book.
—Erika Mailman, author of *The Witch's Trinity*.

Fire. Abuse. Pain. Hurt.
Hope. Healing. Friendship. Las Vegas.
Jordan E. Rosenfeld takes on all these subjects and more in the beautiful *Forged in Grace*. Inhabiting her diverse characters with ease, delving deep into language with obvious skill and care, Rosenfeld brings a lot of love to this story. She grabbed me with the first page of *Grace* and didn't let me go until I'd reached the satisfying ending. This book is at once an escape, a square-off with the forces of evil, an antidote to hate, and a recipe for how to love each other. Don't miss this well-crafted, moving tale from a rising literary star.
   —Rebecca Lawton, author of *Junction, Utah*,
      the forthcoming *Sacrament*, and the best-selling
      Reading Water: Lessons from the River (Capital)

Jordan Rosenfeld's *Forged in Grace* has a narrator so immediate and revealing, one wants to protect her – from her hoarder mother, from the averted eyes of her neighbors, from potential heartbreak of a man she wants to love. Grace's burn scars overlie all her relationships, and leave her both feisty and fragile. Manipulative friend Marly steers Grace into corners, and truths, she wouldn't otherwise face. Rosenfeld's debut novel tears open this tragedy and finds the core of healing – a marvelous, stunning read.
   —Julia Park Tracey, author of *Tongues of Angels*

FORGED in GRACE

A NOVEL

JORDAN E. ROSENFELD

Forged in Grace
Copyright 2013 Jordan Rosenfeld Pedersen

Cover art by Chelsea Starling
Book design by Maureen Cutajar

ISBN 978-0-615-75078-1

Distributed in the U.S.A. by indie-visible ink
www.indie-visible.com
510 Farallon Drive
Morgan Hill, CA95037

Forged in Grace is a work of fiction. The characters and
events are figments of the author's imagination. Any similar-
ity to persons living or dead is coincidental and not intended by the author. Real companies, places, and persons mentioned are also used fictitiously.

*For my two great loves: my husband Erik, who knew
what he was getting into by marrying a writer
and did it anyway; and our son, Benjamin,
the greatest "story" of my life.*

Prologue

I feel swimmy, high, adrenaline on full tilt, though I haven't consumed a drop of alcohol. "We need to subdue him first," I hear myself say. "Can't just slap a hand on his face and hope it knocks him out."

Marly nods, though she is too encumbered to move quickly, and me—there's no guarantee of what I can do.

"I have pepper spray," she fidgets with her purse as though she's about to withdraw it. "And it's not like we have to break in, Grace. He'll let us in, when he sees it's me. Think I'm coming to talk."

"Okay, then," I say, before I lose my nerve. And we get in her car and drive.

We park and walk four residential blocks. The streets are lit by yellow halogen lamps, but there's also a nearly-full moon. Its bold light makes me feel bolstered, sanctioned. Marly points to his condo, one square box among many in a beige world of homogenous residences.

"This could have been my life," Marly whispers, her face a portrait of disgust. "I should be in that kitchen right now making dinner, then go spread my legs for him. I can't *believe* he thought he could get away with what he did to me."

The guilt surges through me again. If only I hadn't healed away the evidence. But we didn't know. Nobody could have known.

"Let's do it soon, before I chicken out." My palms have begun to ache with heat.

"Damn straight," she agrees, and the toss of her hair is so familiar it's like we're fifteen again.

Simultaneously, we take a deep breath.

Marly repeats her lines, "I'll say we're here to talk—that I brought you as my friend and witness. That will put him on his best behavior. And you?"

I choke a little on my own saliva, cough, and answer, "I'll ask for a glass of water, say I got too much sun today. He'll take one look at me and have a hard time refusing, right?"

Marly pats her purse. "Let's go."

She's always one step ahead of me.

I

Chapter One

Drake's Bay

This morning my hands are so hot, sweat slides my mug out of my grasp and coffee spills down my right leg, like liquid fire. On the way to the bus in the pre-sunrise dark, a voice from the past drifts to me, as though I am a radio tower. *"Grace, you're mistress of your destiny."* Marly's voice. *"Come on! Tell the flame."* Whether the memory has been summoned by the pain or something else, I go to work cavalier as always, as though my heightened senses are not a portent, as if everything is not about to change.

༺☙༒❧༻

At the office, Dr. Lieb—Adam to me—is hunched over the fax machine, jiggling it, the paper jammed. The thrum of its electricity beats inside me, like blood in my veins. If he tugs too hard, the fax—thin as laboratory-grown skin—will rip, and he'll say "shit" and then look around as though he's killed someone's pet kitten. I marvel at how capable he is with patients, such steady hands, and how inept he is with the simplest of office equipment (and women).

He hasn't caught sight of me yet. I'm about to impose myself between him and the machine, to keep him from breaking it, when Helen, party pooper on any moment that resembles intimacy, hurries into the office and flicks on the fluorescents. I cringe against their light.

"Oh, good lord, you two scared me," she says, but scowls at *me*, as though her fright is my fault. She steps up so close to Adam that if he were to turn too quickly they might kiss. He frowns and almost hops backwards, which pleases me. When Helen has something to deliver to *my* desk, she drops it in a hurry, as though I am leprous. *You can't catch this*, I want to tell her. But sometimes, I wish I could disfigure people with the slightest look.

"I'm glad you're here early, Dr. Lieb, I need to consult with you," she says, and touches a hand coyly to her businesslike bun. Behind her is a poster of the human musculature system, the body looking like a victim of torture, flayed down to tender bits.

He scowls at the fax and looks quickly at me with a plea in his eyes.

"I've got it," I say, a knowing smile twisted on my lips. "Go ahead."

I expect him to attend to Helen's insistence—but to my surprise he pushes his dark brown bangs, always an inch too long, out of his eyes and sighs. "Helen, if it can wait? I need to talk to Grace."

The princess snubbed for the toad. I try not to do a victory dance. Helen buttons it up and strides into the front office like a third place runner-up in a beauty contest.

I put my hands on the fax machine as a cue that I'm going to take over, and he slides his own away, before we can chance a touch. And oh, the kinds of touches we actually make are nothing like what passes through my mind: his callused fingers on the few smooth places left on my body: between my thighs, at the back of my neck as it curves into my spine.

"You're here early," he says, jarring me out of my fantasy. This is one of those moments when I'm glad it's hard to read the expressions on my face. His smile etches a groove into his forehead, fanning out crow's feet deeper than a thirty-nine-year-old man should have.

"I wanted to say goodbye to Hera before I got here," I say, thinking of her keen eyes, the way she gazed calmly at me as though we were more alike than not.

He shakes his head in sympathy. Sometimes, a bird, even one as wild as the bald eagle, refuses to go from the Drake's Bay Wildlife center, and I'm secretly glad even though I know that a life locked in a mesh-covered cage is no life for a wild animal. I see enough of their bloodied carcasses during my weekly volunteer visits. Surrounded as we are by reckless bird and rodent life in our little town, I'm glad I don't drive.

"I'll watch out for her," he says. This makes me nervous; he's already a distracted driver, the kind prone to missing his exit and running over curbs (though no people, yet) because he's focused on thoughts of his work.

Before he has to ask, I pop the button, releasing the jammed paper, and his face softens with gratitude, as though I've laid a cure for cancer in his lap.

"What did you need to talk to me about?" I ask then, recalling his dismissal of Helen.

He dims whatever he's viewing on his inner scope and turns his focus on me. "I said yes to a low-cost vaccination clinic next weekend. I was hoping you'd come keep me company, though I know you prefer the beasts to the people," he says with the hint of a grin.

"You're lucky you need me." I shake a fist in mock-anger.

He does too much. It's why his dark hair is tufted with early gray. My hands itch to smooth the wrinkles gathered at his shoulders, but I don't dare for many reasons, psychosomatic pain and visions notwithstanding; sometimes I'm afraid of my own impulse control, that it will start as a dusting of lint and the next thing he knows I've got his torn open shirt in my hands.

"Oh come on," I say, "It's not that you want me there so much as you don't want to sic Helen's Imperial Attitude on the undeserving public."

His smirk is a smile fighting itself, then quickly becomes a chuckle. "I'm awful to laugh," he says.

What am I, then?

"Well, your taste in employees is a little questionable, I mean look at me." I wish I could nudge him in the shoulder as casually as any other co-worker.

"Come on now," he says. "You keep us all in line."

Is that all? What do I expect him to say: *"I can't live without you"*?

"Actually, there's something else," he says, and an old man's worries shine through his young face—like his father handed down decades of anxiety along with his practice. "Do you know Jana Horowitz? She used to run that little consignment store downtown?"

I do know her—she has wild fly-away hair and lip-stick that is never confined by her lips, always handing out home remedies and folk cures along with cheap clothing. I nod.

"She's technically a patient here," he says.

"What do you mean 'technically'?"

"Well, she never comes in. But when pain in her abdomen got to be too much, her daughter goaded her into a blood panel and a CT Scan. Turns out she's got cancer. Bad cancer."

"As opposed to the kind and gentle version, you mean?"

"Haha." He sticks his tongue out. "The problem is, she intends to treat it with vinegar and trips to her energy healer." If Nurse Helen could see him like this, maybe her love of order would protest; maybe she'd stop standing so close to him.

"Oh yeah, those terrible energy healers with their mighty crystals and all-powerful chakra clearing kits," I say. Yet I suddenly picture hearty Jana Horowitz whittling down like the flayed-open muscle man in the poster, a skeleton with a tumbleweed of hair.

Adam is used to my irreverence and knows when to press on to finish his point. "Her daughter wants me to talk her into treatment. I just... Grace, I'll never get used to this Northern California attitude, where people think of medicine as a last resort. And I'm not saying it's all crap, but this is cancer. She needs chemotherapy."

"So what can I do to help?" I ask.

He smiles. "Talk to her."

"Me? I'm not even a nurse."

"But you could do your thing where you crack a little joke, break the ice, and then lay the seriousness on her. Let her know that all the folk remedies in the world won't cure cancer, and what the consequences look like."

It's a painful death. I know this much from patients who pass through our doors, happy to have appointments for things that don't involve radiation or poisons pumped through their veins. But I'm stunned he's asking this of me. After the fire, I read all the stories I could find of spontaneous healings among monks and yogis and even civilians in near-death accidents. There were nights when I tried to conjure that same energy, holding my mother's cats down, determined to heal their fight-born wounds, half serious about trying it on myself next.

The office phone rings then—a horrible seventies jangling sound, because Adam-the-Frugal still refuses to upgrade the phone system his father put into place.

"Don't answer it yet," he says, his hand reaching out as though to stop me but then he reels it in, remembering, and I swear I can feel the heat of his hand where it nearly caressed me. "We're not open for another half hour."

I nod, liking the way we feel in cahoots.

There's a mechanical click as the old-fashioned answering machine begins, and we look at each other gleefully, as though we are hiding from someone, like Marly and I used to do after antagonizing a local boy.

"I'm calling to inform your office that my grandmother..." The woman's voice splinters, and in its husky timber I swear I know her. The air in the office suddenly feels heavy. I remember the way my hands were hot this morning, and now all the patchwork parts of me light up with similar heat.

The woman clears her throat. "I'm sorry. My grandmother, Oona Donovan, has passed away." Her voice is husky with grief. "Obviously, she won't be able to make her appointment today. And you can cancel any others. Also, um, if anyone from your office wants to uh, pay regards, the funeral is tomorrow. Anthem Church. 5:00 p.m."

Oona Donovan. That name, or more specifically the voice speaking it, burrows straight through me, unearthing Marly Kennet, and my last glimpse of her thirteen years ago through a veil of flames.

I am surprised to feel tears at the backs of my eyes, as I lean into the counter for support. For the eight years I've worked for Adam, Oona Donovan has come in for run-of-the-mill medications to battle the ailments of aging; sat, fidgeting in the waiting room, casting glances my direction but saying nothing, her face full of unasked questions. On a couple of occasions I came close to asking her if we could have tea, so I could put my hands on hers and see if the truth of where

Marly went and why she never contacted me would come rushing through her skin.

"Grace? Did I upset you by asking you to talk to Jana?" Adam inches his hand toward me as though to stroke mine, but of course he can't offer the kind of comfort I need. No powerful hug, no tender placing of his palm on my shoulder. The doctors say the pain I feel upon contact, and worse, the visions, are all just psychosomatic, PTSD gone unchecked, but it feels damn real to me.

"No, it's just, I knew that woman," I say. "The one who left a message about her grandmother. Marly Kennet."

My former best friend. She's in town. She must know I work for Adam; her grandmother would have told her. That phone call was meant for me: a coward's invitation. This knowledge of her presence is an almost chemical feeling—like we are magnetic particles destined to scuttle together. *What is it about that girl that she says "leap" and you're already in the air?* Ma's voice from years ago.

I walk away from Adam and drop into my chair, dragged far away from this moment. I'm no longer twenty-eight but fifteen. *Marly, staring down an oncoming car, wild blonde hair in stark silhouette. Me, tugging on her arm, pleading for her to move.* In recalling her, I can remember what it felt like when my skin flexed with ease, when the pores on the top half of my body could sweat. When I had hair and both eyebrows.

"Marly. Why does that name sound familiar?" Adam says.

I've never spoken to him about her, not even to the people in my burn group. I used to say her name to myself, the 'M' a smooth ride, tasting the 'R' on my tongue, her name a wave rolling over me just like she did, knocking me down, then righting me again.

"She was the one," I say to Adam. "With me, the night of the fire."

The only one who really knows what happened to me.

Chapter Two

When I get home from work, the front door will not open all the way. My heart beats high in my throat thinking that it's Ma on the other side, slumped in the little walkway between door and living room. I shove a little harder and the door gives, revealing no lifeless body but a stack of slick magazines gushing over in a waterfall, releasing a stale odor of perfume from their pages. It was only a matter of time; when I leave in the morning I tell myself I will align the *Vanity Fairs* and *Vogues* with their cousins, *People* and *Entertainment*, but I never do, always too eager to get out of the crowded hallway into fresh air, not interested in a showdown if Ma notices.

I shove enough of the magazines out of the way to get in, mentally reaching for the sticky roller propped on my dresser to extract the tufts of cat hair that will collect at my pant legs by the time I reach my room. Beatrix, Alpha feline, still unspayed, and the oldest of the six cats who are all her progeny, raises her smoky blue head from a container on the dining room table. The fur at her jaw is slick with something indistinguishable, her little pink tongue rasping madly at the black plastic. I'm afraid to check if the frozen dinner is new or old—hope my bare foot doesn't later step in a regurgitated pile of it.

Ma should be home, but the house is quiet save for Beatrix's almost lewd-sounding licking. "Who needs insulation?" Ma joked last week as I rifled through a stack of *Drake's Bay Gazettes* as tall as I am, the squint of her brow and set of her jaw warning me not to reorganize them.

Then I hear it, the thump-sigh-exhale of my mother trudging back and forth from her bedroom to her bathroom. The noise interrupts the slow-building dialogue in my head. *Does Marly really think I'm just going to show up to that funeral? I don't owe her anything.* I'm torn between the anger—how dare she think she can leave a message like that at my workplace!—and forgiveness: surely she's grieving; she *did* call me, if indirectly.

The anxiety is making me restless. Me, Ma, and the cats pacing our space-challenged two-bedroom house will cause a traffic jam.

I slide my jacket back on, and heft my bag up onto my protesting shoulder. Early evening is my favorite time to walk around town—no insistent sun to spotlight me; fewer people on the street, especially any I'll be obligated to stop and talk to. As my hand grasps the front door knob, Ma's voice snaps down the hall like a lasso. "Grace, can you come here please?"

One hundred and fifty pounds overweight, with painful varicose veins, my mother suffers from greater disabilities than the limp in my right leg. Our roles of patient and caretaker have long since reversed.

Atop the stacks in the hallway—I imagine them as Roman columns, ruins of a once great civilization—she's begun to place empty cans of generic diet cola. Gold and red, arranged in interesting patterns, they are almost pretty. But they force me to move painfully slow, or else an elbow to a column sends the displays crumpling loudly, scattering cats and bringing Ma out to wail about the disorder I've created.

I peer into her room with trepidation. Her bedroom is dark: grey brocade curtains always closed, their bottoms rimmed with dust and whorls of cat hair, since four of the six cats spend their existence in perpetual sloth beneath her bed. Piles of clothes surround her, many of them never worn, the tags still on, all layered in a fine fuzz of feline dust. She's bent forward over her bed, where three big brown boxes sit gaping open. Before her are white bottles with green lettering. I try to retreat but she turns too quickly.

"See what I got, honey," she says, beckoning at me with a ring-laden finger. Most of her fingers bear two rings each, bought on late night shopping binges.

"Oh Ma, please tell me it's not more Skyn Solutions?"

She sinks down onto the bed with a heave, its

springs squawking in protest, her thinning bangs floating up with the force of her exhale.

"*Improved* formula, Grace, for smoothing out roughness. And other things we need, body lotion, wrinkle solution, shampoo."

My hand goes protectively to my head, where hair grows only in fitful, thin patches. I haven't used shampoo since I was vain enough to hope that a product could change what genetics had given me: fine, copper hair that hung straighter than straw—an abundance I came to appreciate too late. My shower is already cluttered with bottles; she replaces them before I can finish the old.

"I'm about to go out for a walk. Is that all?" I hear the impatience in my voice but don't have the energy to curb it.

Ma's face looks drawn, her cheeks sagging. She turns back to her boxes, freshly unwrapped, ordered off the Internet, her voice suddenly soft. "So sad," she says. It sounds as though she's talking to herself. "Such a nice woman. I always meant to visit her—all alone in that big house."

It takes me a minute to determine if we're talking about something she read or watched, but then I realize she means Mrs. Donovan. Marly's grandmother. In a town as small as Drake's Bay, we know most of the folks who die. I don't believe she ever meant to visit the woman, though—just one of those noble versions of herself in her own mind. My heart makes an arrhythmic skip as Ma turns back and gazes hard at me. In her eyes I understand: she knows that Marly's in town. I haven't decided what that means to me yet, but I know what it means to her.

"Thirteen years is a long time," she says, folding her hands into her lap, her rings creating the illusion of a strange jewelry box. "But it doesn't mean that a person has changed all their colors."

"Oh Ma, you aren't saying you think Marly's the same?" Here I am, defending her as though I'm a teenager again.

Ma purses her lips, the shake of her head almost imperceptible. "Let's add it up, Grace. She never came to see how you were, in the hospital. Never wrote you a letter after she left!" Ma's voice cracks and rises a little, the same tone she uses when she learns I've taken out the garbage without her, as if I might have slipped a leaky pen, a moth-chewed slipper, a scrap of something she deems precious, by her. "If she's changed, why didn't she put notice of Mrs. Donovan's funeral in the paper? Or better yet, send out some personal invitations?"

I'm tempted to make a crack about how it's probably still in the mail mountain piled on the living room couch. Everything important I have sent to a P.O. Box near work, but Ma and I are not entirely on opposite sides of the issue of Marly's trustworthiness. Still, I have a teenager's urge to withhold Marly's phone call to Adam's office.

Ma presses on, "For goodness sake you've seen Mrs. Donovan more than her own granddaughter ever did."

I'm no saint when it comes to helping other lonely people, usually in a hurry to rush home to my own burrow. "Mrs. Donovan and I exchanged 'hello's and 'how are you's' in Adam's office, not exactly deep conversations, Ma. This is what you want to tell me, to watch out, Marly's still the same?" My sigh sounds petulant, even to me. "What, what do you think I'm going to do? Go stand on a street corner and shout her name like Brando?"

Tempt fate at the railroad tracks? See how long I can press a lit cigarette into the unscathed flesh of my arm? Swim naked in the creek?

Ma makes a kissing sound, calling for one of the beasties to come up on the bed. After some rustling, the smallest cat, Jemima, finally emerges, a calico whose unfortunate pattern makes her look like she's rolled in dirt, her whiskers laced with subterranean dust bunnies whose composition I don't want to consider. She leaps into my mother's lap, a place I no longer remember the comfort of.

"I just thought you'd want to know that Mrs. Donovan died," Ma says.

I slip into the floral chair that's littered with beading and knitting magazines, all crafts Ma abandoned years ago.

"You're ruining them!" Ma shrieks, and when I stand with a snort of impatience, she snatches up a tiny package of tissues, smoothing it with her hands as though it is an ancient scroll portending enlightenment. A decade of this behavior has whittled down my shock.

"Ma, I already know Mrs. Donovan died."

Ma merely raises an eyebrow.

And suddenly my palms are slick, the base of my neck tight with the tension of exhilaration. I remember this yearning toward the forbidden, of being unable to turn away no matter where Marly beckoned. She could turn the wasteland of Drake's Bay into a playground. *Let's hide in the abandoned shack, scare the assholes with their stolen beers. It doesn't hurt to just look through other people's mailboxes...they won't miss this shit.*

"A funeral is no place for a reunion," Ma says. Her face is pressed into Jemima's scruff, so I barely hear her muffled answer, "I just don't want to see you get hurt again."

If I believed my mother, I would feel grateful. She was my bulwark against rude glares and stupid questions for years after the fire made me into town's most noticed resident. My father tried, too, I suppose, but his efforts at my defense leaned toward the use of expletives, and then his fists, and then he was gone.

She doesn't call me back when I leave her bedroom without a response. She doesn't need to; it's as though she has an invisible thread attached to me, a leash that ensures I can never go far without feeling her fear for me as a constant tug at the base of my spine.

I need to think, which means I need to walk. My thoughts are crowded into my brain like too many trinkets shoved into a bulging cabinet. Tomorrow I could wake up and choose to see Marly after thirteen years, simple as strolling into a room. A public place would force her to acknowledge me. But then what? I am not the type to make a scene.

Even though the sun is already on its way down I cover my head with my favorite hat—black felt, its bell shape almost a bonnet, my face set deep within its hollow. I light out for Francis Park, a kid's playground, emptied by early evening, where I like to listen to the creek trickle below, and breathe in the sweet smell of redwood mulch, escaping the odors of rotting garbage and filthy carpets.

Normally I take the back streets that run between our house and the park, a tunnel of anonymity, but the thought that Marly might be in town makes me bold. She could easily be refilling a thermos of coffee at Drake's Java, hand on one hip, chatting up the barista, making mundane events seem like epic dramas. Then again, maybe she's a bitter woman now, more like her mother, with constant frown lines and rigid hair. Maybe time and loss have carved away some of that wild leaning toward the forbidden.

I walk with head down, marveling at the clean streets of our town, once flanked by seventies Volvos in tasteless condiment hues and now sleek with silver and black Mercedes and BMWs. I marvel where all the money comes from, money that my parents never knew how to hold onto. Ma still working as an under-paid CPA's assistant in town. My father? Who knows.

The downtown nerve center, as Ma calls it, is etched in periwinkle and mauve as the sun goes down, as though Edward Hopper painted Drake's Bay into being. Scruffy surfer boys—and a few grown men—smoke at the fringe, poised and pretty, waiting for someone to make a postcard of them.

By the time I reach The Parkade, I realize I've made a mistake—the street is teeming with bodies. It's Tuesday evening, when all the bars and restaurants do happy hour, booze for cheap. I duck my head and press forward, focusing only on the swath of green in the center of town, hands tucked into my pockets.

I breathe through my nose. Try the mantra a psychiatrist once gave me: *The visions are movies in my mind. The pain is not real.*

I narrowly avoid a woman with a halo of blonde hair and a swath of red lipstick whose laugh is so eerily familiar that I stop and stare. It's not Marly, but I've given the woman a direct view of my face, and it stops her laughter cold. She pulls her soft black jacket up higher and turns quickly away.

I'm almost through the throng when it happens. A thud into my back, pushing me forward. My back is the least sensitive part of my body, but a hand whips around to steady me, a blast of alcohol hitting my nose. A person now stands before me, dark pelt of hair, well-deep eyes, wobbling as he—wait, no, she—apologizes.

Pain is a molten flow traveling from the spot where her unsteady fingers grip me all the way down my arm, transforming into a movie that unfolds in my mind: *Marly and me, stripped down to bras and underwear behind the "bum shack" to keep the heavy waft of pot smoke off our clothes—her bra is neon pink, like Cyndi Lauper, mine white with yellow daisies—hiding evidence of what Gabriel Diaz once referred to as "tic-tac-tits" before Marly kicked him in the jewels. Feet crunching broken bottles into smaller bits. Marly shot up straight;*

I scrambled to find my shirt. Too late. Poking her head around the corner was Sasha Lerner, long dark hair tangled like she'd just woken up, six-pack of Peach schnapps in her hand.

"Thought I'd find you here," Sasha said.

One look at her read neglect: clothes rumpled and pulled dirty off a floor, dark rings beneath eyes that cried too much and didn't sleep enough. Marly shot me a betrayed glower.

I'd told Sasha where we'd be, I had. Marly let her tag along once in awhile, when we could get a ride or a drink off of her. I didn't see the harm; I felt so sorry for her. She had nobody—not even her mom anymore.

"Sorry," Marly said, eyes drifting to the six-pack, "We were just leaving."

Sasha looked between us, understanding dawning— she had genuinely thought herself invited. "You don't look like you're going anywhere," Sasha said, pulling out a sweating, wet bottle.

Marly circled in tight, grabbed me by the back of the head. I didn't realize what she was doing until her lips were on mine and then it was too late. She pressed her mouth to mine, her lips hitting my exposed teeth, then pulled away and grabbed one of Sasha's wine coolers and cracked it open. I stood staring at Marly wanting to ask "What was that?"

Sasha shook her head and grasped a lone bottle to herself as though it could save her. Before she walked away, she turned over her shoulder and said, so low we could have missed it if we hadn't been listening, "You think she actually cares about you."

"Marly!" I said, once Sasha was gone. "Why are you always so mean to her? And what was with that kiss?"

Marly's voice was cold gravel. "Don't feel sorry for her, Grace. She looks pitiful, but she's a snake. As for the kiss..." She looked at me with a quick stab of the eyes, then away. "I guess that was my version of pissing on a tree and calling it mine."

Sasha-of-the-Now coughs, pulls back, and the booze on her breath assaults me. She stumbles away from me with a light, "Shit, Grace, watch out," and then she's off so fast I don't have a chance to ask her if she saw it too, the movie that just played out in my mind. I know that's ridiculous, but they are so real I want to know I'm not alone.

Sasha's avoided me in town all these years since the fire, and sometimes I want to apologize to her, but I don't know for what exactly: for Marly's behavior? For something I did? She'd already taken Marly's hint by the time of the fire and stopped trying to hang out with us. And yet, at least *she* sent me a get-well card.

Suddenly I don't feel like walking anymore. It seems absurd, considering Marly's long silence, that I should want so much to see her again. Yet I can't help but wonder: if bits of my memory are still housed in people like Sasha Lerner, what parts of me does Marly still hold?

Chapter Three

"I'm sorry to make us late," Adam says.

I get into his car with a swell of elation that he is here, that I don't have to do this alone. I pull in my stiff, right leg with my hand. My limp is another thing the doctors have told me isn't real. There is nothing physically wrong with my leg, save for the patchwork scars where skin was removed from it for grafts. If we'd had better insurance I could have been sent to one of those fancy, plastic-surgery heavy Southern California burn centers, maybe added a little spa therapy into the mix, but what I got at San Francisco General kept me alive, left me with thumbs—no matter how ugly—and I'm grateful for what I got. People have suggested over the years that "plastic surgery has come a long way" and "you'd be amazed what one more surgery can accomplish." As though going under the knife again, only to resurface as someone I still don't recognize, would be a lark.

"Can't say I'm ever in a hurry to get to a funeral," Adam says. He isn't smiling like usual.

My stomach undulates pleasantly that we're going out together, even though being in public with him means weathering a few more second glances than usual.

The little bungalow house Ma and I live in is the smallest on our street, surrounded by thick pines and dense bushes; I always feel like I'm emerging from some animal's lair. "I could have taken a cab," I say.

Adam grins, revealing what he likes to keep hidden: one of his top teeth crosses jaggedly over the other, like a gawky boy who's going to need braces. "What aren't you telling me? Who *is* this friend? Is your past more checkered than I realized?"

"Please," I say, leaning back and closing my eyes. "If we're going to talk checkered pasts let's talk about that brassy girlfriend of yours a few years back. The cougar who smacked her gum when she talked..."

"Fran? She was only a year older." It could be the light, but when I glance at him, he appears to be blushing.

We roll down Main Street, a small crowd pushing into The Sleeping Lady for music. My parents hung out there before my accident. One of Drake's Bay's eternal old hippies, with a long gray ponytail, always dressed in painters' whites, dashes across the street, thinking he can make it. Adam slams on the brakes and I am thrown against my seatbelt.

Adam flings his arm out, bumping my collar bones, his fingers grazing my right shoulder. Suddenly my chest is hot, and an aura of light radiates like a migraine coming on. Worse, I see him in that flash of contact: he is thirteen years younger, holding a pair of metal scissors to my face, gauze and flesh merged together, cutting me free of my cocoon after a week's healing.

The car is already in motion when I emerge from the vision, my heart beating at a runner's pace that my body can no longer match.

"I'm sorry, I'm so sorry," he's whispering. "It was a reflex. My sister used to do that to me when she drove."

I rub my clavicles and look away. "No, I'm sorry. I wish I wasn't...." It doesn't matter how often it happens, I always feel mortified by my body's betrayal, reminded of a kid named Lance that Marly and I went to school with, who once had a seizure in the middle of History and woke up in a puddle of his own urine.

Adam's starting to protest that I shouldn't say such things when I realize we are about to miss the street the church is on: "Oh, turn right here!"

Anthem is a Unitarian church, and though I don't know much about religion, I do remember that Marly's grandmother called herself a "spiritual pilgrim" though she didn't attend church. I remember because I felt that Ma could use a dose of that—though in Ma's version it would probably involve sending all her extra money to big-haired TV evangelists. In contrast, Mrs. Donovan often went on Buddhist retreats and women's goddess weekends that made Marly and me laugh until we thought we'd pee our pants, imagining a bunch of grown women running naked through the desert, painted in mud.

"Damn it, there's no close parking," Adam mutters after we've circled the church several times. "Let me just drop you at the curb, Grace. I don't want to make you hike from several blocks up."

Nobody's walking in, so I know the funeral has already started. My knees feel jittery at the thought of going in alone, but then, I reason, this whole effort is about mustering courage.

I nod, pulling the strands of my longest, most full-coverage wig around my face as he drops me at the curb. At least finding something to wear was not a problem; most of my clothing is black.

I stand outside the church, hand poised to push open the door. *What will she think when she sees my face? Will I terrify her?* There's a moment of dark pleasure at the thought, payback for her abandonment, but it's replaced by something else, something older: the urge for her approval, a leech of a feeling I wish I could shake off.

I can't recall the moments leading up to my accident very well, and almost nothing afterwards until I was in the ambulance. The times that someone has mustered the nerve to ask me what happened, I've envisioned a row of candles multiplying, surrounding Marly and me like dominoes lined up for miles. Hypnotically, fire leans tenderly in, leaps from fabric to flesh, and burns every part of me in its reach. There is only one spot above my belly that it didn't lick like a rough puppy—a large oval of unscathed skin below my right eye, cheek and half of my lips. Turn me one way, tuck my ruined brow under a swoop of wig, cover my chin with my fingers and you might think, "What a lovely girl," as long as the lights are low. The lower half of me is a tithing ground where I offered every available scrap of virgin skin to reconstruct a version of my face that nobody recognizes. Least of all, me. Marly, however, I'm told, barely suffered a scorched hair.

It's been thirteen years since I last saw Marly, since I moved with arrogant ease in my teenaged limbs, thinking I had it so rough. My real self has been sleeping inside me, in my very cells, this whole time, like all I had to do was click ruby slippers or turn my ring three times and Marly would appear, and life would start again. But I didn't conjure her; her dead grandmother did.

My pulse is like an engine revving. The sweet-acrid scent of Marly's old AquaNet is suddenly in my nose, though I know it isn't possible. I press my hand to the cool wood door and push, moving slowly to attract as little attention as possible.

The church is small. Thankfully, the mourners have just burst into loud applause for whomever has concluded speaking—most likely one of Mrs. Donovan's students from when she taught high school English. Photographs of her looking regal and intelligent are projected onto a screen on the stage, massive bouquets of flowers heaped on either side. The photos all show her smiling, draped in her favorite shawls, hair down— she never really looked like an old woman.

The pews are packed—no way I'm going to shove myself into an already crowded row, so I stay in the shadow at the back of the last pew. A woman rises and ascends the dais to the stage. For a moment I think it's

Sonya, Marly's mother, but this woman is too tall, too pretty.

When she clears her throat into the microphone and then laughs at how loud the sound is, I realize it *is* really Marly. She still has the sunny beauty I remember—as though she's lit by a special light. Smooth, poreless skin that time hasn't touched. Curves that flowered too early but now look exactly right on her tall frame. Blonde hair that doesn't need highlights. Hers is a Midwestern beauty, winner of pageants and a poster girl for milk and eggs, as though she might smell like wheat fields and fresh air.

"I'm terrible at this kind of thing," she says right away, and a few titters lend support. "As many of you know, Oona Donovan, my grandmother, would sooner spend a Sunday morning nude sunbathing on Stinson Beach than listening to a sermon."

Marly looks up from the papers in her hand and out at the audience. A thrill of anxiety rumbles through me. I will myself smaller, hugging closer to the wall.

"So when my aunt Helena insisted we have the service in a church, I almost asked her what she'd been smoking." She raises her brow into a wicked point. *Oh my god, this IS the Marly I remember.*

"But then I thought about what Gram herself used to tell me, when things were dark in my life. And they were really, really dark more than a few times. Gram and I had a lot in common, and I spent many a weekend at her house, oftentimes with my best friend Grace."

I swallow, feeling like I might choke. She's scanning

the crowd, looking for me. The shadow is suddenly not big enough as I try to scrunch into it.

"Gram said, 'Honey, people believe all kinds of bullshit.' Her words, I'm not being rude. 'It really doesn't matter what they believe—in Jesus or Buddha or drinking fermented yak butter—so long as they have a common group to believe with.'"

Cool air rushes in behind me, and I know it's Adam coming in, that his sudden entrance will draw Marly's eye and there's nowhere for me to go. Adam makes his way to my side, and Marly's eyes follow him the whole way.

"I think what Gram intended for me to take away," she says, eyes sliding ever closer to me, "is that the only way we get through the crap of life is to somehow, through whatever means, believe we're not alone. Well, Gram was one of a very small pool of people who gave me that sense of safety, of being loved that much. Now she's gone and I'm afraid that I might not ever feel that way again." A sliver of softness enters her voice.

Marly has been subtly looking at the person to the right of me, then Adam: now she stops and stares at me. Her breathing is loud and ragged.

"Grace fucking Jensen?" she says loudly into the microphone. The entire church of mourners turn to look with harsh glances. "Grace, I can't believe it's really you!" She drops the microphone and a man in a dark suit steps up to replace it as she leaves the stage.

Hundreds of pairs of eyes now stare at me as though I've wrecked the funeral. I only realize I'm not breathing when Adam says, "Grace?" in an anxious voice and does something he has not done since I was a burned teen in a hospital bed—he grabs my arm, because my knees are buckling.

Where his hand grips me, I reel back at a sharp stinging pressure, blurry images flooding behind my eyelids, light-shapes that don't have time to become full images. A keening sound rings out in my ears, and then Marly is in front of me. I'm waiting for the recoil, but she doesn't even flinch. She pulls me from Adam's grasp only to envelope me in a tight hug so firm that for a moment all I feel is a strange relief. Then prickling heat clutches my torso and a wave of nausea passes through me. I pull away.

"My skin," I explain, pulling back, "hypersensitive." And yet I can't remember the last time I was clutched in someone's embrace; I'm reluctant to let it go.

Adam frowns, mouth open in a horrified gape, as though he is responsible for what has just happened to me. Marly shakes her head the way you do when a grand coincidence reveals itself, though this reunion is the farthest thing from a coincidence, and bursts into tears. Then she laughs and dabs her eyes with a corner of her gauzy navy sleeve, leaving behind a streak of flesh-colored makeup on the fabric. Marly—vague figure of both bad dreams and the only really good memories I have, is really standing in front of me.

"Please tell me it's you," she says, "Tell me this is real."

"It's me," I say. But I can't tell her it's real. It doesn't feel real—it feels disjointed and strange, like those times we smoked pot she scored off Gavin Green and my head felt detached from my body.

Marly looks prepared to launch into a soliloquy of apology but suddenly people are moving toward her from all sides. She must have been the final speaker—it would be like her to organize the world's shortest funeral—everyone is sweeping out of their pews. Frowning older ladies clutch at her arms, circling her, and in a moment we are separated.

"Come to Gram's house, in an hour," she shouts over the bodies, and then she is absorbed into them like a drop of water into a sponge, as though she was never there at all.

Chapter Four

I make it a point not to come this way. The sloping Y of the streets where Bolinas merges into Cascade inspires a feeling of vertigo, as though I am suddenly at the top of a hill on a bicycle without brakes. The road is still flanked by redwoods that I remember being half as tall.

Adam parks, and we stare up the column of stone stairs, the ivy robust and shiny after winter rains. A diffuse yellow light shines out from one room in the big house. I have not set foot here since the night my childhood burned to ash.

"Should I wait?" He frowns and glances up at the house as though it might be haunted. "Are you sure your friend is in there?"

"If she can't give me a ride, I'll take a cab home," I say.

"Don't be silly, Grace, call me. I'll come back. I'm less than ten minutes away."

"I appreciate it." I feel him wanting to say more, but the pull of the house is so strong I forgo politeness.

Once out of the car, I want to dash up the stone steps like I did years ago, but my body doesn't move with effortless ease. I pause halfway up the steps to wave to Adam, self-conscious of him watching my slow climb. Adam waves back at me and starts the engine, leaving me alone to face the final steps and the front door that feels like a barrier between me and the past. I knock as the sound of Adam's car rattles off in the distance. There's a deep moment of silence and then the clatter of dishes abandoned in the sink, followed by footsteps echoing along a wooden floor, and finally, at the top of the half-moon window, a dome of honey-blonde hair appears. Marly wrenches open the door, sniffles as though she's been interrupted crying, and waves me in.

The air inside is thick with a mixture of cedar chips and dime-store perfumes; the latter, Marly and I once spent hours daubing along our bodies. The couches and chairs are still draped in bright, Mexican textiles and the walls are hung with colorful masks, frames, and mirrors—a riot of ripe fruit colors. Marly's grandmother had called herself a *bon vivante*, and now, my adult self finally understands.

"It's...exactly as I remember it," I say. The click of the door behind me sounds final; there's no turning back.

She sighs heavily. "I know. I still get dizzy looking at it all. It's getting sold or donated. It's too much memory, or

I'd take some of it back home with me." She bites the cuticle of her thumb and then I can barely concentrate; what I wouldn't give to have a thumb cuticle to bite. I force my hands deeper into the pockets of my sweatshirt.

"Back home?" I ask.

"Vegas." She looks away, rolling her head on her neck as though working out a kink, but I wonder if she just doesn't want to maintain eye contact. My own neck tingles with the urge to do the same.

"Are you thirsty? Hungry? I can make us a drink. Wine? Vodka?"

"Uh, whatever you're having," I say.

She flips open cabinets expertly, whipping out a tall clear bottle of vodka, brand new, which makes me sad, as though Oona Donovan was waiting all these years for visitors who never came. Marly splashes red juice pulled from the fridge into two glasses and then passes one to me, downing half of hers in a flash. I've never liked hard liquor, but I take it anyway.

"Was that your boyfriend?" She gestures toward the street. My own heart thumps a question.

"My employer," I say. "He was a resident at the burn center when I was first admitted. Gave me lots of moral support. Eventually gave me a job." I realize she's never met her grandmother's doctor.

"The burn center," she says softly to herself, as though confirming it to be true. She finishes her drink, and I force myself to take a sip of mine—sharp and sweet—as though it can bolster me for all the things I want to ask her.

"You left that message at Dr. Lieb's office for me,

didn't you?" My voice is barely audible, and before she can answer, I ask the thing that's been choking my heart all these years, like the items in one of Ma's cluttered cabinets. "Why didn't you contact me before this?"

She bites her lip, as if weighing versions of the truth. She was never really a liar, just a selective truth teller, a reframer of events. "You know, Gram told me how every time she went in there you looked like you were waiting for something. She asked me several times if she could bring a message. But I just...what could I say?" Now her eyes find mine with their old openness and she bites the inner wall of her cheek, an old gesture I remember well. "You can't believe I've ever stopped thinking about you all these years." She opens her palms as if to offer me something tender and small cupped there. "You have no idea."

No idea, no contact, no word. "You didn't even visit me in the hospital..."

Her shoulders tighten up. "I wanted to!"

"So why didn't you?"

"Your mother..." Her eyes rove past me, then land on me, sharp and direct. "She said, in her own way, that you'd rather I never show my fucking face again."

Her words are a fist against my chest, stealing breath. "I never said that! Ma told me your stepdad got the job earlier than expected, that your family moved away a week after the fire." Her stepfather, Bryce was short and handsome in a young ruffian kind of way, and a decade younger than her mother. Marly always forbade me idolizing him. "Gross! He's like my dad," she'd say in a scandalized voice. I'd persist, to get a rise out of her.

"What?" Marly rears back as if slapped. "We moved *two months* later. This wasn't like her turning me away at your hospital bed, Grace. Your mother called me, the very next day after the fire, and told me that if I ever came near you again, she'd file a restraining order. After our near-arrest, I guess I can't blame her. But she should have told you the truth."

My skin seems to be vibrating in her presence, heat radiating off me despite the cool February weather. The betrayed look in her eyes sends a thunder of guilt through me, even though my mother, not me, is responsible for it. I know better, but I step forward and take her hand. First comes pain, sharp and blade-like, followed by an image—the night of our "near-arrest." *Marly's hand steady as she drags red lipstick across my lips, her fingers firm on my cheek. Sasha skulking in the corner. Drinks in our hands, shots of stinging liquid. A wave of giddiness, the world soon undulating. Marly pulling me to her, dancing against me, all eyes on her. And then our sudden escape, rushing after two strangers into the night, with only the slightest thought of leaving Sasha behind.*

I break contact from Marly, and both of us gasp, or maybe she just coughed, it's hard to tell what's in my head, what is real.

Marly sighs, then says, "When I came by your house Friday, to tell you about the service, to see if you would speak to me, your mother said that your feelings toward me hadn't changed. It's cruel of her to tell you I came if she doesn't want you to see me."

I press my index fingers into my temples, my jaw

tight, a sick twisting working through me from belly to throat. *Why would Ma lie to me?* Instead of voicing this question out loud, I simply say, "My mother doesn't know I'm here now."

Marly grins, like we're colluding, as if we're teens again. "It's good to have secrets from your mother, trust me. Look, I just figured she can't get over the past. I'm the old bad influence, back in town. She wouldn't even let me into the house; made me stand on the stoop like a salesman."

Suddenly the stack of magazines in the foyer makes sense, why it had shifted to near-toppling when I'm always so careful coming in. I can picture Ma at the door, flustered, facing off with a grown version of Marly, Wild Girl, the last person to ever see me as I was before the accident.

We lapse into a loaded silence and then Marly jumps up, taps me lightly on the shoulder. Her four-teen-year-old self rises like steam in my mind, in her favorite black baby doll dress with the velvet bodice and neon green tights, flopped onto my bed clutching a magazine cut-out of Johnny Depp to her chest. *I'd let him do whatever he wanted to me.* Behind her, there's an image of me, all gawky knees and freckles.

How I've missed her.

Marly begins to putter around the living room, pointlessly tidying what I know will all be packed up anyway.

"Where's your mom?" I ask.

She raises her head sharply, eyes hard. "Didn't come to her own mother's funeral, Grace. Would have hired strangers to pack this all up, can you believe that?" Tears hover at the rims of her eyes.

"So you're still not close?" I pick up a long orange and yellow scarf, finger its softness. It is all I can do to keep from grabbing her to me, hugging her.

Marly laughs, almost a bark, then gazes at me with such direct eye contact I look away, at the scuffed toes of my black boots. I want to ask her how she can do that: take me in without cringing.

"So you moved to Vegas two months after the—" I can't say "the fire."

She plumps a couch pillow and then sits on it, exhaling as though she's suddenly exhausted. "No, we moved to Seattle first, for Bryce's job. I hightailed it to Vegas when I was eighteen. I actually slept in my car on the night before my birthday, a kind of 'fuck you' to the folks. What was my mom going to do about it?"

I want her to ask me about the hospital, about my recovery, but she doesn't. And beyond that, I realize, there's nothing to ask me. I've done so little, my whole life confined to a radius of less than two miles. My face feels tight and hot. I press my hands to my cheeks. "God I don't think—"

"What?" she demands, eyes flitting to my disfigured thumbs, twice the size of normal ones, then away again.

"It's nothing..." *Look at you. Didn't everyone always look at you?*

I'd always wanted to be beautiful like her, from the age of seven. When our friendship blossomed over hopscotch, I was all knobs and angles and she was confidence embodied in an eye-bursting package. I'm ashamed to realize that nothing has changed.

"You're still my Grace," she says, a sad smile forming before she pulls a cigarette out of her pocket and lights it. The smoke smells oddly good, but tickles my throat, gives me an instant cough. She frowns at the cigarette as though it has done something unexpected. "Shit. Come outside?"

I follow her through the long hallway past the kitchen, now full of open boxes. Pans lie side by side with rusty old cookie cutters, and fistfuls of silverware spill out of tall mugs. I have a strange urge to gather these things, caress them as though they are parts of Oona Donovan, whose house I longed to escape to as a kid—a house of flow and openness, color and joy, unlike the dank nest of clutter that I call home.

We ascend a staircase to the second floor deck, overhung by two tall eucalyptus trees whose long, scythe-shaped leaves give off fragrant menthol. The wood of the deck is faded and pocked. As it creaks and groans beneath us, I suffer a moment's anxiety at how sturdy the whole contraption is.

Marly stands, her back to me, blowing smoke rings into the distance. "I loved it here."

"Me too," I say. "Remember when your gram let us wear her old vintage dresses if we'd read Shakespeare scenes to her?"

Marly claps a hand to her mouth, smiling, an eyebrow—dyed dark, I see—rises to a delighted arch. She lifts a hand theatrically into the air. "The quality of mercy is not strain'd/ It droppeth as the gentle rain from heaven/Upon the place beneath: it is twice blest/

41

It blesseth him that gives and him that takes..."

"Wow, that's impressive. I don't remember any of it."

Any of it. For a second, I'm ready to ask her: *what do you remember of that night*, but Marly's lips veer into a pout, a cloud shading her face, like she's had a terrible thought.

I feel unsteady for a moment, dizzy, then it passes.

Marly's voice is soft when she speaks again, "Gram was the only one, you know, that I listened to, told things to. That I trusted. Other than you. But I haven't been able to cry yet."

Her grandmother was a woman who spoke in hyperbole and hugged tightly. She gave us sips of champagne, made us ice cream sundaes, and let us sleep under the stars. Marly's tone suggests she has more to say, but she doesn't offer and I don't press it. She stubs out her cigarette at last. "Come on, I want to show you something I found yesterday."

I hobble after her, back downstairs and inside her grandmother's bedroom, which she's mostly packed up. All the perfume bottles of my memory are gone, the curtains pulled down to show layers of dirt on the window, and the closet is emptied. From an open box she pulls out a thick, dark green album and lays it on the bed. When she opens it, grainy old photos with rounded edges spill out, the kind of miscellaneous family pictures my mother no longer leaves in plain sight. I often wonder if Ma keeps them under her bed and pulls them out to remember her little angel.

"Ah-hah!" Marly plunks her manicured finger down on a page. There we are, two spun sugar darlings, our skin fresh and glowing, our cheeks flush with summer sun, at age seven in yellow bathing suits, dipping our feet into a kiddie pool with looks of surprise on our faces, as if the water must have been icy. My face is a lightly freckled peach, my eyes a lovely, lucid green. Then another: Marly and me holding giant wheel-like lollypops with Mickey Mouse ears at Disneyland—her gram took us; Marly and me vamping for the camera circa 1990, wearing red lipstick, high heels and mini-dresses, mouths open in croons to Madonna.

"Oh, I just love this one, look!" Marly peels away the plastic coating and lifts a photograph of our faces pressed cheek to cheek. Our eyes are closed, mouths cracked in grins that reveal matching gaps where teeth had fallen out. It's been years since I've looked at photographs of myself before the fire. I've grown accustomed to the rough landscape of my skin, the gradient colors of my patchwork self.

The beauty of that other me is so real I feel it like a thumb gouge to the diaphragm. My chest is tight, as though once again stuffed into the pressure garments I wore for years, air catching in squeezed lungs. I push myself away, maneuvering off the bed, and bang my shin against the frame. Marly calls after me, but I scurry out the door, away from the image of that younger self.

I find myself at the backdoor off the kitchen and out into what was formerly a tame garden. Now it is a wilderness. It takes me a minute to realize what I'm staring up at—the ancient oak tree, its tree house long since burned to cinders, its trunk scarred with great black char marks from the night that razed me to the core.

My breath hitches higher, as though there is once again a fog of smoke crowding out the oxygen in my lungs, heat rushing up the sides of my face, so intense it wants to melt me, consume me, cut straight to the bones and reduce me to ash. Colors lick at my vision— the bright yellow of candlelight, Marly's eager face of thirteen years ago straining toward me.

Marly finds me folded in a forward crouch gasping, my muscles locked up. "Oh Honey." Her fingertips rest briefly on my back before she pulls them away. "I didn't think. Can you forgive me?"

I nod but don't raise my head. *A memory of heat on my skin, my own shrill keening...* I can smell the egg-like odor of burning hair. Marly puts her hand on my chin and tilts it up, like a lover about to kiss me.

"I thought I'd put it behind me," I manage.

She pulls her hand away quickly. Her eyes are wet. "Nobody puts something like that behind them."

The weeds feel soft as I sink into them and fold my hands in my lap, tucking my thumbs in my palms. She sits down beside me; she is wearing leggings, bright purple, under her soft jersey dress, just like when we were girls.

"Grace, for years I had nightmares. The wake up screaming kind."

I look at her gorgeous, unblemished face, her eyes imploring. I believe her. In a strange way it helps.

"But I'm a coward. I know that even my worst nightmare is nothing compared to what you went through. Even if your mother hadn't warned me away, I didn't think I could look you in the eye. I'm a coward. That's the whole reason I never called or wrote."

I take a deep breath. "I wish you'd found a way. I needed you."

"I know." She looks at me meaningfully as though she's about to say more, then leaps up off the ground so effortlessly I am breathless at the thought of such freedom. I lean unsteadily forward and begin to ease myself upwards, my right leg protesting at the sudden expansion from sitting to standing. I'm too proud to ask for help. Marly watches me, her hand twitches and lifts off her thigh as if she is going to offer it to me anyway, but she must see the determination in my face because she lowers it again. Before I gain my balance, she puts out her arms. I am not getting through to her about the pain that touch causes me.

"I'm so glad you're here, Grace. I really missed you. I'll be gentle, I promise." The look on her face is so plaintive that I lean in for a brief moment and let her enclose me.

She smells like jasmine and cigarette smoke. Lights dance behind my eyes and as uncomfortable as it is to be clutched in her embrace, it is also the first time in ages that someone has hugged me in a way that doesn't feel obligatory or careful. An image forms in my mind's eye, that of a man jogging on a tree-lined path, like a fragment of a dream you suddenly remember without context. Something about this makes me shiver and pull back quickly.

"Stay here," she says.

"Why?" But she is already gone, racing off to the back of the house. When she returns she dangles a large ax in one hand, swinging it back and forth perilously close to her tanned thigh.

"What are you doing?" But as soon as I ask it I know. "Marly, you can't chop down an enormous tree with that! You need a chainsaw at least."

She bites her lip as she hefts it over her head. "I know. But we can hack away some of the evidence."

She bee-lines to the tree that was witness to my awful transformation and swings the ax into the charred spots, making jagged little bite marks.

I watch, fascinated.

"Come on, Grace!" She pulls back again, and the ax makes a satisfying thunk into the flesh of the tree. "It feels good," she says. "Really. Better than therapy, and I should know—I spent years in it." She swings again and again as if the tree has taken something from her, too.

I come closer but refuse the ax when she hands it to me. "Marly, I can't."

"Sure you can. You're strong. Don't let this memory own you, Gracie!"

I realize I will have to be blunt. "I can't raise my arms over my head." I demonstrate, lifting elbows to ear level, where they will go no further. "Fourth degree burns. Some muscles were damaged."

Marly releases the tool with a soft thud.

"It's okay. I *would* chop down this tree if I could."

Her lips tighten even though they're still curled into a smile. She stares for a long minute. From up in the house the jangle of an old-fashioned telephone rips through the air. Marly's head snaps up as though she is guilty of something. "Shit. I just talked to my mother. Only one other person that I know has this number, and it's too late for estate business."

The phone rings on and on, the sheer persistence of it sounding urgent, demanding.

"Go," I say. "Answer it, please."

As she runs back to the house, I take one last look at the tree. Like me, it is still alive despite what it's been through. Then I make my way slowly after her.

I reach the kitchen as Marly slams the phone down. She kicks a box, dull utensils spilling into a jumble.

"What's wrong?"

"Nothing. It was just The Loser, my ex." She stares at me, her mouth parted with what looks like a heavy explanation, but then she closes it. "Grace, I have to go back."

"What? But you just got here. I only just..." I wish I could squeeze her hand again, like when we were girls.

Marly tilts her head and pulls out her full-wattage smile, the one that raises her cheekbones to high peaks. "Come with me."

"What?"

"Come with me, Grace. Why not? Just for a couple of weeks. Tell me you aren't just dying to get away from here?"

It's true—sometimes the mere sound of my mother shuffling in her pink house slippers from the kitchen to her bedroom at night, the plaintive mewing of her cats at her heels, makes me want to climb the walls. Not to mention the feeling that I am another of Adam's pity causes, a wounded animal never to be released from captivity.

Marly eyes are shiny as she grins at me. "Seriously." I can tell she wants to grab my hands, as though touch is necessary to convince me of something. "Vegas is a

Mecca of...the widest range of people you'll ever meet anywhere. It attracts variety. It's a place where it doesn't matter what's happened in your life, how bad you feel, or what you look like." She claps her hand to her mouth "Grace, I'm sorry. That came out wrong."

I force a smile.

Marly shudders and clutches herself, looking almost nauseated for a moment. "This town is so damp and cold. Doesn't it ever get to you?"

I shrug. "That's the least of the things that get to me." The truth is, other than Adam and sometimes Ma, all I'd miss otherwise are a handful of damaged animals and birds that wouldn't even know that I'd gone.

"I need to think about it."

Marly nods, still clutching herself. "Of course you do."

She drives me home, talking the whole time about Vegas and her life there. By the time we reach my house I can see this strange and beautiful world of showgirls and billionaires, picture the restaurant where Marly manages a team of "underwater mermaids" in a bar that caters to the patrons of fancy casinos, and a few times a week, dons the fins herself, in a floating performance.

"I'll be calling you in the morning, Grace."

"Ok. Don't pull up all the way. I don't want Ma to see...us," I say.

Marly nods, but says nothing else as she drops me in front of the movie theater. The Marquee is fritzing, and in its flashing pink light I walk toward my house, like the girl at the end of the movie who knows exactly what she wants.

Chapter Five

Marly's headlights recede behind me as I let myself into the house. I force myself not to turn back, as if, like Orpheus, or Lot, I stand to lose her altogether. Images of Vegas—gleaned from Godfather movies, and the one where Nicholas Cage drinks himself to death—dance through my mind. I step onto dingy brown carpet, once beige, but see swatches of red velvet casino carpet under sequin-studded heels; as I pass the nearly-dead fern that reeks of cat pee in the dining room, tall, hearty palm trees wave exotic fronds in my mind. I navigate my house mostly by memory, our lights dim, picturing a lit path around a too-blue swimming pool with happy tourists playing in it. In the gloom of the microwave, sallow light leaks out from the kitchen, and Ma's person-high piles of J. Jill catalogs—which she has long since ordered from—resemble library stacks. Not that

I'll ever be allowed to go searching for a lost copy of National Geographic, as it threatens to ruin the order that makes sense only to my mother.

From my room there comes a rustling, like one of the cats searching for a leftover bite of food in a cupboard. My door is cracked open, my desk light on.

With an unusually swift and powerful urgency I shove hard on the door. "Ma, what the hell?"

She's half-squatted, half hunched on the floor at my closet, leaned forward into it as though balancing for a last taste of honey in a hive. The way she throws her head over her shoulder at me, then tries to get up without success, hunkering, makes her seem like a cornered beast.

"I've told you not to put anything of yours in my closet." The words trip out of my throat with choked rage. My hand trembles on the doorknob.

Shoes I never wear tumble out onto the floor, a few shirts have fallen off their hangers, making my clothing seem foreign, as though maybe it really isn't my closet after all. She continues to shove and fix a pile of...something. "Stop it! I'm going to throw out whatever you put in there, don't you get it?"

"You wouldn't!" she cries, as though I've threatened to harm one of her cats. She struggles to stand up, and though one half of me is already twitching forward to help her up, I resist, pull myself back. How dare she! At last she heaves herself onto my bed, sweating. Something reddish, knit, cranes out of my closet like a strangled creature. It's probably more clothes that neither of us will wear, too small for Ma, too attention getting for me.

"This is the only space I have, Ma, that's mine, that I can...that isn't..." To tell the truth is to risk hurting her.

"Well I have nowhere else to put them," she says softly, almost childlike. I think of all the closets that I can't open for fear of being crushed beneath their contents, child safety-locks holding back the avalanches. All the cupboards that should hold dishes but are crammed full of odds and ends that should be thrown away—the empty roll inside paper towels, bottle caps, chip bags still dusted with crumbs. Even the dishwasher itself is a home to wayward pop-tart boxes and other recyclables.

Ma fidgets with something small in her hands. "I knew where you were as soon as you didn't come home after work tonight," she says, surprising me. "She was over here a few days ago looking for you and I could see it in her eyes—she will bring you nothing but heartache, I promise you. I don't want you to bring her to this house."

I toss my bag onto the bed near her, barely resisting the urge to throw it at her. "You kept Marly away from me after the fire—it makes no sense to me. Why did you lie to both of us?"

Ma cringes up at me. "I had good reasons—"

"Don't you think that while they were scrubbing the burned, dead skin from my body, I needed a friend? How about when they cut chunks out of my legs and stitched those onto my face and neck? Think maybe I could have used a friend then?"

Ma shakes her head slowly, as though she can ward off both the past and the future. Then she stands up, signaling she's done talking, but I can't let her go. Though I know I will suffer for it, I grab her wrist and bite back a cry at the scalding sensation against my palm.

"Gracie, please," she whispers.

Still I hold on, and it comes—an image dark and hideous—my face burned past recognition. A child, a daughter, reduced to a swollen raw mess in a hospital bed. I drop her hand.

Tears cloud my vision and pain rockets through my body as though looking for a landing spot—wrist, shoulder, neck, arms, then it's gone. "You should have told me the truth," I whisper. "I thought she abandoned me."

"Gracie, they didn't know if you were going to make it through the night. Who do you think sat by your bed-side while you moaned that you wanted to die when the drugs started wearing off? Not your father, not your little friend. No, it was *me*. You don't have any idea what I had to do for you..." Now she's crying.

I cradle my head in my palms, breathing through my nose. She's still trying to trump my pain with her own. "We'd all have been better off if I'd just died, right?"

Ma points a meaty finger at me, her eyes blazing with a look I remember from the years when we fought about me hanging out with Marly. "How dare you say that to me! I chose to fight for your life—and I didn't ask for your gratitude."

"And you *chose* to take Marly from me, the only person who can look at me like this without cringing!"

My palm still tingles from where we touched.

Tears cluster in the corners of her eyes, but she wipes them brusquely away. "Well, don't you think for a second I made that decision lightly. She was not a healthy person—I didn't want her influence on you when you were so vulnerable. I put you first. All that driving to San Francisco and back—I stopped painting. Stopped talking to your father. I put it all on hold."

Inside the extra flesh of her face I almost see the lines and angles I once shared with her, our slender Norwegian heritage disappeared in each of us by different forces. "She wants me to go back to Vegas with her. Stay awhile."

Ma gasps, clutches her heart, and looks so pale that for a moment I fear I've given her a heart attack. My own pulse is going at a breakneck speed.

She laughs, a guffaw I haven't heard in years, since she used to host a woman's painting group, heavy on cocktails, at our house. "You're just going to up and leave, are you? Pack your bags and go to Las Vegas—"

She slaps her thigh.

Perhaps she sees my determined expression, and on my face, it must be somewhat horrifying, because she stops laughing.

"What is it you hope to do there?" she asks then, in a softer tone.

I look away from her, to the vanity dresser that belonged to my great-grandmother, the only antique in this house that hasn't met with ruin. Its mirror has been covered with a thin grey veil for years. Through it I can still see the faintest reflection, like someone swimming underwater. Now, that reflection is trying to gaze back at me, as though my old self is still there, wondering how to get out.

"I want to remember what it feels like to have friends, fun, go out," I say. *Rush against a horizon of excitement.*

Ma purses her lips.

"Vegas isn't so far from Arizona. Maybe it's time I contacted Dad, too. At some point I have to suck up my pride."

Ma's eyes reach out from the density of her face. "Oh Grace, do you really want to dredge all that up? You know it's just going to make you feel awful."

"Me? Or you? I'm twenty-eight! Should I just keep waiting until it's all over? Just wait until Dad's dead, and I'm too old to try anything? I know you're afraid for me, but you can't protect me from everything."

Ma sniffs, looks away.

"Come on, please don't cry. It's only for a little while. I need to do this."

She nods, and though I know I'll pay for it, I come around behind her and lean into a hug. "You don't have to, Gracie," she says, but I stay there, and let it come, heat, a throbbing ache, my vision going hazy at the edges.

What comes is not anything horrible, but Ma and my father, Harlan, his hair still dark and thick, Ma almost thin, bent forward over a bassinet, looking at a downy, swaddled infant. It's a lovely image, something that would sell diapers and stuffed animals, but images of things-as-they-used-to-be give me more of a shiver than my own charred reflection.

I pull back, heart thudding, and Ma heaves a sigh so big I can read the resignation in it.

"Just be careful with that girl."

I don't know if she means Marly, or if she's talking to me, the girl I still am in her eyes, forever frozen at fifteen by a molten snap of bad luck.

ကြို

In bed that night, the house shifts noisily around me, like a restless sleeper. It is probably just the cats navigating the few unpacked pathways between and around spaces we humans cannot possibly squeeze ourselves. Dare I leave Ma to all of this? She can barely rise off the floor without my help. In an earthquake, none of us would be safe in this house, but we pay our earthquake insurance and try not to think about the big fault line that lies less than a hundred miles from here. Marly and I tempted fate a hundred times as girls, and survived. Even the fire, an ironic accident in our spate of daredevil antics, didn't take me out. If I stay, I'm squandering a chance. I can feel it. If I leave, I'm abandoning Ma, the only person who stayed by my side.

But memory comes rushing in like ocean waves, taunting me.

We hit the stretch of Drake's Bay Boulevard where black tar road merges into inky ocean. The moon has undressed further at the shore, enhanced by a huge bonfire that shows signs of having been raging for a while already. Cars line the road, and, below us, dark silhouettes writhe to a bass beat.

This. This is what Marly offers me.

Parties that appear out of nowhere.

Marly slings a ratty gray back-pack over her shoulder and grasps my hand tightly. "Isn't this fucking awesome?" she says. Her words are full of heat. As I clutch her hand while we make our way down the hillside, I feel momentarily imbued with that essence of hers that makes strangers give her their numbers on buses and men gawk at her right past their wives.

"Oh wait, I forgot." She stops and opens her pack, pulling out a small red piece of cloth that could be a bandana, it's so small. "Put it on."

I clutch the shimmery spandex material in my hand and it unfurls into a tank top.

"You'll freeze, but it will be worth it," she says.

She wears a hot pink baby-doll dress, its deeply v-neck revealing ample cleavage. "Go on. No one can see us up here," she coaxes. I look around nervously, at the ant-like people cavorting below us, and quickly pull my long-sleeve black T-shirt off. The chill ocean air raised goose bumps across my chest, my nipples hardening painfully.

Once encased in red, I feel bolder, if not exactly transformed. I leave my soft copper waves down from the hasty bun I usually keep them in, and they tumble just barely to my shoulders. In another few minutes we scramble and thump down onto hard, wet sand.

Wherever we look people wear face masks and capes, cat tails and white sheets. "I totally forgot about costumes," I say. It's Halloween night.

"Who fucking cares," she says, and struts directly

toward a crowd of people.

"How can you tell who anyone is?" I ask.

"It doesn't matter," she says. "So long as they know who you are."

The crowd parts to let her in, and then to let me in. And there's dark-eyed Gabriel Diaz who will later put his fingers into my underwear, smother me in weed-scented kisses, before insulting me when I don't put out.

I suppose I should remember that night with shame or misery. It was the night Marly told me they'd be moving soon, the night the boy I liked rejected me. But tonight it comes into my mind viscerally, bringing the brine of ocean and the tang of beer, the smell of my own arousal, the feeling of possibility, of something magic hidden around a bend in the road if I'm only brave enough to go that far.

II

Chapter Six

Las Vegas

I watch the earth recede as we lift into the sky, feeling the anxious swoop of sudden buoyancy. The last time I flew out of Oakland International Airport, I was ten, on our way to visit Ma's dying father in New York. My one and only encounter with my grandfather. Now, I stuff a pillow to the right of me, to ward off any accidental contact of Marly's and my knees.

We have barely made it past the unfasten seatbelts sign when Marly's face pinches and she tears the items out of the seat pocket ahead of her, grasping onto a paper rectangle. She holds it to her mouth, eyes squeezed shut. I look away as she retches, trying not to gag.

She wipes her mouth and turns to the man across the aisle who has watched the whole event, mouth open with accusations he seems to be on the verge of delivering. "It's not the plague, okay? I'm pregnant,"

Marly says, sighing theatrically.

The flight attendant comes and takes away the signs of Marly's morning sickness but I am left with the horrible realization that there is much I don't know about Marly, least of all this.

"Pregnant?" I ask, as if this might be either miscommunication, or one of Marly's outspoken attempts to get attention. Marly's flat stomach does not match the rotund images of pregnant women who comprise nearly half of Adam's business—always frowning and moaning, pressing their hands to their lower backs. A pinch of guilt follows my thought: what if her condition impinges upon our fun?

"It's new to me, too." She leans back into her seat and exhales. "Which is why I didn't say anything." Her hair is in a messy pile atop her head, though it still manages to look artful, on purpose, but it also reveals vulnerably exposed ears and neck.

"Are you undecided?"

She folds and unfolds a tissue in her hands. "There's something insanely hopeful about a child, right? Fresh start, the sweet smell of baby skin, a person who loves you more than anyone else on the planet." She closes her eyes.

I can't contribute much to a conversation about children. I've only spent time with them at a distance, at parks, learned to avoid close contact with them. They're pointedly honest, their clothes always smeared in food and dirt. "I think Ma's big hope is that I'll find a husband so I can have children that will look the way I used to," I say.

Marly doesn't respond, and I'm left feeling like I

used to in school when I spoke the answer before all the other kids.

"Where's the father?" I prompt.

She shakes her head, her long silver earrings shimmying. "It's not about *where* he is. He's not father material. A long story. Don't want to bore you with it. Frankly, I'd rather do it by myself."

Not boring, I want to say, more like important tourist information in the village of Marly, where I am about to reside for two weeks. But she's already pulled out her iPod. "You don't mind if I tune out for awhile? Flying is making me feel super sick."

Even if I do mind, I realize as she pops in her earbuds, the question was rhetorical.

∽✦∾

We touch down in Las Vegas at just after 1:00 p.m. I'm quickly shucking off layers from clammy Drake's Bay; the air is temperate and dry here, even for February. "I can't believe that!" I say, pointing to a middle-aged man playing a slot right past the baggage claim, a look of urgency in his red-rimmed eyes.

"Lady Luck might be anywhere," Marly says with a silvery tone. "First time I came here I swear I felt it in the air, this heady anticipation of things to come."

"And now?" I ask. "Do you still feel it?"

Marly pats her belly and shoots me a smile.

After we fetch my luggage Marly walks us expertly to a line of travelers standing with their suitcases on the street—as we get closer I see they are girls, young women really, wearing short dresses and sandals, ponytails, and dripping with dime-store jewelry like previous incarnations of Marly. One of them gives me the quick head snap glance that tries to say she didn't even notice anything unusual. I hunker behind Marly, grateful for her height.

Marly's smile is amused as she looks at me crouching behind her, perched on the top of my suitcase, and for a second there's a clutch of annoyance at my breastbone that she doesn't have to think about which way to stand facing people.

"Don't mind them, Grace," she says. "All those girls care about is booze and hooking up with hot guys who won't remember their names at the end of the weekend." Her words are laced with the acid of experience.

The girls crowd into cabs three-deep, and though I know Marly is right, a part of me envies them for the ability to sit so close to each other without consequences.

When it's finally our turn, sweat drips inside my pants, sweater, and boots. I'm relieved to sit in the dank smelling cab. Outside is a dry, dusty terrain that does not allow any secrets.

Marly tells the cab driver her address, adding, "Take us down The Strip, avoid the tunnel, please."

The airport rolls away until, before long, The Strip rears up like an acid trip, revealing a lit Roman dome and a fancy version of the Eiffel tower. A giant globe outside Bally's looms over everything, promising to glow moon-like at night.

"Wow. You'd think Vegas was a scheme a rich person dreamed up to compensate for their lost childhood."

"Isn't it?" Marly shrugs. "It's a place where people get to re-live their lost childhoods, too," she says, then too quickly adds, "Do you know there are show girls and casino employees that work all night and sleep all day for years? They literally don't ever see the sun. Have to get fake tans and take Vitamin D in a jar."

"That sounds awful."

"Oh no, Grace, it's exciting. Think of life lived during the stretch of time when most of us are asleep—it's the witching hour all the time."

Though I know we'll return, The Strip passes too fast—I want to run after it like a child after a train.

It takes twenty minutes more to reach Marly's apartment, a tiny glass rectangle glimmering above us in an enormous gray column of condominiums. I can barely make out the little planter boxes of red geraniums she tells me to look for on her balcony. Twenty-third floor.

I roll my suitcase behind me through the lobby, which is decorated in gold and green that still sings of the seventies, into the elevator that's mirrored on all sides. As Marly presses in a code, then hits "23" I don't know where to look because I don't want to stare at myself for so many floors. As we start to ascend, Marly fidgets next to me.

The elevator is so hot that beads of perspiration perch on Marly's brow and nose. "You okay?"

"I don't know." She shrugs and holds her shoulders up at her ears for a moment. "I thought I was going to find closure in California and come back here feeling...renewed."

"But you don't?"

"Well, I found *you*, but...I'm knocked up, my only relative worth giving a shit about is dead, and I have to figure out how to get *le sperm donor* off my back. I'm just glad to be home."

Home. Hard to attach that word to this mysterious place of desert rock and fairytale oases. "You really don't have any connection to Drake's Bay anymore? You never miss it?"

"Grace, I don't know how to explain this to you. I know it's still your home. But for me, it's like the past is stored in the redwoods, grouted into the sidewalks when I walk around town. I feel memories jumping into my body like parasites." She clutches herself as if suddenly cold. "When I'm away, it's like someone just cut the strings to a thousand weights hanging from my body, and none of it has to live in me."

Not having been away from home long enough to experience what she's describing, I do like the way the Vegas air seems to fill my lungs, to shake out the old, stale air of Ma's heavy corners.

I look away from her only to catch my own nervous face in the mirrored walls. It is one thing to look at Marly, a whole and perfect creation. But to see us standing together, my bald head poking out of my sweater like a Q-tip, is like looking at a goblin come to collect on his favor from a queen. I close my eyes.

I try to think of something I can say that will improve her mood, but then Marly shakes her head and claps her hands together as the elevator dings at floor twenty-three. "Quit your bitching Marlboro," she instructs herself, then turns to me. "I've got you!"

"You call yourself Marlboro?"

She shrugs. "I was a chain smoker for awhile. It stuck."

I remember her, years ago, pulling out a glass jar full of cheap cigarettes from the bush outside her bedroom window—the harsh tobacco scent exciting, dangerous. Its promise of a "powerful buzz" always dissolved into coughing and nausea for me, but Marly could take long, deep drags and then lean back as though the smoke changed her into something more than human.

My suitcase clacks behind me as I follow her down a long burnt orange hallway, past a row of identical orange doors. Marly has only a small carry-on bag with her. She stops in front of lucky number thirteen. The hand that holds her key out is suddenly shaking, and it takes me a second to figure out why. The door is already open, cracked a few inches wide.

"Oh fuck," she says, low and husky. "Wait here Grace."

My hand hovers at the edge of her elbow, to pull her back, but I can't. "No, you don't know who's in there! It could be a robber or something."

Marly's shake of the head is like a lion tossing back its mane before a meal. "You can't break into this building. You have to know the code on the elevator to get it to go up and have a key.

"Well then, I'll go in first," I say, more bravely than I feel. I came here to have adventure, after all.

"No, together, at least."

Side by side, we step into her apartment. Whatever I may have expected—a colorful palette like her grandmother's house, a riot of collaged magazine pictures like her teenage room—I am not prepared for this: just about every piece of furniture is upside down or on its side: lamps, couches, dining room table, chairs, etc. This vandalism was not done in a fit of passion, but rather with calculated care, items laid on their sides just so. No perpetrator waits in sight.

More alarming to me is the blinding whiteness. All of it is white—the walls, carpet, bookshelves, sofa and matching loveseat, picture frames, her Formica table and its chairs, the few dishes set in the dish drainer, as if someone came in with a big air gun of white paint and sprayed everything at once. I feel like I've entered a set for an existential play. "So...white," I say.

"Helps keep my head un-crowded," she whispers.

Un-crowded? On tip-toe I shadow her through the living room, past the kitchen. "Why would someone do this?"

"I told him I'm knocked up," Marly whispers, craning her head around the corner. "I just didn't confirm that the baby is his. This is his answer to me. I guess he's planning to turn my life upside down. So original, fucker."

"So the baby isn't his?"

"Oh it is," she says, peering into her bedroom. "But it doesn't give him claim to my life."

Her logic defies me. "Okay, but this is creepy. Aren't you afraid?"

She sighs, squinting at the living room as though deciding what to set right first. "It takes more than tipping over my furniture to scare me."

"We should call the police."

Marly shakes her head with a sigh. "Police don't make things better, Grace. Especially when a guy's got a temper—calling the cops on him just aggravates things. Anyway, don't sweat it okay? I've got a deadbolt on the inside."

After we've done a thorough inspection of the apartment and are sure it's empty, Marly cracks open the freezer and withdraws a tall bottle of vodka and pours it into two clean, white mugs sitting in the dish drainer. Then she bends down and sets the kitchen table chairs back on their feet.

I sit primly staring at the cup of vodka, the scent conjuring the film developing chemicals my father once kept in the garage. "Well," I say, as much to myself as to her, "Life is already more interesting here than in Drake's Bay."

"Oh yeah." Marly smiles and knocks back her drink.

"You think you should be drinking?" I ask. Not the actions of someone with the intent to keep a baby.

She looks at her glass with raised eyebrows, as though surprised to find alcohol in it. "No, I should not be drinking. Or smoking. What I should be doing is figuring out what I'm going to do about the unexpected spawn, but..."

She stops her explanation and stands up, stretching out her lower back. "I have an addictive personality, or something. Perils of life—and work—in a town bent on hedonism. You're going to love Beneath the Waves," she says quickly. "My mother thinks I'm a stripper, or a hooker, which is so like her, never giving me any credit. But wait until you see it, the illusion is pretty spectacular. I could have had a million waitress jobs, working in casinos or hotels, but this is something special."

"It has to beat working at a doctor's office," I say, though I feel a rush of regret for leaving Adam to his blood drive without me. He'd tried so hard to hide his disappointment by looking busy, but he couldn't hide the frown, the heaviness that weighted down his voice. Whether he meant to or not, we forged a bond from that first day thirteen years ago when he came to my hospital bed with gentle derisions of the nasty nurses, making me feel as though I was still the same old Grace, no matter who I see in the mirror now.

Chapter Seven

That night we head out to the casino at the Bellagio, which, like many of the hotels and casinos on The Strip, stands tall and looming with a Roman sort of imposition—the setting for a spectacle or an alternate version of reality. Inside it's like I've stepped into a child's carnival brought to life—art and whimsy merging into objects that are either larger or smaller than they should be in real life: a gigantic poppy flower that towers over us, hot air balloons fit to carry Thumbelina off. It's mesmerizing and dreamlike in the best of ways, and the air smells of the perfect marriage of food and perfume.

Marly was right about one thing: nobody looks twice at me in the neon-light of the casino, which is bustling with high-dressed women bearing spray-tans and heels one can only teeter in. I'm wearing the only dress I have that is not an effort at full-body conceal-ment—eggplant colored rayon that drops to my ankles in a full skirt, cinched at the waist with a patent leather black belt. Knee-high, black going-out boots that I rarely go out in. It's a far cry from the form-fitting numbers on most of the women we see around us, and even from the short, pale pink flapper style dress Marly's wearing that makes her look Amazonian, but it accentuates the parts of me that Ma is always telling me to play up—my small waist and long torso.

"The first time I played slots at a casino," Marly says, standing as close to me as she can get without taking my arm, "I blew three hundred dollars in an hour, half of what I brought with me."

The rows of slots look like tiny glittering robots, but nothing that would cause me to lose time or money. "Is it really that addictive?"

She nods. "Be careful." She taps my arm and smiles. Beneath that tiny tap blooms another Marly—eyes too bright with liquor stolen from her parents' cabinet. *Just a taste, Grace.* "But not too careful."

Marly orders herself a Shirley Temple but encour-ages me to have a real drink. "It helps you sink into the experience," she says, handing me the cocktail. One gin and tonic morphs into two. I am surprised to find I am not, in fact, immune to the anticipation that comes just before pushing the slot button. Is this frizz of possibil-ity what Ma feels at night when she orders from the shopping channels, the promise of a shiny new bauble compressing the truth of the disorder that sits layered around her like the rings of ancient trees?

In the dark of the casino, surrounded by people immersed in their own private gambling, I feel a sudden urge to join them, to walk amongst them and run my hands along their shoulders, touch the seams of their shiny dresses and smooth, silk shirts. I'm confident that from a distance, with my bad side pointed away from the machines and the rest of my face obscured by my wig, I look like a perfectly ordinary girl who could get away with such a thing.

Because I should, I try a slot, feel the electric sense of possibility when I drop in my coins, and a rush of elation when the numbers spin. It's only after I've played nearly all my change that I realize I have, indeed, become caught up in the hunger to win something. Marly flits in and away, coming and going, as she has friends all over the casino.

"Hey," she says in a slurry whisper some hours later, "that guy is looking at you." She points to the poker table where a man does appear to be looking my way.

"He's been staring at you every time I've come over here," Marly insists. "He's checking you out." A nearly metallic burst of alcohol exudes from her, and her words have an inebriated slither. In her comings and goings over the past hour, she's been drinking, and heavily.

Words, for a moment, elude me. I'm upset that she's *drunk*—and also insulted by her gleeful tone.

"Marly, even if there was a *chance* he's looking at me because he finds me remotely attractive, what should I do, go take him back to a hotel room somewhere?"

Marly purses her lips and folds her arms. "You're not being open-minded," she says.

Her words poke something old and tender, and my tongue is loosened by the liquor. "Okay, if we're going to call things like they are, you should cool it with the drinking. Or study the effects of nicotine and alcohol on a fetus."

Her glazed eyes seem to flash fire, though I know it's only the reflection of the casino lights. "Oh thanks very much Nurse Jensen. I'm the one who wakes up every morning feeling like I swallowed shit, who has to pee every five minutes. I don't need to be lectured by you. There are lots of different ways of being in pain, Honey. And trust me when I tell you that yours is not the worst."

The alcohol makes me feel underwater, numb to the outrage just under my skin. I stand there gawking as Marly storms away from me. Not six hours in Las Vegas and we've already had our first fight?

My ears suddenly feel assaulted by a million pings and beeps, an ever-growing drone of conversation that swells and swells around me. My breath comes in gasps, and my chest feels heavy. A large man in a cowboy hat roughly brushes past me, his body scraping my side with a rush of pain and light. He spins me into the orbit of three young women who put out their hands defensively, their fingers like hot pokers repelling me. I try to murmur apologies but my tongue is glued to my mouth. My purse feels like a bowling ball in my hand and I reach for the nearest thing to lean on—a tall potted tree. It gives way beneath my weight and the next thing I know I am slumped on the floor, bruising my hip and back. I sit there, mortified, an object on display that pull the slavering gazes of gamblers my way for a moment. I want to pull something over my head. But before a well-meaning security guard can help me, Marly is suddenly there again, eyes wide in something like horror, I hope, at her own behavior.

"Oh Gracie, I am so sorry!"

She puts her hand out but I wave her away and help myself up to standing, painfully.

"I behaved like a total cu—" she begins.

I wave at her to stop, then grip my purse more tightly to me. "Let's just get home. I'm exhausted."

"Of course." She nods vigorously. She seems to have sobered up, or maybe I was imagining she was drunk—I don't want to dwell on it. The idea that she could have said those things to me while sober is worse.

Marly drives us home after agreeing to my lay person's sobriety test—walking a straight line and reciting the alphabet backwards. I almost forget everything that happened as we hit The Strip now, the gin in my veins making me feel as though I'm floating. The first thing that registers is light, neon and...moving. It pulses, shimmers, glows from the mammoth buildings like the world's biggest candy jar full of colored light, announcing shows and services, girls and adventure.

"It's like a bizarre dream full of symbols that add up to a meaning I should be able to understand," I say, almost to myself.

"Mmm-hmm," Marly sounds deep in thought herself.

Most of our ride back to the apartment is silent. We

both wince getting out of the car, though for different reasons—the parking garage smells like urine and garbage, assaulting my nose after the strangely perfumed scent of the casino.

"All kinds of shit shifts in your body when you're preg—"

A man is suddenly standing behind Marly, taller than her. I scream and he darts forward, grabs me sharply. Pain disproportionate to his grasp assaults me, as though someone is jabbing me with a sharp stick. "Don't fuck with me!" he says in a high, strained voice, and pushes me. Suddenly I am face-down on the hard cement of the parking garage. Terror flares an urgent pressure to my bladder. Marly's scream sounds more angry than afraid, but it is soon muffled, as though behind a hand. *I hope she bites him!*

Marly shrieks, "The baby's yours, okay? It's yours!"

I hear fists or feet making contact with flesh, a guttural cry that is his and then his echoing retreat, footsteps slapping concrete. In the tepid amber light of the garage Marly looks down at me in a daze of blood and tears. The tears look painful as they squeeze out the ravines between her swollen eye, down the slope of her misshapen, probably broken nose, and flow into the turgid river of blood that forms a gelatinous line down her neck. Fingertip-sized red marks bloom on her arms. Her hands protectively cradle her belly.

"We should go to the ER," I say, sounding shrill and breathy.

"No!" The word sounds painful; the top of her lip is split. I remember the pain and effort of trying to talk through my own burned lips.

"At the very least, the police should photograph you. This is...this is a crime, Marly. You can't let him treat you like this and get away with it!"

Marly only sobs harder at this. "No hospital. No police."

"Then let's get upstairs." I can always call emergency if I have to, I reason.

She nods. "I just feel so stupid."

I am never more thankful for the elevator in the garage.

"Are there security cameras?" I ask, craning around for some.

Marly shakes her head. "Been broken for ages. Cheap fucking place."

I get myself up to standing without her help, still bruised from my fall at the casino. She wobbles as she walks, one shoe on, the other dangling from her finger, its heel broken. We ride up to our floor in the silence, neither of us looking into the mirrored walls. She doesn't ask me for help, but I guide her nonetheless into bed, and fetch absurdly inadequate supplies: wash cloths (all unfortunately white), ice, Neosporin, and a bowl of lukewarm water. Wiping blood off her face and neck, the water in the bowl turns a disturbing crimson. She winces each time the cloth nears her nose.

Without much thought, almost in a trance, my hands move toward her belly; I want to reassure the baby inside that someone is looking out for it. When my hands make contact with Marly's skin, a sizzle that is at first as painful as always, becomes more like a vibration, as if I've laid my hands on the hood of a running car. At first, I chalk it up to the complex biology of pregnancy—all that extra blood and fluid, but rather than my usual urge to pull away, my hands want to keep moving, like a command ending directly in my finger tips. The images ripple, too fast to fully understand: the beat of feet on cement; a glinting sharp steel edge; a foot kicking a gray metal door, a smell of sulfur and then just a dark gray watery surface. My hands move, smoothing across her belly in soft strokes, then up toward her face. When I cup her cheeks and nose in my palms she sighs and melts into relaxation.

My hands continue down the sides of her ribcage, following this trail of energy that is serpent-like in its movement. It feels...other than me, though familiar, is the only way I can explain it to myself. She sighs, closes her eyes, and her heartbeat steadies, so I keep it up, as though pulled by an invisible cord, no idea how much time passes. Eventually though, fatigue rushes at me like a sudden tunnel and I collapse inside it, too tired to bother going to my own room.

꙰

Marly's shriek of alarm wakes me. I am alone in her bed, still in my clothes. On her night table sits the bowl I cleaned her face with, the bloody water now a murky brown. Marly shrieks again, the sound coming from the bathroom. My leap is so fast that the skin of my right leg stretches painfully in indignation. In the bathroom she is turned sideways inspecting herself in the mirror.

"Don't look. It makes it hurt worse when you look." I know exactly what it's like to wake up totally changed from your former self. I can remember Adam as a young resident in training, holding a mirror tilted upward at a careful angle so that all I could see in it were the tiny pinhole dots of ceiling tiles—a galaxy of symmetry. Thirteen years before I raised that mirror with terror, bits coming into view as foreign as if I had stepped off the plane onto Mars. There was no *me* in this view, only raised, raw, red mounds of flesh. *Chewed, ruined, scourged, masticated, swollen, raw.*

"What did you do to me?" she says now in a tight, low voice.

Why didn't I call 911 and make them take her to the emergency room? What kind of a friend am I? "I'm so sorry Marly. I just didn't want to fight you..."

Slowly she pivots toward me.

"That's...not...possible," I say when I see her.

No bruises. No swelling. No traces of blood. Her few chicken pox scars are gone and her skin is truly glowing. I am grateful to have so few hair follicles, for those remaining are all standing painfully on end. Marly walks toward me and I have the urge to back away, like she has been made undead.

"You healed me, Grace." Marly's eyes are wide and bright. They unnerve me.

"That's ridiculous." My voice is a barely audible whisper. "That's impossible."

"Grace, I've r*ead* about this type of thing. Marly runs her hands across her face. "I looked like Mike Tyson's handiwork last night. There is a bowl of bloody water by my bedside, so you can't tell me it wasn't real." She runs a finger down her smooth cheek. "You have a gift, Grace." She sounds euphoric, like she is about to fall at my feet and kiss the hem of my skirt.

I'm not saying it's possible but...How? Why now?"

The top of her head seems to grow taller with the widening of her eyes. "What do you mean 'why now!' Grace, you always...always saved my ass." She bows her head, and I have a bright and unwelcome flash of memory: *Marly in a yellow dress, smeared with blood.* "You've never *tried* until now, have you?"

I stare at her, forming a protest. *Of course not! Touch is painful to me.* I close my eyes, rest my palms against my cheeks, and take a deep breath, wondering if I'll feel that serpent-like energy again.

Marly circles her right wrist with the fingers of her left hand with a suddenly wistful expression. "Oh," she says softly. "It's gone."

"What?"

She looks up at me with ocean-dark eyes. "Oh...it's stupid."

"Well now I want to know for sure."

"I had a scar from the fire." She sounds afraid of what I'll say.

"I always wondered if you had any, if you were burned." A laugh, slightly hysterical, wants to escape but I bite it back.

She keeps rubbing the skin, as though burnishing a piece of silver. "It was a part of me I was used to. But it's gone now."

There's something more under the surface that I can't

read, but I'm so shaken by what's happened I can't begin to sort out her unspoken feelings, too.

I stand there for several minutes, breathing in and breathing out, trying to clear my mind. If I could, if I did remove Marly's scars, what could I do for my own body? I hold an image of my cheeks as they were before...smooth and freckled, my eyelashes long and reddish-blonde. I'd thought myself plain, especially in comparison to Marly. Now, I'd consider myself a supermodel to look that way again. Foolish as I feel, I place my hands on my face. After what must be ten minutes I feel something—the strain of holding my hands up to my face. My shoulders ache and I drop them with a sigh.

Marly looks at me, hopeful.

"Nothing."

"It was real," she says, "what happened. You can do it again."

Her certainty makes me uncomfortable. I want to put our feet back in the real world. "*Whatever* happened, you do realize we have no proof now that *Loser* attacked you. There's nothing to take to the police."

Chapter Eight

Of course I know that the women swimming in serene circles in the blue-tinted water of the "mermaid grotto," are not magical, but even so, I'm spellbound. They're scantily clad in shiny, shell-shaped pasties and eerily realistic fish tails that move effortlessly through the water. They hold their breath for a stupendously long time, as they swirl and swoop, blow kisses and press their gleaming cleavage to the tank's glass. They look real. They look capable of dragging a man underwater and enchanting him.

"Is it hard to do?" I press my face to the tank. A short man cranes behind me on tiptoe to get a better look, but I'm not moving. The tank bottom is tiled in mosaic blue and greens, and all through the water, long green ropes sway and wave like algae. Tiny iridescent fake fish "swim" on clear wires through convincing coral displays, and little cave-like alcoves emanate colored light. A mermaid weaves in and out of this underwater grid, displaying her wares to the glass, wiggling her tail and torso suggestively, then grasps a rope of "algae" and swings herself up to catch a breath of air. The way she breathes is seamless: her head disappears into a silvery-gray "sky" that can't be seen from the tank level.

"That tail weighs ten pounds alone, and you have to seriously work your stomach muscles. While holding your breath and trying to look alluring," Marly whispers.

"They pay well for this?"

"Well enough for the girls. I'm in charge of the team—scheduling, hiring, firing, payroll. So I make a good wage with health benefits. Tips make up for the rest."

One of the mermaids winks at Marly, who chuckles. "Fern—gotta watch out for that one. I think she'd like to parlay this gig into a topless affair if she has her way. It's something in the Vegas air, I think. Makes exhibitionists out of us all."

As if Marly needs any help in that department.

"What you can't see is the 'beach,'" Marly waves at a phantom landscape outside the tank. "There's an area where mermaids go to 'sun themselves' and that's where patrons can stick cash into little nets. But if you don't work it down here, you aren't going to get much up there." Marly sighs and folds her arms. "Truthfully, there's something beautiful about this. I love the illusion. Let me show you the outside area."

Marly gently touches my arm to direct me through an in-door tunnel composed of transparent Plexiglas walls. At her touch, a bubble of memory expands in slow motion, offering a dizzying world of sound and color, a night that changed everything. As girls, when she wanted to convince me of something she always made physical contact—firm fingers finding the soft skin of my wrists, an arm encircling my waist in a collaborative huddle. "*Trust me*," whispered in a hush.

Subtly, I pull my hand back before memory can yawn open and pull me too deeply in. Live, silvery fish swim in artistic clusters over our heads, under our feet, and on either side of us separated only by these thin walls of plastic, an ocean womb. Then the tunnel spits us out into the bright February day, onto a fake seaside. The sound of waves hitting the shore is uncanny. If not for the chill in the air and the sight of pirate clad waiters, I could easily believe that we are at a real beach.

"Here, sit," Marly points to a chaise lounge. "I'll be right back." A dark-haired young pirate comes to take my order—lemonade.

Marly reappears and makes her way to me at the same time that a petite strawberry-blonde with enormous dimples and wearing an aquamarine bikini and sarong comes bounding up. She looks like she's going to bounce right into Marly's arms, but stops short, and Marly draws herself up taller, her body suddenly stiff.

"I'm so glad you came back," the woman says to Marly. "It's been a total clam bake without you."

Marly smiles. "Grace, this is Sabrina, mermaid and barkeep. Sabrina, this is my best friend from childhood, Grace."

To her credit, Sabrina makes only the briefest blink,

as though adjusting her contacts, then puts out her hand. But I swear the thought running through her mind is something like: *Woah, what happened there?* "Nice to meet you."

I fear I'll embarrass Marly if I explain why I don't shake hands, so I take Sabrina's hand in mine with a deep breath. My hand pulses and then I have a vivid feeling of irritation in my bladder. The quick way Sabrina drops my hand has nothing to do with disgust at my ruined thumbs, I can tell; I think she felt something pass between us. I exhale with such force that she stares at me. I don't need to tell her she has a bladder infection; I can tell by the way she stands with legs crossed, that she already knows. I'm stunned into dumb silence for a minute and throw Marly a heavy glance, hoping she'll see that I've felt something again. And this time, it's almost like a diagnostic; no visuals, just a sure-fire feeling that this woman needs an antibiotic.

Marly raises an eyebrow, signal received, but plays it cool.

"There's been so much dirt since you were gone." Sabrina's hands fly out like flowers unfurling. "Fern almost got arrested for going to a customer's hotel room, but they couldn't prove anything." Marly's eyebrows lift delicately, as if she is only feigning surprise. "Leila and Jane came out publicly as a couple, and Hank—" she turns to me and adds, "that's the owner. He's trying to get them to do a pseudo-lesbian number in the tank, and I think they're filing a sexual harassment suit against him."

Marly shakes her head. "I was gone a week!"

"Oh, and..." Sabrina looks at me as though unsure if she should say the next thing. "Your ex was by. He had one hell of an attitude." Sabrina raises an eyebrow and shrugs.

Marly sighs, compresses her lips and nods slightly. "Sorry about that."

A ship's horn vibrates the air around us, making me jump. Sabrina says, "Sorry chicas, I'm on!" and dashes away with a lithe energy I envy.

"As you can see, there are no secrets in this fish tank," Marly wrinkles her nose in the direction of her mermaid coworkers on the beach. Their fishnets are already heavy with cash from men in Hawaiian shirts and khakis.

I shrug, suddenly feeling off-kilter, like I can't rely on gravity to hold me to the earth.

"I get off in a few hours, so we can go do something fun. Maybe tomorrow you can come to work with me, not be at the mercy of cabs."

Fun. That feels further away now than it did back in Drake's Bay. Marly is pregnant. She's under attack by an unhinged ex, and I appear to have turned into a conduit of some kind. "What do you think that was the other night? What happened to us?"

Marly shrugs but her face softens and her eyes have the far-away glaze of someone caught up in a fantasy. "I don't know. Even if I did, it wouldn't change how miraculous it was."

Her certainty challenges me. "I'm sure it was a fluke. We were tired."

Marly chews on her lower lip, a swoop of hair obscuring her cheek, making her look like the girl I knew so well once. "Grace, what about your family—maybe something happened to you as a kid. Didn't your mom go to church for a while? Any faith healing sort of thing go on?"

"We went to AA meetings, Marly. Lots of coffee and cookies, and the Lord's Prayer, but definitely no faith healings."

"Well, have you ever had anything weird happen before?"

The words are hovering in my mouth. *How about thirteen years of weird. Thirteen years of pain without a source and visions without a cause?* Some part of me resists telling her.

"Maybe," is all I offer.

"Maybe?"

I rub the spot between my eyes, feeling the halo of a headache coming on. "After the fire. After recovering a little, I mean...they put me through all kinds of psycho-therapy for my self-image, and on a ton of drugs but...there were, are, little things no one can explain."

Her eyes gleam. "Yeah, like what?"

"Phantom pains. Visions, I guess, except they're often vague, and not always... What does it matter?"

Marly squints, adjusts the iridescent green tank top of her out-of-water uniform. "It matters because I've got an idea."

I stare at her from under the brim of my hat. "What idea?"

Marly tightens her ponytail. "I'd like to be your manager, or handler, of sorts. Look, don't think of it as exploiting you but directing your talent. People charge money for lamer shit, Grace." Her hand grasps mine before I can think to step away.

Come on, Grace, they seem nice. Two tall, handsome guys beckoning us into a night of adventure—what kind of girl would turn down such an offer?

Almost a reflex, I step away from her, as though she is a wave I can keep from crashing on me, and she drops my hand. "I'm not a circus act, Marly! Whatever that was, it was a one time thing. We have no evidence I could repeat it." Yet I recall how my body felt when I laid my hands on her—powerful, vivid, alive with energy, as though I was not contained or diminished but expansive, as big as the universe. "There's no way that my hands are capable of doing more than making people uncomfortable."

"You gave me a look when you shook Sabrina's hand. You felt something, didn't you?"

Now that the moment's gone, I feel sure it was my own imagination. "I don't know, it felt like...okay, like she has a bladder infection."

Marly's smile is big, smug. "Ha! The girl gets chronic UTIs, Grace. She thinks it has something to do with the chlorine water of the tank. Holy shit, see!" She holds her hands out like she's inviting worshippers into a shrine.

It's still not enough to convince me. "What if we were just drunk?"

Marly's eyes narrow, as though she's waiting for me to chastise her again, her tone brittle. "I was not drunk, Grace. Not when I drove us home, and not...after."

Surrounded by all this fake blue water it's hard to even remember the roaming, wild heat that surged through my hands last night.

Marly turns to me. Her eyes beg me not to break her gaze. "I believe in you, Grace. I'm living proof. And there are people who need what you can offer. What could it hurt to try?"

On my lips are words rushing to remind her of a night that began with the promise of dancing, after hours, like those fairytale princesses, pulling the wool over our parents' eyes, and ended with the two of us in the back of a police cruiser. But that was different. Wasn't it?

Chapter Nine

My one flexible finger is the right middle one, which I find ironic. I dial, the phone rings ten times and, though most other people would hang up, I know she's there, perhaps trying to find the phone muffled beneath a pile of clothing, or prevented from quick access by one of her mounds of unworn clothing or a tower of boxes still spilling out packing peanuts. After fifteen rings, worry is a ball on the roulette wheel of my body, pinging my nerves. What-ifs offer themselves to my mind. What if the big quake hits and Ma is trapped between ancient *Drake's Bay Gazettes* and the pouty-faced covers of *Entertainment* magazines? What if she trips over one of the wily felines who have learned to twist through the house like little snakes, out of sight, scavenging?

My fears are allayed after twenty rings.

"Yeah." My mother never says hello; whoever is calling must want something from her.

"Ma. It's me."

Ma sucks in air. Then her growing silence manages to feel loud. "Well," she says at last, "Are you having a *good time*?" All of a sudden I want to hug her, if only for a sense that something is normal.

The monochromatic box of a spare room where I'm staying, thanks to its whiteness, has a sharp, cold feeling. I long for a warm color—mauve, even an eggshell yellow—and I wouldn't argue with a pile of laundry or some messy plants full of spiky tendrils. Marly's empty, sterile spaces have a too familiar hospital-like flavor to them.

"I'm not sure yet," I say.

"But you're well?" she asks. She coughs loud and raspy.

Am I truly going to explain to my mother that I have suddenly discovered myself to have healing abilities? Then again, Ma has spent years buying creams that promised to make my scars disappear, vitamins that would heal me from the inside out, "magic" makeup that suffocated my pores. Of course I eventually rejected all magic elixirs. After a bracing breath, I spill it out as plainly as I can—telling her limited details of Marly's injuries, claiming they happened after a fall.

Ma is quiet again for so long, I wonder if she hung up, except I hear no dial tone. "Gracie," she says at last, "is this some kind of punishment because I didn't want you to go? Think it's funny to make things up—"

"I'm not making this up! I don't even *believe* in this

kind of thing. You think I would call you just to make fun of you?"

Ma drops into loaded, breathy silence. I imagine the cats, like demon familiars, purring in her lap, plotting to claim my bedroom in my absence.

"Look, I'm calling you because I couldn't think of anyone else who would believe me. Who would be able to help me understand this."

"You want my advice?" Ma asks. "God forbid I should ever offer it unsolicited."

"I am soliciting it! Marly thinks I can use this...ability, whatever it is, to help people—"

"To help people, or for some selfish reason of her own?"

"She has her issues, but that doesn't make her evil."

"So you say, Gracie. Maybe she staged that fall down the stairs so she could get your sympathy. Maybe none of her injuries were as bad as you thought."

My lie about Marly's "fall" works against me. "Ma, listen to me. I know what I saw, what happened. If you don't have anything useful to offer me, I'll go, then—"

"Fine, fine, don't get in a huff. What do you want me to say?"

Ma coughs again, and I wonder if this is a stalling tactic. "Gracie, since you don't believe in God or a higher power, this is hard for me to answer. But if what you've told me is true, then you *have* to believe in *something*. If it really was you, and not Marly concocting a scheme—"

"Let that go, Ma." My mother has the power to still make me feel, and whine, like an indignant teenager.

"You don't just wake up with the power to heal for a lark!" My mother now sounds excited, as though, between breaths, she's had an epiphany.

Feeling somewhat stupid, I try to say a little mantra of thanks in my head to whatever force has bestowed this upon me. What I picture, oddly enough, is a big flame goddess extending tendrils of blue fire to my forehead like I'm knighted.

"I mean think of what this could mean for YOU," she persists.

It hits me what she must be thinking and I wish she wouldn't. "Ma, I've accepted being the way I am."

"But if you *could* heal yourself—"

Her words are like steel-wool against my heart. "Ma? Get over it. I'm sorry I bothered you."

I hang up on my mother.

୧ଚ୨

I'm just coming out of the bath when Marly gets home. Showers are a thing of the past for me, with all those prickling drops of water like tiny needles on my skin. By the time I've dried and dressed she's sitting on her soft white couch, holding something small and flat in her hand, paper, I think. Her hair is wet and she smells faintly of chlorine, a chemical smell that I've always strangely liked. It was the smell of my father after his weekend morning swims, coming home just as I was readying for cartoons and cereal, a towel wrapped around his neck, that stinging scent rising off his strong shoulders.

Marly's face looks bare, free of makeup, except for a faint stain of red on her lips, and a pinkish oval around her eyes, which I guess is a casualty of swimming for a living. Her shoulders are rounded forward, and on the small glass coffee table in front of her she's set a bottle of vodka, still capped.

It takes me a minute to realize she's crying, so silent is she, only the nearly imperceptible heave of shoulders upward in a hiccupping motion.

"Oh Marly, what's wrong?" I come around and sit on the big white lounge chair opposite her, realizing at once that it's a mistake, as its soft gravity sucks me uncomfortably into its center.

She holds up the photograph in her hands, a Polaroid, and tosses it at me. It lands on my lap. I expect something from our youth—maybe one of those happy family plastic-smile pictures before we knew how badly things would go for us.

But the photo is recent. In it Marly's wearing a slinky white dress that barely comes to her knees, high silver heels that look impossible to walk upon. A man has his arms around her, a square-jawed, dark-haired guy, taller than she is in her heels, kissing her cheek.

"What is this? It looks like a prom photo." But it can't be; I can all but hear fourteen-year-old Marly's scorn as she turned down another Senior, *"I'd sooner die than go to a prom."*

Marly nods, her cheeks crimping with the effort of holding back more tears. "That's Loser and me on our wedding day. Three months ago."

Despite a well-honed reflex against staring at others,

I stare at her. "What?"

Marly's shoulders shake with unhappy laughter. "I sent my mom the other picture we had taken at the chapel. I was just screwing around with him, never meant to get serious. He's one of those guys who blows into your life in a cloud of excitement, promises, bringing you gifts and telling you how beautiful you are, then sleeps with your friends and stops calling."

"Oh yeah, I know the type," I say with as much sarcasm as I can muster, but Marly doesn't catch it.

"So why'd you marry him?"

Marly looks at the vodka with yearning, as though it's her therapist or savior, though she doesn't touch it.

"To piss off my mother. It was a joke, at least I thought it was—we were going to have it annulled, no big whoop—just a silly prank, and hey, when you live in Vegas, getting married at a chapel is just like walking across the Golden Gate Bridge in San Francisco."

Though one part of me thinks that's a silly reason to marry a person, another part of me gets it right away. You don't live with your mother your whole life without mastering the fine art of pressing her buttons.

"So, can't you get it annulled or something?"

Marly tosses her hands up in the air like they could fly away from her body. "I got pregnant. Stupid, stupid, stupid." She smacks herself lightly on the forehead. "I got off one birth control pill to try a new one that didn't make me into a crazed bitch who porked out, and, well, here I am."

Here she is, revealing personal details like when we were girls, only I have nothing to offer in trade. Other than the short spell of dating Gabriel Diaz, the last few times I've been touched by a man, it was a doctor, usually peeling off bandages and pronouncing me 'healed' with a squinting look.

"And Loser now thinks that because he planted his seed in my soil or some such bullshit, that I am his, that our marriage is real, and that if I won't listen to reason, brute force will wake me up. I'm in a fucking bind. And all I want to do is pour a big old glass of that Grey Goose right there. I want to drink it so badly, because I keep telling myself that I can still decide not to have this baby, you know? What does it matter if I drink or smoke—it's just a cluster of cells that accidentally wound up in my body, right?"

"But it won't be for long, Marly." The shaking in my voice surprises me: I'm angry at her even considering taking another drink. "Soon you will have to make a choice."

Marly's face is so drawn and pale I'm overcome with an old feeling of rescue, a late night phone call, panic in her voice: *Grace, I think I did it this time. They want to send me away.*

With a deep sigh I heave myself out of the chair and come around to sit next to her, not quite touching her.

She makes a pitiful attempt at a smile. "When you had your hands on me, Grace, I felt it, the baby, for a flash. You gave me something I would never have felt. You, and your gift, are the best thing to happen to me in years, Grace."

I sink into her words like perfect bathwater. "That's really sweet." But it is so much more than that.

"I told a good friend of mine about you. His name is Drew. If you'd consider it, Grace, he could set up the circumstances for you to try again, in a neutral setting—no expectations, what ever happens, happens."

Her eyes are wide, imploring. I feel her need like a bright rope of light twisting its way from her through me.

Would it kill me to try?

Chapter Ten

I close my eyes the entire drive to Drew's house. Marly doesn't ask me why my eyes are closed, and even turns the car radio down to a low hum. In the theater behind my eyes I picture a billowing tent, a tuxedoed man hawking tickets to a freak show. I don't realize we've stopped until Marly whispers my name softly.

When I open my eyes again we're parked in front of an unassuming white house with a tamed wilderness of a garden—tall flowers wave over soft, fragrant herbs. A little bridge arches over a delicate stream.

"You okay?" Marly pats my knee so quick and light I barely feel it.

"I feel like a fraud." My hands feel heavy in my lap. "I don't know if I can look at people in pain and pretend that I can help them."

Marly nods, as if she could possibly understand

what I'm feeling. "You're not pretending. You're be-ing...Well, don't be anything you're not." Then she ap-plies a coat of ruby gloss to her plump lips.

With a sigh, I adjust my strawberry curls in the car mirror. My skin is dusted in mineral powder, something I rarely do because it leaves my face feeling like a de-sert-scape, dry and hot. Marly bought me a white cot-ton dress that covers all of me, except for my ruined hands. It's downy and soft and I feel ethereal in it, like some spirit girl in a séance. Perhaps the power of sug-gestion alone will heal the masses.

We cross over the little stream, where bright orange Koi nibble with hungry, gaping mouths at the glassy surface, and walk up to a dark red door. Marly knocks, and my bad right leg suddenly throbs as if I've been walking all day. Every crevice that can, sweats. Pressure ripples around me, lifting those few hairs that remain, prickling at me like an impending storm.

A tall, man with dark blonde hair and gentle eyes opens the door. "Marly! Look at you," he says, touching her belly through her dress as if he knows her secret. His hand lingers there a second longer than I consider polite; do they have a history together, too? What he thinks of my appearance is hidden inside his placid expression.

"I'm Drew," he says, extending a long-fingered hand. "We're grateful you came, Grace."

I reluctantly disentangle my own hand from the folds of my dress. *If I am here to heal, I can't very well refuse to shake hands, can I?* What I expect to feel—the images, the lights—is eclipsed by the sensation of his soft skin. No pain follows.

"We're all gathered in the back garden," Drew says. "There's plenty of shade," he adds, and exchanges a worried look with Marly. *She's clearly mentioned my sun sensitivity, but what else?* Drew leads us through the house to a back garden that is even more profuse and lovely than the front. Baskets of hanging flowers drip from the eaves and green plants lurk at the edges of a splendid pond.

But more startling than the garden is an audience—about twenty people—seated on blankets and in white Adirondack chairs. At first glance there is nothing visibly ill about any of them. People you'd never look twice at. The longer I stare, however, the more I see. One woman's face bears the greenish shadows of cancer. In others, there are sallow cheeks and bloodshot eyes, spindly limbs and bandaged hands. I have the absurd thought that these people are like the wild animals I work with, trying hard to hide their illnesses for fear of being easy prey.

My bad right leg bends with the threat to buckle entirely.

Perhaps Drew senses I'm overwhelmed, for he's quickly at my elbow, leading me to a chair under a large umbrella. Then he places a cold glass of what looks like iced tea in my hand, water beaded on its slick surface as though it, too, is nervous. Marly looks dazed. *Did she expect such a turnout?*

"Grace, listen. We don't want to push you. Just make introductions, that's all," Drew crouches at my knee, his face in shadow.

People in the audience close enough to hear him, nod.

"I thought if each person here just stood up and told you, in brief, a sample of their story, then you could see if anyone strikes you. And go from there."

Just to have something to do, I sip my iced tea and then set it down before I drop it. "I've never done this," I say quietly. "Except for Marly, and that was...I don't know if I can do it again."

Drew gestures out at the crowd as if to say *look at them, at their misery*. "They have nothing to lose," he says. "Tell them about you."

Drawing in a deep breath, I sit forward in my chair, searching for words that sound comforting. "I don't know if I can help any of you." My voice is small and dry, cracked. "But I know what it's like to experience the kind of pain that makes death sound better." To my surprise, I hear myself chuckle. "And I guess the truth is, you do get through it, and then you kind of forget it. Still, I remember what it's like to wish for things to be different. All I can say is that I will try to help you. That's all I can do. Just try."

Their eyes assess me. I close my eyes and the murmuring of the crowd is almost comforting, as if they're encouraging me. I feel called in a direction, and open my eyes to find myself facing a robust looking woman who introduces herself as Flo when I point at her. She's overweight, her eyes are narrowed to dubious slits; she reminds me of my mother. She limps up at my request and over to the seat that Drew has positioned next to me, where she sits with a wincing smile. Her hand is in mine before I realize I've picked it up. She looks at the ruins of my thumb against hers without disgust. We sit there, holding hands like schoolgirls, both of us probably thinking the same thing: *Is there any way on earth that this can possibly work?*

What happened when I touched Marly that night she was attacked? I had simply wanted so badly to take away her pain. So I wonder what Flo's pain is like. I wait for the images to form, the heat, the sensation of that curious serpent to appear.

The only thing that happens is that our hands grow sweatier and the song Sweet Home Alabama starts to run through my head like I'm picking up a bad radio station.

At last, I let hers go and shake my head. She sighs and nods and I feel a collective shiver of disappointment rush through the group.

"I'm sorry." Shame makes my cheeks hot. "I really wish I could have helped."

Flo bends her head and keeps it there for a long moment. When she raises it again, tears glisten in the corners of her eyes. "Hey, we're asking for miracles, after all," she says kindly. "They don't come easy."

Marly is suddenly at my side. "Maybe there's someone else you'll connect with in the audience," she whispers. "Maybe you can't heal every wound or illness?"

That has got to be the understatement of the century.

"I can't believe we got all these people's hopes up," I say through clenched teeth. My stomach feels suddenly queasy. "Where's your bathroom, Drew?"

He jumps up and directs me inside to a guest bathroom fragrant with fresh roses and lavender. I slump down on the lid of the toilet and place my head in my hands, which come away shiny with mineral powder. With a damp washcloth I take off all the makeup, then strip my head of its curls. I don't know how long I'm in there, but when I emerge, Drew is gently herding the last couple of people off the lawn. Marly sits on the ground frowning, running her fingers through the grass. I can't tell if she's disappointed in me, or guilty for setting this failure into motion.

The last few people to leave include a woman who looks to be in her thirties helping a frail elderly man limp across the grass with a cane. The sun causes a strange dappling of light just above her right breast. It takes me a minute to realize the sun is angled in the completely opposite direction. There is no light source. "Wait, stop!"

She turns around. Faster than I thought possible, I stride across the lawn, barely even registering the complaint in my tight right leg.

The woman's eyes widen at the sight of me up close; the wig and makeup shrouded the truth of me from the distance at which she sat.

Panting with exertion, I manage to ask, "How far along is it?" when I reach her side. "Your...cancer."

Her hand goes to her mouth, eyes a horrified width. "My, no, my dad's the one with—"

Without asking permission, I touch my index finger to the top of her right breast and it's like pressing into hot tar. She recoils, but my finger stings after she's pulled back.

"I'm not sick," she says firmly. "I came here today for

him. He's the one with cancer. He's the one who needs help!"

Her father frowns at her. "You've had those chest colds you can't shake."

"Oh this is bullshit," she looks at him with the weary frown of the constant caretaker. "I came here because you begged me to. Because if medicine hasn't figured out a cure, surely some new age charlatan will!"

Her father's smile turns down, an apology hidden in it. "I am a lot of work."

"I don't blame you for being angry." I clutch my hands together. "I barely believe myself."

The old man holds out his hand. "Thank you for trying." He purses his lips. "Believe it or not, I feel better just from spending one day thinking that I might actually beat this thing."

"What's your name?" I ask.

"Ray."

"Thank you, Ray." Uncharacteristically, I take his hand and at the same time we both gasp as a feeling like an electric charge passes between us. The serpent of energy I felt when I touched Marly slides up his arm until it changes direction and creeps toward his midsection. I follow the serpent with my left hand, which I place right below his belly button. He doesn't speak or move but stares past me, off into space. I follow the energy deep into his bowels, until I feel it—a dark rotted place that makes me nauseated. His daughter has let go of him and is staring at us as, gape-mouthed, as if we are insane.

"Lay him down." My voice sounds husky and thick

to me. Drew and Marly get to task; they lay him on the grass and I see the dark place, a shadow spot, that my hands want to follow. "I have to unbuckle your pants," I say. "I have to touch you skin to skin." He gives a kind of half-nod, half-shrug and I place my hands against the flesh of his belly, soft and wrinkled. Though I know my hands only rest on the surface of him, it feels as though I am dipping them into pudding. From the outside, what I am doing probably looks obscene, though I don't touch lower than the top of his pubic bone.

After wading through the pudding I arrive at a hard stone. I close my eyes and see myself lifting the black pulsing stone and tossing it into a bottomless well. Ray groans and his daughter paces around us as though she wants to intervene but can't bring herself to.

Beneath the "stone" is another stone, and another one. I mentally lift, and toss, at least a dozen, Ray groaning beneath my hands each time, until finally he rolls away from me and throws up into the grass.

"What are you doing to him?" his daughter shouts.

The connection broken, I now feel like a fish flung out of water onto dry land, breathless and dazed. My hands are heavy and I could close my eyes and sleep right then and there if they let me.

Ray shakes his head over and over, though he doesn't seem to be able to speak.

"Stay close to a toilet," I say, my throat parched. "For a couple of days. You won't be able to keep anything solid down. Lots of fluids, soup, water." I don't know where these instructions come from, but I am sure of them.

His daughter helps him to his feet with a scowl at me I interpret as suspicion, and leads him, stumbling off to their car. He looks wrung out, barely able to make his feet walk him to the car, and I want to offer a hand but am too spent. Drew and Marly watch, seemingly paralyzed, as though too afraid of the man's daughter to help, either. Just before she buckles herself into the driver's seat, I see her look down and touch the spot above her right breast.

Then the blackness comes.

ᏅᎾᎧ

When I wake, I'm in a four-poster bed. The scent of roses perfumes the air around my head, and weak late afternoon sun scurries toward the horizon. Every surface of me aches, as though someone has spent an hour poking me vigorously all over. I expect to find bruises to back this up, but when I turn back the downy coverlet and sheets to investigate myself I find nothing but my usual lunar surfaces.

I am still at Drew's. At my side sits a tray with a thin, yellow soup and a glass of water with ice and a sprig of mint. I gulp the water. The ice crashes into my teeth and makes my gums throb, but I don't care. I haven't been so thirsty since the hospital, when medications stole any moisture the fire hadn't licked away.

Slowly, I rise. When my bare feet meet cool wood floor, I wonder which of them removed my shoes. Was it Drew? Did he stop for a second to admire the smooth pedestal of my toes, which bear neither calluses nor bunions because I don't walk barefoot or wear high heels? I haven't jogged since I was fifteen. I feel a tingle of embarrassment at the thought that he might have undressed me.

I weave my way out to the living room, and find Drew and Marly leaning forward on the couch, whispering. Though their bodies are not quite touching, they're looking at each other with a tenderness, a familiarity, that suggests they share more than platonic feelings. When Marly spots me she calls out, "You're awake!" and shifts away from Drew as though intentionally putting more distance between their bodies.

"Thanks for the lovely nap," I stretch my arms out in front of me. "I really hope neither of you carried me."

Drew frowns. "You don't remember getting into bed?"

"I don't remember anything after Ray and his daughter left. It was like being taken under by a wave."

Drew makes a thoughtful sound, and Marly says, "I knew it would work!"

"You don't know that anything happened for certain," I say. "I made the guy puke, and pissed off his daughter. That's all we really know." In truth, though, I know something more happened this time—an echo of that dark, stone-heavy source in his body hangs over me like a pall. Relief that something happened, that perhaps the pain and the visions of all these years have a purpose runs up against something else. Responsibility. Is this what Adam feels after he administers help to ailing patients? I can picture him flopping onto his bed at the end of the day with the burden of all his worries—and I have a sudden absurd wish to be there, rubbing the tension out of his shoulders, offering a drink.

I ease myself into a blue armchair so soft it feels as though it is digesting me.

Marly shakes her head. "I *know* it worked. Drew can check in on him. Maybe he can offer testimonials for the next one?"

I struggle to sit upright. "What next one? I'm done with this, Marly."

Marly's flawless face crumples with disappointment. "Grace, every one of those people came to see you work. I was staggered by their faith."

I want Drew to rally for my side, to point out that I collapsed after doing one short healing. If that's what it was.

But Drew says, "I wish you could have seen it from our perspective. It was like you were *one* with the man. I know how that sounds."

The two of them sit there nodding like religious zealots.

"Grace, do you trust me?" Marly asks.

What runs through my head is: *Lie! Lie! Lie!* "Of course." These are the most painful words I've said today.

"Good," she says. "That's all I need to know."

Chapter Eleven

Marly paces back and forth in front of The Mirage with its campy palm trees and volcano grotto. It rises like a strange storybook in a dream behind her, intimidating and powerful in its gaudiness. I stand hidden beneath the brim of a hat so encompassing in its protection—from sun or unwanted glances—that Marly refers to it as my "sombrero."

A small crowd has gathered nearby, when suddenly the fake "volcano" gives off a great rumble, and disgorges murky red lava into the air. Marly shrieks and stares at me as if she's expecting me to run screaming.

"Don't worry—it's not real enough to freak me out," I say.

"So the anxious look on your face," Marly says, "Is it because you're nervous?"

Prior to Vegas, it's been a long time since I've had

anything to be nervous about—and suddenly I've got tons of new opportunities. I suppose they call this living. "A couple days ago I sort of hoped I couldn't repeat what happened, but now…"

She stops pacing. "Look, it's no big deal if nothing happens; we don't make any promises. But don't you have just a little bit more confidence in yourself now?"

I know she's referring to the phone call we received several days ago from Ray, the man with the "cancer stones." The tumor, he said, had shrunk in a dramatic way that only chemo and radiation usually achieved. My first bit of medical "proof" that perhaps I helped him to heal. Or so I have to believe.

"I don't know what I'd call it, but it's not confidence."

"Well just pretend. We're due to go in!"

I follow Marly into The Mirage lobby, jittery with nerves, but unable to turn away.

At the front desk Marly angles herself between me and the well-coiffed young man with an impeccably square jaw. He peers around her shoulder like she's concealing someone famous. Then he rings our host to let him know we're here.

Ten minutes later a woman of an age I find hard to determine emerges in a two-piece suit. She's the kind of small that gets called 'petite' and smells of a lily-scented cream I associate with old ladies. She guides us to the elevators.

"Marly, Love," she says, and she appears to grow an inch when she smiles and takes Marly's hands.

"You know each other?" I ask. Marly didn't mention that detail.

Marly smiles at me. "Mariam and Calvin let me rent a room when I first moved to Vegas."

"Oh goodness, when Calvin first started working for Cirque," Mariam says, lips compressing as if she's spoken a dirty word.

She passes the politeness test when looking at me, no tortured effort to make eye contact, just a sweet smile.

Before we move on, Mariam pats Marly's belly with a knowing look. "Children are such blessings," she says. "You'll work it out." Marly steps back, confused. I know in that moment that Marly hasn't told Mariam about the pregnancy. Do Mariam and I have more in common than meets the eye?

Their suite is not extravagant, with the lived-in signs of people staying awhile: clothes tossed in heaps, books stacked by the bedside. From the other room comes a heavy sigh and a groan. "He's in there," Mariam says, as though the agonized sound didn't give it away. She points to an open suite door, where I can make out a long limb and big foot draped on a couch.

She keeps talking, "He promised me retirement by now." Her voice is choked, and tears ring her eyes. "I was supposed to be in a bikini on Greek islands by now, not hunkering in dark rooms while he gets the thrill of the crowd. And for what? Does anybody know his name? Is he famous?"

Marly nods and clucks under her breath. She takes Mariam's hand. "You've given up a lot," she says as though she empathizes, though the woman sounds petulant to me.

"He thinks I agreed to this because I've seen the

light and am supporting his work," she says in a low voice now. "But he doesn't know I'm making him an ultimatum after today. It's me or the show!"

Marly's nods continuously. "You deserve some time. Can I make you some tea?" She looks toward the cluttered little kitchenette with an eye of uncertainty.

Mariam's sniffles become fully fledged tears as Marly leads her to a little sofa that looks out through a large window onto the glowing shapes of The Strip. The view is like looking out onto a planet of its own with unusual life forms. Marly signals with a nod that I should head into Calvin's room. My heart makes a skittery thump before I brace myself and walk in, feeling apologetic, as though I'm interrupting him.

"I'm working in two hours," a deep bass voice says when I enter his room. My gaze starts at his electric blue and silver wing-tip shoes. From there my eyes walk the length of emerald green trousers, up and up the expanse of legs to a barrel chest smocked in an electric blue vest and white frilled undershirt, up further to a large head with penetrating green eyes and a vividly white mustache. "So I hope it's okay I've got my show-clothes on."

"Working?" I can't imagine what he does. Reaches things in tall places? Then I remember Mariam referring to "Cirque."

"Cirque du Soleil," he says. "A lot better than the old days of Barnum and Bailey." He smooths his vest in long strokes, as though he's proud of it, and what it stands for. "Mariam give you a hard time out there? She's sure hoping you can do something about my knees," he points to them. They seem an impossible distance away from his ankles, big blocky lumps, kin to my bulky thumbs in some odd way.

"I—I'll try." My voice does not convey the confidence I hoped it would.

"The doctors want me to take drugs, for inflammation, but they make me woozy and then I can't work." He props himself up. "How should I sit? Or lie, if that's better?"

I stand staring at him, slightly surprised; whatever discomfort he feels looking at me is invisible, as though he is trained not to show it.

"Um...well, how are you most comfortable?" I gesture at the bed, which turns out to be a lucky guess.

"Probably lying on that bed, propped against several pillows—if that doesn't seem weird to you."

"Not at all." I'd rather not tell him that I have no protocols, no clue what I should or shouldn't do.

He rises, unfurling upward almost impossibly high, like a giant praying mantis. From the other room I hear Mariam's voice rise to a shrill crescendo, then ebb down beneath the steady flow of Marly's words. I can't hear what they're talking about, only the static and chatter of it.

He tilts his head in the direction of the voices and frowns. "My wife is a high strung thing. Not her fault. It's her brain chemicals—never have been right. Keeps things interesting, I guess," he says with a shrug.

I don't know how to respond, so I close my eyes and take a deep breath. "So it's your knees?" I rub my palms together. "The pain, I mean?"

He shrugs. "All my joints, actually, but my knees the most during performances. And standing. And walking up stairs. Even lifting off the toilet, if that isn't too much to tell a lady." He cracks a lopsided grin.

I suppose I'll have to get used to such confidences if I keep this up. "Not too much," I shake my head. He stares at me a long minute, as though he's suddenly just realized that my face is ruined, and I'm expecting a question about my accident on his suddenly parted lips, when he shakes his head. "Will it hurt?"

I don't mean to, but I laugh. "I don't think so. But I'm not going to lie to you, I really haven't done this much. It's all new to me."

He nods and inhales deep. "Okay then, we're on equal ground—that seems right. It's you or surgery, so I'm willing to try."

Sitting in a chair beside him fails to give me a comfortable reach, so I opt to sit on the edge of the bed, side-saddle, and rest my hands upon the first knee in question. His limbs seem made from something denser than bone. With Ray, I felt an instantaneous pull of energy. Now, all I feel is a hard lump beneath my hands.

I am about to tell this man whose wife may leave him, that I can't help him, when Mariam's voice rises in intensity. Every time her voice hits a shrill peak, tiny lightning storms explode in Calvin's knees. That's all it takes to draw my serpent out of his cave.

While cancer felt like dark stones, whatever is going on in Calvin's knees and other joints feels more like hot cement, like a sidewalk on a summer day. It's clearly inflamed. I imagine little jackhammers made of ice chipping away at the cement-like texture, cooling it as I go, until it feels to be breaking up beneath my very hands. It's like I'm working through layers of protection that have been built by his body, a wall built as if against an enemy. Mariam's persistent voice in the other room clues me in. The more I chip away, the more he seems to relax into the bed, until he seems as soft as marshmallow.

"Rest now," I whisper to him, unsure how much time has passed. It could be minutes, or hours.

"Thank you Miss," he says softly. "It could be the mind over matter but I swear these knees feel lighter already."

When I stand, I feel leaden and tired, as though something of him was transferred to me now. Fatigue curls my vision in at the edges. In the next room, Mariam has composed herself and is sitting tall, small hands folded over an envelope laid upon her knees. Marly stands, gazing down on the Vegas-scape.

"I know you can't cure him of what really ails him," Mariam says. "He won't live to be a very old man, but if you help the pain, maybe I can get something like a golden retirement out of him. She rises and holds the envelope out to me. I see it twice, everything multiplying by two as my eyes blur. I am vaguely aware that there is money in that white rectangle. I almost feel like a prostitute.

"You're a miracle," she says in a whisper meant only for me.

Or a fake, I want to add.

"You, too," she says to Marly. "I'm sorry for losing it.

New medication helps a little, but not enough."

"Don't sweat it," Marly says. "Let us know how he's doing."

Mariam nods, and then we say our goodbyes.

I lean heavily on Marly as we re-enter the elevator, which brings us quickly to the lobby. Marly holds me up as we exit and the crest of a vision begins to form. I want to pull away from it but I don't think I can stand up straight on my own.

Marly, fourteen years old, stood on the thin railing of the bridge over Lagunitas creek. A strong breeze could have pushed her in.

"Please don't," I cried. "Be careful."

"Careful?" She walked heel to toe down its length and I could feel the beat of my blood in my ears, could all but feel the shattered bones in her body dashed across jagged rocks. "Careful is boring. Adults aren't careful, Grace."

She leapt. I screamed and closed my eyes.

When I opened them again, she was standing in front of me on the bridge. "I'm fine," she said, touching the tip of her nose to mine. "For now."

The light of day has dimmed to a watery indigo that bleeds into night. A second crowd of people has formed in front of the hotel, but this time they aren't paying attention to the volcano. Something hot and fast whizzes by my head, but I know that lava is fake.

It takes me a moment to make sense of what I see: nearly naked dancers entertaining the crowd by spinning ropes of lit flames. Though I'm not near enough to these spinning flaming objects to feel any heat, my body *remembers* that moment when flame launched from fabric to flesh—the back of my neck alight and scorching.

Sparks explode into the darkening sky as the crowd "ahhhs" as one. My entire torso and head grow so hot I fan myself. Breathing makes my lungs feel full of liquid rather than air. I drop to a crouch, arms over my head, nose touching knees. Marly's voice calls my name, telling me everything is okay, followed by a noise like a thousand grasshoppers rubbing their wings together.

I don't know how long I'm like this before a man yells, "paramedic." He shines a light into my eyes, and then helps me up to sitting. He's short and freckled, with a buzz cut of hair very much the copper color of my own former hair. "I'm fine," I say, though my hands are shaking.

"Are you taking any medications?" he asks. "Have you eaten today?"

"It's PTSD," Marly says to him, sounding annoyed.

The paramedic feels my pulse, checks down my throat, and gives me a long look before nodding at Marly and stepping away. I imagine his thoughts: *Charred girl watching fire dancers. What was she thinking?* "Well, keep her warm and hydrated," he says before turning away. "If she has trouble sleeping, can't keep warm, or has short-term memory trouble, take her to the emergency room."

Marly gives a terse nod, as though she's insulted that anyone would tell her how to care for me. "Let's go home," Marly says softly. "Can you walk, Grace?"

I stand, unnerved by the sway and buckle of my

knees before gravity and I become reacquainted. "Yeah, but I'm really tired."

"I know. Poor Grace."

᙭

When I wake, through slit lids I see Marly is at my bed-side.

She tips a straw to my lips and cool water flows soothingly down.

"You didn't move in your sleep," she says, her eyes wide, moist. "I had to lean in close several times to make sure you were still breathing."

"Yeah, I learned that trick in the hospital. It hurt to move so much for so long that I just found a position and willed myself to stay there, even while sleeping."

"How did it feel?" she leans in closer.

How did it feel to be stripped of half my skin, soaked in caustic, anti-bacterial astringents, pumped full of pain-killing drugs, and then, after countless surgeries, to be stuffed into pressure suits that felt as though life was being squeezed out of me? To have my most personal and basic needs attended to by strangers, some of whom made it clear they would rather have been anywhere else.

"How do you know when the healing is working?" she prods.

"Oh," I say and shift up to sitting; she wasn't referring to my recovery. The base of my head throbs. "It feels like..." Like energy that seems both *of* me and outside of me. "I don't have words for it yet," I say instead.

For an instant, I'm afraid Marly's going to cry. Then she says, "We found each other, Grace." She squeezes my arm for a moment. "All is right with the world."

I want to agree with her, but I don't say anything. In the early morning light she looks tired and washed out. Is she right? What do I want from Marly? And even more confusing, what, really, does she want from me?

Chapter Twelve

A week later

I buzz up a flower deliveryman who has arrived for me.

Marly peers through the peephole before opening the door. "Roses!" she says and twists back to look at me. "Who would send you roses, Grace?" I know what she means but it comes out just the tiniest bit like an insult.

She opens the door to a delivery boy in a red baseball cap who shoves the vase into her hands and doesn't wait for a tip. The vase is crowded with buds, and a tiny card sticks out from a plastic stem.

Grace,

A person can learn to live with anything. For me, it's been pain from as long as I can remember. Until you laid your hands on me. Not even a

*twinge in two weeks. My blessings aren't big
enough to thank you for what you did. I'll spread
the word of your miracle, though.*
    —*Calvin Snow*

I stare at the card, then bury my face in the roses.
"It still could be the placebo effect." I set the roses on
the kitchen table. I feel a bold pleasure at the flowers'
shocking flare of color in Marly's all-white apartment.

She shakes her head as she fluffs the roses. "You
and your placebo effect nonsense. Don't you want credit
for your hard work? I would, if it was me."

I shrug. What I've done so far barely feels like work.
"This was so sweet!"

"Well, it is an auspicious beginning to our day,"
Marly claps her hands together, and I revel in how good
I feel.

"You sound like you have plans," I say, realizing
she's already got her makeup on.

"We are going out. I thought you deserved a cele-
bration for your hard work, and Drew has a discount at
this really cool spa oasis place about an hour from here;
we'll have a fantastic brunch, then maybe some spa
treatments." She all but dances into the kitchen to pour
herself some orange juice.

"Drew?" What I feel is childish, old. The asymmetry
of three never works.

She sets her juice down, frowns. "I just thought
you'd want to do something pampering."

"I'm guessing that spa treatments include massage,
body wraps, hot water?"

Marly leans into the counter, cheeks slouching. She turns away from me, ostensibly to put the orange juice back, but I figure it's so I won't see her hurt expression.

"Things that other people enjoy remind me of medical procedures, Marly. I don't even like the feeling of a shower on my skin, much less a massage. I don't mean to be a downer."

"What about just lunch, then?" She speaks into the fridge, her food-rummaging a perfect excuse not to look at me, not to let my words sway her. "They have a mineral pool, too, and an awesome cactus garden."

She's set on it, I can tell, and I have a sudden feeling that it's less about taking me out to celebrate, and more about something to do with Drew.

We meet Drew on the street outside Marly's apartment. He waits, leaning against his grey Acura with a confidence in his stance, no slouching, face perfectly at ease, dark blonde hair gelled into place. Somehow he manages to look at both of us as we come toward him, or so it appears, so I can't tell if his easy, wide smile is pleasure at seeing Marly or friendly toward me. In contrast to the overpowering chiseled picture of Loser, Drew, who is handsome in a lanky, cute professor way, doesn't seem like Marly's type.

"Ladies," he says simply, opening car doors for us. Marly hesitates only a moment before offering me the front seat and then glides into the back.

"I thought we could leave a flier, some cards at the

Oasis," Drew says, shooting a quick look at me. Suddenly I regret not sitting in back. He's forced to look at my ruined left side. "People that come there are, you know, often into alternative forms of healing and what not."

"I don't have either," I pat my pockets as though maybe I forgot something.

"Well," Marly says from the back. "I was going to wait to surprise you—" She reaches over the seat and swats the back of Drew's head lightly. He reaches back and grasps her fingers for a moment, almost as though he's going to swat her back, but then lingers holding her hand, until Marly pulls away.

I pretend not to notice, but I'm keenly aware of loaded energy between them, like another passenger in the car.

"What did you put on my cards?"

Over my shoulder she slides a card—all white of course, with dark blue lettering.

"Oh this has got to be good." I take the card. *GRACE JENSEN, HEALER.* She's left her own voicemail as the number. I am simultaneously embarrassed and gleeful at the sight. It might as well say: *GRACE JENSEN, HAS PURPOSE AT LAST.*

෧෨ඌ

We drive nearly an hour out into the desert, the conversation staying on safe topics like mermaid politics and Drew's job as a concierge at The Bellagio, which celebrities are rude and which ones surprisingly considerate. We eventually park in some sort of dirt enclosure.

"Sheesh, you did say this was a spa, right? You didn't mean walkabout?" I get out of the car slowly, stretching my tight right leg. All I see as we exit the car are more rocks and pebbly dirt, scraggly little patches of juniper and cactus here and there. A bird of prey circles overhead and shrieks, a beautiful, eerie sound. The air smells fresh but enters my nose with a dry rasp.

"That's right, Grace, welcome to your vision quest. Get the peyote, would you Marly?" I want to squeeze Drew's hand for his humor.

Only about a hundred yards further the road bends around a curve, at which point I can make out a small compound of some kind—several cabin-like green buildings. The closer we get, I see a big rock fountain in the center of the circle of buildings. Bronze sculptures of Hindu deities sit perched on rock slabs amidst landscaped but wild-looking grasses.

My ears are teased by the gentle clinking of wooden chimes, the burble of more water, and delicate birdsong.

Further past the fountains stands an enormous hanging gong in a wooden frame, golden and shiny, as though it's polished daily. Marly lifts the smooth wooden mallet and rings the gong once, loudly. Its vibrations travel right through me, leave me buzzing.

"Does that mean I have to leave the stage now?" Drew asks. Marly raises an eyebrow and scrunches her nose at him with a mock-frown, and I feel as though I've stumbled upon a conversation that's been going on for a long time without me.

Not a minute later a man appears, some kind of Arabian Bedouin from the look of his white turban-swaddled head, who announces himself as "Chris." He wears a long, beige linen tunic and blowsy pants, his feet capped in soft brown moccasins. A copious brown beard drips down to chest level.

"Welcome Miss Marly!" he booms, coming forward and taking Marly's hand.

"I thought you were the one with the coupon," I say to Drew.

Drew smiles and whispers, "One of the things I love about Marly—she knows everybody, everywhere."

Up close I see that despite his Eastern get-up, our host is as Caucasian as we are. He nods and bows to Drew, then he bows to me and says, "You must be Miss Grace."

I stand unsure if I should bow back. "I must be," I say at last, casting suspicious looks at Marly. "Chris, did you say?" I am half-afraid I will be led to a cottage and offered a chakra realignment.

He shakes his head good-naturedly, "No, Krish, with a 'sh'. Let's get you checked in."

"Sorry we're late," Marly manages a perky frown that is both apologetic and charming.

"No, we don't run on Western time here." Krish makes a prayer sign with his hands.

I lag behind as Marly and Krish chatter in that familiar way that tells me she knows him from some other context, one hand continually touching his arm, walking closer to one another than strangers would. Drew doesn't take his eyes off their backs, but he banters with me as though it doesn't bother him.

The rest of the grounds of this little oasis are all

neatly manicured and staged—for that is the only word I can think of—to provide a sense of lush tranquility out in the desert.

We enter a low-ceilinged green cabin to find a mandala inlaid into the wood floor. There are abstract watercolor paintings on the bare wood walls and a big hot water carafe with glass mugs lined up on a long wooden table. The room looks out onto another smaller courtyard with a fountain and an aviary—a big cage full of brightly colored tiny birds. The strangers reclining with towels on their heads glance up and find my face and then whisk their gazes away again.

As we wander off to the restaurant for lunch a group of people with solemn expressions follows a yogi-like woman in a flowing beige dress down a winding stone path, out as though toward the desert. Everyone is dressed in loose clothing that looks a little thin for the weather.

"What do you think they're doing?" I ask Marly, who glances at them with a casual flick of her head. "Dunno. Apparently they are not about to eat a scrumptious lunch like we are."

Drew glances at me. "Probably where the virgin sacrifice takes place."

"Haha, dork," Marly smacks him on the shoulder.

Lunch is served in a covered outdoor patio, the floor a mosaic of beautiful natural stone in the shape of a labyrinth, with heat lamps to keep off the chill that I don't feel. Marly and Drew sit next to each other, close, leaving me to decide whose side I'm going to sit on for an uncomfortable moment, though they're chatting so intimately they don't notice. I finally decide to sit next to Marly, with a good couple feet of distance between our knees.

"How'd you guys meet?" I ask, once we've placed orders for the lunch special.

"Marly was looking for a job," Drew says, with a raised eyebrow. "Before she became the underwater queen."

"So...a while ago, then? You've had your job for a few years, right?" I ask Marly.

Marly frowns. "That was a weird time," she says softly, and shoots Drew a hard look, as though he's revealed something embarrassing. I'm left wondering what I'm missing.

Drew cocks his head. "I interviewed her," he tells me, leaning forward past Marly, who's gone uncharacteristically silent. "Would you believe she was very serious and I had to prod her to talk?"

Marly wrinkles her face. "I was trying to impress you, you know, to get the job."

"And so...what, you didn't hire her?"

Drew puckers his lips then blows out air. "Oh she got the job. She just got a better offer before we could hire her on."

"And thank God," Marly grasps her Diet Coke straight out of the waiter's oncoming hand. "Or I'd have been stuck behind a desk all day, rather than in my tank, free!"

After salmon and wild rice, two staffers appear at our table. Marly turns to me. "You sure you don't want to try a mud wrap with us?"

"No, it's ok, thanks. I want to check out their cactus garden and aviary."

She and Drew are ushered off to put on sand colored robes, and I can't help myself—there's no one overseeing my actions. I wander off, casually, in the direction of that group of pilgrims, with a frowning look of "oh, sorry, I'm lost" on my face.

The people are gone, though footprints in the sand remain, and I follow them around a bend, to a large open pit, lined with tall, flaming tiki torches, glowing red.

Red hot ovals of coal flex and move, like baby dragons about to hatch. Several burn survivors in my support group had done firewalking to "heal" their fear, to empower themselves. One—a patient of Adam's—collapsed on the coals, burned her legs, had a total relapse and wound up in a mental hospital after the experience. I watch the coals ebb and reignite as though by an inner life. Skin is barely more than a tease to fire; it protects for a moment, and then yields like a virgin, offering up fluids and sinew. Fire takes what it wants, eats through nerves and melts away more, turning to ash the soft, moist inner marrow of bones.

My fear of fire is not consistent—a campfire no more inspires dread than a faucet, though the crackle and pop of a burger frying in a pan will have me flinching. If anything, I became more fascinated by fire after the accident. Only when there's threat of it inching near my face, I think, shuddering at the recent memory of the fire dancers, does it cause alarm. I'm hopeless around birthday candles, candle-lit dinners, candle vigils, but coals—I can see the appeal: fire, contained and localized.

"The coals demand a lot of us," a voice says from my back, startling me a step closer to the pit than I intend. I turn and find Krish, removed of his turban, eyes soft in a way that tells me he spends a lot of time meditating.

"*Life* demands a lot of us," I hear myself saying.

"You want to walk them, don't you?" he asks.

The coals' gentle pulsing glow is hypnotic, all potential, no actual flame, yet it holds me in a kind of thrall. As I look at the glowing embers, a foreign feeling of courage flexes inside me. A little like when the healing energy begins, the serpent merging with my skin, my bones. Maybe the only thing that can really heal me is more fire.

I only realize I've nodded when Krish answers, "Don't run. Just walk briskly, with purpose. Know you can do it. Offer yourself to—"

I snap a look of irritation at him and he shuts up. I have given enough of myself to flame.

I slide out of my sandals and let a foot hover over the top of the coal-bed, just to feel its warmth. It sizzles, crackles, the coals shifting with a sound like glass beads clinking together. Something about it reminds me of those high school physical fitness tests—like some cruel version of survival of the fittest, the weakest of us discovering we did not have the strength to shimmy up a rope or make a long jump.

All I feel is silly. It doesn't feel right unless I know what I'm offering, or better yet, what I hope to receive in return.

"Thanks," I say softly, unable to make eye contact, "maybe another time." I slide my foot back into my shoe.

I follow the spiral path back with a slight sense of urgency, as though the coals can somehow chase me down,. I pass a tall row of lithe flowering plants and around to a little cabana where I see Drew and Marly's backs, their feet disappeared inside a hot tub, steam rising like a shroud around them.

"So what are you going to do, just wait for him to strike again?" Drew says, loud enough for me to hear where I'm standing. I don't move. "There's only one way you can get him fully out of your life."

There's silence and then Marly takes on a heavily sarcastic tone, "Oh I get it, you don't want to be with someone who's carrying the seed of another man. You men are all alike—harking back to your Neanderthal roots. Why don't I just wait until it's born and you can smother it in its sleep."

"Shit, Marly—you always take it way further than I'm going with it. But you can't deny it gives him a claim to you, to your child, a way in."

"Well maybe you should have gotten there first."

Drew groans. "You didn't want anything serious."

"Oh right, now it's my fault."

"Well I sure as hell didn't make you get married and pregnant." Drew splashes his foot hard into the water.

I want to interrupt them, if only to keep the mood up for the rest of the day, but whatever glory I felt from my success with Calvin Snow is ebbing like the ember of those coals I didn't walk on. I'm a fraud, a nothing, not brave or beautiful. And Marly's life is riddled with secrets, revealed on a time-release.

I don't interrupt them but take the path around to

the mineral pool, even though I have no intention of stripping down to a bathing suit, though the pale jade water does look inviting. A woman with buzzed black hair is hunkered down in the water on one of the natural stone steps, arms crossed over her knees, an off-in-the galaxy stare making her seem carved, not human.

She does a double take when she sees me, and I cut her the slack of surprise.

"I'm sorry, I don't mean to disturb you. I can go."

She shakes her head. "No, no, of course not. Stay."

Her voice is hollow, like she's whispering to me from the end of a long corridor. Inside the vaguely sulfurous whiff of the water I smell loss, a stark, metallic scent that seems to be wafting off her body. I can't very well go over and put my hands on her, so instead I slip off my shoes and socks and dunk my toes into the water. It's neither cold nor hot, more like a bath left to grow lukewarm.

"I'm Grace," I say, voice reedy. I need practice at being the one to speak first, to willingly call attention to myself.

"Janine," she says, and I'm tickled that she holds out her hand. I give her wet hand a firm shake, and though it's faint, I have a quick image of tangled roots, white skeins of scar tissue wrapped around a pink surface.

"I can help you," I say, before I mean to. She retracts her hand, eyebrows narrowing into one dark isthmus, surely expecting a religious or commercial pitch of some kind. "It's endometriosis, isn't it? My mother has it."

Her eyes plump from raisins to licorice drops and her voice is a whisper. "How could you know that?"

It's not without some pride that I answer her, "It's just what I do."

🙰

By the time I come back to find Marly and Drew, they've smoothed over their squabble. If I hadn't over-heard, I'd never know now that they had shared so much as an ill word. They're sipping what looks like iced tea with mint leaves and reclining on lounges.

"Grace, there you are! Did you see the cacti in all their prickly splendor?" Drew asks. "Or build yourself a sand mandala?" I appreciate the irony in his voice, but I also feel cut off somehow, like they're putting on a show.

"Drew and I have been talking about ways to get our next client," Marly says. "*Your* next client, I mean."

I hold up one of my new business cards, indented with wet finger prints and Janine's phone number scrawled on the back. "Thank you, my friends, but I have done just fine on my own."

"Well look at you!" Marly says, sitting all the way up now.

Her eyes flicker, and I can't tell if I'm reading hurt in them, or something else altogether.

🙰

That night I wake, sweating, from a dream that Brown-ie, the big old bear, a resident of the Wildlife Center since I was a child, died in his grotto, and they called me to resurrect him. His hulking form rises from the ground, eyes dead white, fangs bared. In the sliver of moonlight penetrating Marly's curtains, it doesn't seem so scary, though my heart is at an aerobic pace.

Ma's voice rents the stillness in my mind. *What are you still doing there, Gracie? You have a life back home, a job.* This conjures the slopes of Adam's kind face, his unruly bangs, shirt collars never ironed quite flat, hands reaching out to his patients with tenderness no matter their ailments. My three weeks is almost up, so what am I doing setting up another client, handing out business cards?

The clock—its red digital numbers the only color in the room—tells me it's 3:00 a.m., but there's no way I'm going back to sleep now. I lie in bed for another ten minutes when I hear Marly visit the bathroom, shuffle around in the cupboards and refrigerator. I rise and tip-toe out to the kitchen. A box of Cheerios is toppled over on the counter, and she's standing at the kitchen window, bowl in her hands.

"Hey," I say softly, but she still jumps, sloshing milk and wayward O's onto the floor.

"Shit, did I wake you?" She puts a hand to her mouth.

I shake my head. "Weird dreams."

"Full moon." Marly gestures to the sky with her spoon. Even though she's not showing much yet, her nightgown billows out as she moves, creating a gravid illusion of a swelling abdomen. "Always does that to me."

"Are you okay?" I ask.

"Yeah. I just wake up a lot. To pee. To eat. To think about what the hell I'm going to do."

What a coincidence. "You know, today, at first, when you handed me that business card with my name on it, I felt this amazing sense of purpose, excitement. Even at work I don't have a card of my own, no specialty. But—"

"I know, 'healer' is a flaky term. I couldn't think of anything else that sounded better," Marly says, then shovels in two big bites of cereal. "Drew wanted to put Priestess as your title, I kid you not."

I laugh at the thought. "No, the title is fine. It's just, we're acting like I live here. Like this is my work, my calling, like I don't have to go back home."

In the dark of the kitchen I can't see her expression, only a subtle shift of her shoulders. "You don't," she says, as though it is a command.

"But maybe this gift—I mean, maybe I can help Adam, and the animals at the Wildlife Center."

"Help Adam," Marly repeats, voice hard, and sets down her bowl. "Grace, I guess, wow—" Now she heaves into a chair, and though I can't see her eyes clearly, within a minute I hear her crying.

"No, don't cry, please. Of course I love being with you, too."

"It's just," Marly says, sniffles punctuating her words, "I'm having this baby, Grace. And I'm scared. I don't want to do it alone."

I come over to her, put my hands on her shoulders; within three weeks all this hand-to-person contact now helps me control the visions. So I'm not expecting this one: *a strong muscular back, flexing, an intimate heat that is both pleasurable and suffocating.*

I don't want to pull away quickly, but it feels too personal so I gently remove my fingers, aware that my heart is beating faster, heat crowding my thighs. I sit down across from her.

"What about Drew?" I ask, sensing my opportunity.

Up close, I can see the surprise in her eyes. "What *about* Drew?" She pushes her cereal bowl away from her.

"There's something between you, right? You're seeing each other, aren't you?"

She sits up straighter, lips pressed tight together. "It's complicated."

"That's what you said about Loser back in Drake's Bay."

She slurps milk out of her cereal bowl, then answers, "Together, they are one big complication."

"Well, seems to me that the one who takes you to day spas is a better deal than the one who beat you up in a parking lot."

Marly smiles with only half of her mouth. "See how much I need you? I can barely sort this stuff out by myself."

I sigh and walk to the window, my sock soaking up the spilled milk, squishing on soggy Cheerios. Strange to think that healing is my purpose, in this land of alternative universes and fake prettiness. Stranger still to think it's the friend who saw me burn thirteen years ago who would lead me to it.

Like some screwed up version of toastmasters, I talk to my indistinct reflection in the bedroom window, over and over again the next morning. "Hi Adam, it's Grace!" No, too cheerful—he'll think I don't miss him at all. "Hi Adam, Grace here, I need to talk to you..." That sounds too morose. The more I practice the words, "I don't know when I'm coming back to work, to town," the more they sound final in my head, the more impossible to speak, the more heartbreaking. Of course, I don't even know if he misses me.

And I've never been good at speaking my mind. Even in my burn survivors group, which I attended for two of the worst years of my recovery, with feelings swelling like a sac of poison just behind my throat, I could not tell anyone how it felt. I was in awe of a man I called "Kuwait Guy"—one of my defense mechanisms, not to learn anyone's name. He was an optimist. A "Beauty is Internal" believer, even though his face literally melted away after a bomb blew his platoon to shreds. He always started the same way for the newbies: "You've heard them call you lots of things, but take it from me... you're a burn *survivor*, not a victim."

When Kuwait Guy was done with his speech, and the new ones were dabbing their eyes with tissues, the group facilitator would venture around the room asking if anyone else wanted to tell their story. Like me, one half of her face was spared the flames, but her reconstructive surgery pulled her skin down into strange puckers so that her right eye threatened to droop into the heavy cowl of sweaters hiding the territory of her neck. At least they're honest when they call it "reconstruction" I remember thinking. No matter how good the surgeon, we'd all been counseled on the unlikelihood of getting back our old faces.

Every time she came to me, Sally or Selena, whatever it was, tilting her good side toward me in a way I would come to mirror, asked the same, pointless question: "How about today, Grace?"

I had never been able to explain that I came to group only because Ma had fits if I didn't, as though I'd turn into some kind of deranged fire-starter without counseling. But the truth was, I didn't feel seen or purged or less alone, the same way the special ed kids at our school probably didn't feel "integrated" stuck away in portables at the back of the school. As a sixteen and seventeen-year-old who just wanted a normal life, coming to those meetings was just a reminder of how much I didn't want to be among these "survivors."

What I wanted was to be able to navigate the world of regular, unscarred people with hardly a second glance, to live a life promised to me in the literature of my English classes and the feminism of my mother's generation.

The kind of life I can have now, here in Vegas.

And trying to put that into words to the people who've helped me *survive* the years in between seems unfair, and impossible.

Chapter Thirteen

April

This patio is lush with flowering green ferns, their spiny tendrils like fingers all craning toward me, wanting. I'm holding the hand of a woman named Hawa. She couldn't bear to be inside the small apartment she shares with her young husband. Her bright blue head scarf is so threadbare, well-loved, one of a few possessions that made it out of Darfur with her to America when she fled. Her face bears wrinkles and hollows of fear and trauma, aging her—she could be anywhere between sixteen and forty. Her eyes are hollow, hidden. Her left hand shakes as if with a palsy.

The woman, Aina, who speaks for her is tall, with skin several shades lighter than Hawa's deep umber, says she is Hawa's aunt. "Hawa was raped." The woman gets straight to the point in thickly-accented but clear English. She delivers the words as though we are talking about getting one's hair done. "All night. Lost the baby she carried, and the husband—he was killed. She want have another baby, with the new husband, but she have trouble with the..." She looks over Hawa's head, squinting, searching for the words. "With the love. There is pain, down there." She points to Hawa's lap.

Marly is sitting on the far end of the patio, my overseer. When I glance at her during the story of Hawa's injuries—men using their bodies as weapons in a war she was a casualty of—Marly's face is almost green, her shoulders hunched over, like she will be sick. She shakes her head repeatedly. I look at my hands with concern; are they up to the task, am I up to the task of walking with this woman's body and its abuse?

But I look into Hawa's eyes, and she looks back, and does not cringe. Her expression says: *Ah, so you know suffering, too.* And my serpent makes an appearance, slow, gentle, inviting her out from the darkest place to which she has had to retreat, into the light.

ᲗᲒᲔᲑ

When I open my eyes, black spots float across my line of sight against a light so dim, I can barely make out my own hands. A cool cloth is instantly pressed to my forehead.

"Here, take these—" Marly's voice. She puts two pills in my hand and I swallow them down with a glass of ice water without bothering to ask what they were. All the cooling helps. She gently massages the source of the headache. I scoot backwards and up to a sitting position.

It feels late to me, as though I've slept many hours this time. On a bedside tray she's amassed a mountain of French toast that oozes syrup, scrambled eggs, and fruit. A pitcher of orange juice accompanies it. Before I can speak she offers me forkfuls, and I am so starved, I eat.

I'm not sure if I'm eating so fast because I'm famished or because Marly is shoveling it in rapidly, but when I'm stuffed I begin to feel restored. "What time is it?"

"Nine-thirty at night," she says. She bites her lip and bounces one leg in the chair. "You slept all day," she says. "I was worried." She fidgets with the fork from my plate.

"That's a record."

Even after two months of this work, it still amazes me each time a person allows me access and opens the "gate" that lets the serpent do its work. Without that permission, nothing can happen.

I am vaguely aware that it's a beautiful April day outside, and I should take advantage of the tiny window of "mild" Vegas weather before the bulldozer heat bores down on us, as Marly has warned me it will. I reach over to a list I have on my nightstand. Marly peeks over my shoulder, reading aloud: "Cancer (colon), Cancer (breast), Kidney stone, Stomach Pain (Chrone's Disease), Cancer (ovarian), Cancer (breast), Diabetes (trouble balancing blood sugar)...keeping score?"

"That's last week alone, and I know that's not everyone. I'm...sick of sickness," I say. I look at her belly, which is a miraculously round protrusion. The effortlessness of Marly's pregnancy gets me thinking of Ma and her lament that she never had more children, which brings a sudden, unbidden memory of my parents.

My father saying in a slightly slurred shout, "Why keep up the sham any longer, Roseanne? We don't love the same things, we don't believe the same things...Just because we've been together since we were sixteen doesn't meant we have to keep doing it. Grace will understand."

"I don't care what she understands, Harlan Jensen. You took a vow to me, and I to you."

I raced down the stairs afraid to let this conversation run its course.

When I entered the living room, Ma was red-faced and sweating with anger. The Christmas tree looked as though it had been attacked by a gang of small animals. The twinkly lights hung at the base of it like a woman's skirt roughly stripped; the antique glass bulbs had been tossed on the wicker couch beside the tree, though two were in shards on the carpet, as though crushed in rage. Pine needles littered the floor.

"What did you do?" I whispered. Ma shook her head. "I am trying to make the season happy. Buy presents to make it a beautiful holiday..."

"Roseanne, it's more than a few presents. You've got a problem," he shouted. "We can't live like this. We can't afford it, and we can't...you're crowding us out!"

"Can't we just have a nice Christmas?" I asked, my voice shrill, childlike. "I don't even care about presents. Let's just act like a happy family."

"You call this a family?" She pointed at my father. "I was going to have so many babies! My body failed..."

My father's face softened a little. "Roseanne, you can't be blamed for that—"

Ma actually stamped her foot. "That is not for Grace's ears. You know what? Take it all back. All the presents, the tree, all of it!" Ma kicked the tree. "I'm going to my room."

"Hey, where'd you go?" Marly's voice draws me back into the present. Before I can answer, she says, "Do you think there's anyone you can't help, Grace?"

For a moment I wonder if she's saying I'm a fraud, or asking if I have an expiration date. "I don't know," I say. "I mean, there always seems to be something I can do."

Marly chews a cuticle, holding her Deep in Thought pose. "I wonder if you can heal emotional wounds," she says lightly, almost as if she's not ready to share the thought aloud.

༭ཡ६

I've gotten used to Marly's style of deciding what we're going to do, so I am not surprised to hear her tapping at my bedroom door before 7:00 a.m. "Come on, Grace. Up and at 'em!"

I'm still groggy from the last healing, despite my inordinate amount of sleep. I don't understand how she can always be so full of energy, her body busy making new life, working full time, and fostering me in my strange new venture.

"What is it?" I demand, sleep still web-like around me, dream fragments resisting the pull of morning light.

"Something very important," she says, her hands flying around her like birds as she pushes her way into my room, pulling the curtains wide. The sunlight grinds in on me and I squint away. "Woah," I say. "Too much!"

Marly doesn't seem to hear me. She paces my room, finger tapping her top lip. "Dress nicely, maybe that white dress you wore to the first healing."

"Are you going to tell me what we're doing today?" A headache beats out a steady pulse in between my brows.

Marly flings my closet doors open. "Where is it?"

Though it's actually her closet, and I have barely a handful of items tucked away in there, I'm suddenly filled with naked dread that she's about to see into some dark corner she shouldn't—half afraid that a tumble of Ma's junk is going to come crashing out onto Marly's pristine floors. "I'll get it. Go make yourself something to eat," I say. "Please?"

When I'm dressed and steady, coffee in a travel mug and ibuprofen on board, I follow her down to her car.

"I just want you to know that I'm onto you," I say, trying to sound somewhat teasing.

She whips her head around to look at me as though I've accused her of a crime. "What?"

"I just mean that when you want me to do something you don't think I'll agree to, you don't tell me the plan—you just swoop me up and away, toss me into the mouth of the beast, so to speak."

Her eyes look downcast, and her smile tumbles into a frown.

Now I feel guilty for taking the steam out of her idea. "It's ok. I like it. Let's go on with this big surprise."

Marly considers me from beneath her cleanly

brushed hair—which is pulled back in a headband, not her usual look.

"Ok," she says, but the steam that was there a moment ago seems gone, and I feel like a jerk. I sip my coffee to stop myself from saying anything else.

When we pull up in front of Las Vegas Hospital I'm baffled. It's a tall, clean building, with no landscaping other than tanbark and a few non-spiny cacti.

Marly is so quiet as we traverse the hallways of the hospital that waves of anxiety start to ripple through me. Either we're here to see someone very sick, or she's arranged for me to meet with some kind of plastic surgeon, a false promise of change that I have no faith in; insurance companies are all too happy to consider reconstruction an "elective" surgery. I exhale, looking around at the once-familiar, sterile supply stations and beckoning rooms.

It's only as the scenery changes to include wallpaper with colorful balloons on it, and posters of Sesame Street characters that it hits me what she's done.

"No, Marly—I can't go in there." I stop at the doors where the sign announces Pediatric Unit.

Through the doors, at the end of a long corridor, are two forty-something people slumped in chairs. They rise when they see Marly. They're walking toward us before I can think to run or hide. The woman has long, thin hair piled in a messy bun atop her head. There is a large and alarming streak of white in her otherwise dark hair. The man's face is imprinted with tiny little squares, a pattern from the knit shirt, which he must have been pressing into his face, sleeping on his arm.

"They're expecting us, Grace. Just talk to them." Marly quickly waves to the parents, who smile in the tight but polite way of people whose pain has erased the familiar muscle memory of happiness. "Max, Celia—this is Grace."

"You really couldn't have warned me?" I whisper harshly to her. I know where we are. I know what's coming. What I cannot do.

I wave like a politician, curt and short.

"How's Sienna?" Marly asks as the tired couple approaches. It takes everything in me not to shake my head, not to simply shout, "I'm sorry, I can't!" and turn away.

The mother—Celia—blinks. "Sleeping. Surgery went well. Now it's just fingers crossed, wait to see if her body accepts the lungs. Walk with us."

Marly moves in front of me, so that if I want to run away I'll essentially have to push rudely past her.

I walk with these strangers, past rooms into which I try not to look. In one room the doors are thrust open and a family is gathered on a small bed, two young children gather around an older child—head bald, eyes ringed by the purple of a body in crisis. They're laughing, and it seems staged, as though cameras are about to film how serious illness can be *fun for the whole family!*

"Our daughter has cystic fibrosis," Max says to me, as he follows my gaze. I can see in both of their eyes a darkness that looks like guilt—they made their child, thus, somehow, they must be responsible for her illness. I barely feel my legs beneath me; a numbness has spread up.

145

"She's fourteen," Marly says. "Finally made it to the top of the donor list, got a shiny new set of lungs."

Max and Cindy have to put in a pass code to take us through the next set of doors. The fluorescent lights are giving me a headache—little floating black spots pass through my left eye, and I'm blinking over and over, till my annoyed eye produces tears, which I mop up with my sleeve. Marly chances a concerned look at me.

"Rejection rate is highest in the first few days, then months and then year," Max says, as we finally stop outside a door that has a big yellow sign on it. I don't even have to read the sign; I know what it says. *This is a sterile environment. The patients within have had recent surgical procedures and have fragile immune systems. All who enter must wash hands and arms with antiseptic scrub, and be wearing suits and masks.*

Adam never treated any cystic fibrosis patients, but I remember an NPR story of a girl who survived a transplant, kept an audio journal of her process, everyone involved eternally hopeful. But she died.

The parents look at me with their eyes and I can feel Marly looking too, and it occurs to me that I'm supposed to say something. "What is it you're hoping for...from me?" I ask, at last.

They both look in toward the room at the same moment. Through the Plexiglas window at the top of the door I can see the next door, and the protective plastic sheeting after that—layers and layers, no true protection, really, from a tiny microbe any of us might be carrying on our persons. Though I can't see their daughter from here, I imagine her in there—the scraping whoop of a machine that is breathing for her until her lungs take over. The gut churning smell of chemicals. At first, when the flower bouquets turned up in lieu of people to visit me in the hospital, I hated them. Hated their cheerful symmetry, such an easy way to check me off a list. But only a week or so into my stay I craved their scents—reminders that there was a world beyond the glare of white walls and grey equipment that kept on growing, thriving, despite it all.

Celia gives me a smile, though her eyebrows are frowning and tears pool in the corners of her eyes. "We thought, maybe, you could help the lungs settle. Help her body accept what's happening. It's worth a shot, right?"

Marly's moved closer to me; she's feeling nervous, sensing my urge to bolt.

"I don't know much, well, nearly anything about the disease," I say. "But she's in a sterile environment. I can't just waltz in there."

"You'd get suited up and wear mask and gloves," Marly says in a hostess's overly-cheerful pitch. "They've cleared it with her doc."

I don't know what compels me to do what I do next, seeing how all I want to do is turn tail and run, but I grasp one hand each of Max and Celia. Instantly I can feel the raw edges of their fear, the sharp edges of anxiety that she will not make it beyond this. My serpent merely runs alongside their grief, stroking it, acknowledging it. "I know you're both afraid," I say. "What your daughter needs right now is your faith in her, and your strength. Be with her whenever you can, talk to her.

That's all there is to do."

Celia pulls her hand out of mine. "So you won't even try to help her?"

I shake my head gently, still drenched in her grief, which feels like a hangover crawling through my body. "Consider if I failed?"

Max throws his head back and sighs. He puts his arm around his wife who remains rigid beneath his touch. "She's right, Celia."

"But what about later? If the lungs do take? Maybe then?" Celia persists, her eyes red at the edges, mouth curling up into desperation.

I shake my head, and find myself backing away, though I can't take my eyes off her. "I'm sorry." I back up a few more steps and then quickly turn and briskly walk out of that falsely cheerful department.

Marly mumbles something to the parents and then races after me. "Grace?" She sounds annoyed with me.

"What were you thinking?" I shout, when we're finally out in the stabbing day light, away from burning fluorescence and antiseptic.

She lifts her chin higher, puts one hand on her hip. Her voice comes out strained, "I was thinking that you have a gift that could be put to such amazing use. That you have a purpose, a reason for being—and we're squandering it on people who've already lived more than half their lives—old people dying of cancer and shit. Maybe that's just natural selection."

Her eyes are bright, the pupils pinned as though she's on some strange drug.

I decide not to address that last statement, which

doesn't even sound like her. "Don't you see what a set up it is, Marly? Children? No, I will not be the lightning rod for parents' grief. I will not stand there in the face of sick children with no idea if I can help them! Children, Marly—parents' hopes and dreams all tied up in one little body."

"What about all those doctors and nurses who helped you when you were injured? Where would you be without them?"

"That's a low jab, Marly! That's different."

"Oh yeah, how?" She folds her arms and sets her jaw.

A couple of passing doctors in white coats glance at us suspiciously. "Those are people with training, with medical degrees, and a hospital with legal support for when they get their asses sued. I have no protection, nothing to back me, not to mention no training."

Her eyes are narrowed down to slits. I can all but see her Great Big Hope for curing all the children of the world spilling out of her like coolant beneath a car. Yet she's not conceding that she's wrong.

She looks up in the sky as a cloud of tiny black birds wings overhead in a race somewhere. "I wish we'd known it was in you when we were younger, Grace. I think you have a bigger talent than you even realize," she says softly. "I think that refusing to help anyone who could use your help is..." She lasers back in on me. "Immoral."

The word strikes me like a spear to the throat. I feel choked—saliva gathers there, as though I can vomit it back out of me. My words come out sounding strangled as I fight not to insult her right back. "Well you're one to talk about morality," I whisper—afraid of what will happen if I let myself speak at full volume. "I'm just one person, not some miracle worker." She frowns and stands up straighter, pulling herself up to her impressive stature. "You're forgetting one very important thing, here, Marly. I have no machine or instrument, it's all me—this broken body of mine. Nobody's here to give me a tune-up or fix me up when I crash after healing, when I take in all the darkness of people's pain and then sleep for two days straight."

She flings her hands out. "Who the hell am I, then?" she says. She turns and begins to walk back to the car.

Despite the warmth of the day, I shiver. Images of waif-like children, with bald heads and hollow, green-tinted skin pass through my mind. Babies hooked up to tubes, tiny bodies struggling for breath, writhing in pain. I have to actually shake my head to clear this hallucination—as though the ghosts of that children's ward walked out into the Vegas day, prepared to haunt me.

Chapter Fourteen

For the first time since I came to Vegas, I'm relieved when Marly goes to work that afternoon, though I'm left feeling as though I've been caught walking through a spiderweb; trails of the ghostly children clustered at the hospital and their parents' failed hope cling to me. Rarely have I stopped to consider what it must have been like for my parents as they watched me recover my health.

Marly's apartment feels empty and strangely cold. I have the urge for warmth that comes from the inside, to find a place I can both be with people and be anonymous to myself. A quick internet search reveals a coffee shop called Emergency Arts that appeals to me, and the cab agency's familiar yellow car is soon waiting for me on the curb.

Vegas in the daytime would sell nobody on nothing,

I think as we drive. Drab and masculine, its buildings are not special or fancy without the wild indulgence of The Strip. I suddenly have a palpable ache for the lush greenness of Drake's Bay, the feeling that the ocean is just around the corner—freedom at the edge of the world.

The cab drops me off in front of what looked exciting in the online photos. Emergency Arts is a modern little arty café snug inside an old hospital building. Hidden beneath my most concealing wig—long hair that I can hide behind—I feel almost brave as I step to the counter and order myself a mocha and chocolate chip muffin. The coffee shop is crowded with middle aged people who seem to have nothing but leisure time here on a Wednesday afternoon. I'm just about to take a seat when I realize that a paunchy older guy with a stringy, gray comb-over in a stained white shirt is staring at me. He makes full eye contact, head tilted back and up, mouth pinched, like he wants me to know he's looking. Like my very presence offends him. He shakes his head slightly and mutters something under his breath, grinds his jaw. A shock of certainty travels through me that this is not a person entirely in his right mind, or with good intentions. I pay quickly for my food and then rush out of the café, with no idea where I'm going or what I'll find. I just start walking down Fremont Street.

The guy in the café didn't get up, yet I walk with the feeling of being followed, constantly craning my head over my shoulder behind me, muddy coffee burbling up from the hole in my to-go cup, panic tightening my muscles, my heart beating too fast. It's as though my mind only just realized I'm not in tiny Drake's Bay, where everyone knows me, knows to avoid looking too closely or touching me. I'm in a big city known for its perversions and excess. I remember a story I read in the news, when Ma still let me read the *Chronicles* tossed onto our porch. A woman in New York lived through a small plane crash, lost her husband, her dominant hand, and most of the skin off her face. But she lived and went back to school, becoming a veterinarian. Then one day some very sick guy followed her, accused her of being a demon come to kill him, and raped and murdered her right in the middle of the afternoon with a pocket knife.

Ma found me crying into one of the cats, forbade me to read the newspapers, and to her credit, took out the trash long enough to rid those papers from my view.

I am moving so fast and with such panic that I don't see the crack in the cement until my shoe is tripping over it, coffee flying up into the air and then back down on me like tropical rain.

I'm not injured, just a little startled. Even more startled when nobody on the streets stops to ask if I'm okay.

It hits me all at once then, in a wave of self-pity that morphs into a weird joy: other than the creepy guy in the coffee shop, few people have bothered to look twice at me. I am not Grace-the-burn-victim and helpless wonder from Drake's Bay, who must be treated with kid gloves; I'm just another body among the masses. These tears I cry are of relief.

When I look up, I see that I'm in front of a gallery. The photo in the window display—as big as the entire square of glass, is of a woman, naked except for black underwear, her body classically hourglass, hugging herself as she looks down a row of books in a tiny library, lit by one tiny, mushroom-shaped lamp.

I shake off coffee from my hands, toss the empty cup into the garbage can on the sidewalk, and enter the gallery as though it was my destination all along. Every photo, each one nearly as big as me, is a black and white of people's backs standing in states of partial dress before different corridors—a young boy in pajama bottoms looking down the dark hallway of a home framed by family pictures, ostensibly at night, lit only by the moon. An elderly person in a hospital gown, knobby edges of spine showing through—it's impossible to tell if the subject is male or female—staring down a hallway marked "surgery."

"Do you like them?" a voice at my right ear says suddenly, and I jerk around, glad the speaker is on my good side. The squeak of surprise comes out of me before I can stop myself. I know he's a man because of his deep voice, but I'm looking into a cartoon page, an ancient map—I'm not sure frankly what I'm seeing, so bold and all-consuming are the tattoos upon his face. There's not a centimeter of actual skin left that isn't inked. The design is somewhere between aboriginal and comic book. Bright blue, green and red—black stripes that look like skid marks left by a car, symbols crowding the spaces between the lines. His dark green eyes blinking out of the face make him look as though he's peering up at me from beneath a child's toy chest.

If he's as surprised by the terrain of my face, he

doesn't register it, or perhaps surprise is simply lost in a face like his.

Fortunately, Ma raised me to be polite. My nod is so vigorous my neck muscles pinch. "I do like the photos."

"My show's almost over. Glad you got to see them." He sweeps a hand around the gallery.

"Oh, they're yours!" I point at one dumbly.

The tattoos over his top lip rise to meet those of his cheeks, and I realize he's smiling.

"Gus." He puts out a hand and I chuckle, both because it is so smooth and unblemished by ink, and to hide my own anxiety at showing my thumb.

"Grace." I shake quickly, and detect a strong, kind energy in him that makes me feel instantly at ease, releasing my hand before my serpent gets too curious.

"Why do you photograph them from behind?" I ask.

He gazes at me for a long moment, and I force myself not to trace every image—Egyptian ahnks, God's eyes, the infinity loop, all vibrating just slightly with the life in his cheeks.

"This series is about shame," he says. "Hiding and fear, and frailty."

I consider the image of the young boy again. "So, you're depicting shame, or trying to overcome it somehow?"

He smiles his twisted-picture smile again, and two tiny doves kiss on his cheek. "I'm showing that we all feel it, no matter the circumstances."

The question is on my lips before I can stop myself, "So did you tattoo yourself before or after you started this series?"

A tall blonde woman in a red suit—not a tattoo, or for that matter, a blemish on her—drifts in from a back room somewhere, perches on a stool at a desk in the back of the room. She looks almost like an art piece herself.

"I tattooed myself when I got clean as a reminder of the shit that I wrought when I was high."

"Drugs," I nod, as though I, too, have been there. Ma was militant in doling out the narcotic pain—initially morphine, then downgrading to Vicodin and eventually just ibuprofen—demanding I sweat it out whenever possible.

"Drugs," he barks a laugh. "Gateways to higher consciousness my ass."

"How about now?" I ask.

"Now? Now I'm so busy looking through the lens I don't think a whole lot about my own face. It's a great conversation starter. I don't look at myself very often. I still feel like me beneath the skin."

I'm taking in his words when he tilts his head as though he's thinking how to frame me inside the camera and asks, "Accident, or on purpose?"

For a moment I feel an old familiar beat of indignation that he would dare call attention to me in such a stark way, followed by a quick gust of relief, like pulling off a dead toenail.

"Nobody has ever asked me that," I say. "Accident. When I was fifteen."

He frowns. "Painful, I bet? Has anyone ever told you the shape of your scars is really cool?"

My nervous laugh bubbles out of me. "Uh, no. Most

people avoid talking about it at all."

He takes a deep breath through his nose and then points to the photo behind me. "Shame."

"I'm not ashamed. It's not anything I could control," I say, heat tightening my throat, shrinking my words.

He simply stares at me with an unwavering expression I remember from therapy—the "go ahead and believe what you want to believe" gaze. In my peripheral vision, the blonde at her desk raises her head, as though she wants to say something, then looks back at whatever she's writing.

"I'd like to photograph you," he says.

"Me and my shame," I say, trying to un-pinch the kink in my voice, where defensiveness pools.

He shrugs. "You."

"Why?"

"Because you're interesting. You walk around with a story on your face, one that people are afraid to even ask you about, one that probably defines you in many ways. Interesting."

For a very short moment I realize that this is what it's like for people who do not, in fact, carry a story on their face, to meet, flirt, and date.

"Maybe," I say.

Gus nods, reaches into his back pocket, extracts a card and hands it to me. Since we're doing this, I pull my own little white card out of my purse and hand it to him.

He reads it, his eyes widen, and he smiles so big that he flashes me all of his nice white teeth—a strange effect inside his wildly colored face. "Healer, well what do you know. I knew you were interesting, Grace. Hey Gina, Grace is a healer!" He calls over his shoulder to the tall blonde, who nods and looks at me for the first time.

His wild smile is infectious. "You should come have drinks with me and Sara, my girlfriend. I think she'd like to meet you, too."

"Okay," I say, though I'm a tiny bit surprised that he has a girlfriend; leave it to me to misread flirting. At any rate, I came to Vegas to live more, didn't I? And that means making new friends.

୧ⓔ୧

So emboldened by my day out, I take a cab directly to Marly's work to see if I can catch her on a break.

Sabrina is counting out the cash drawer and two guys stand, spell-bound by the sirens in the tank, one of whom is lazily checking for dirt under her fingernails. I know Marly would have a fit seeing a mermaid out of character, but then again it is only one in the afternoon. A single tail weighs more than ten pounds, Marly told me—and my hips ache just looking at them.

"Marly's not..." Sabrina starts, when she sees me, but Marly herself comes bounding down the long water-encased tunnel bringing that metallic tang of wind to my nose. "Oh never mind, she is here after all," Sabrina says.

"I was at the beach." Marly's hair flies out in a static frizz around her head. "Hi Gracie, you ok?"

Marly misses nothing, her eyes flash to the bored

looking mermaid and she bolts for the tank window. With the flat of her palm she smacks it. The mermaid snaps to with startled eyes, goes up for a breath of air, then back down—suddenly ethereal and delicate, pretending to chase a fish.

"Whatcha been up to today?" Marly asks, pulling out two chairs at a table far from the two elderly male patrons who sit staring, not speaking, not drinking the blood colored liquid in their umbrella-laden drinks. I have this image of them having been brought here and dumped by some residential home for the elderly. Maybe strippers would give them heart attacks.

Rather than tell her everything, I shove Gus's card across the table. The card has the photo of the half-naked woman on one side. "Stumbled across this guy's show at a little gallery near Emergency Arts."

Marly frowns. "Emergency Arts? What were you doing over there?"

"I wanted to go to a cool café. Looked it up on the internet."

Even though we're sitting, her knee is jittering like she's bored or anxious. Her eyes narrow. "There are a ton of cool cafes a lot closer."

"Well that's where I went, is there something wrong with it?"

She shakes her head. "No. Yes. Well...it's just one of the places Loser used to like to go."

"Oh, I'm sorry."

Her eyes are shiny and wide for a moment. "Wouldn't it be funny if you saw him and didn't know it?"

"I didn't see him; remember, I know what he looks

like from your wedding photo."

Marly nods, but her eyes aren't focused on me.

"Anyway, the photographer of this series, which he calls 'Shame' was really cool. He wants to photograph me."

Marly's eyes are suddenly on me with blazing intensity. "What the fuck? That's creepy."

"No—he's tattooed, his whole face...he was a genuine person, said my scars are *interesting*."

"Great line for getting in a girl's pants." Marly's mouth twists into a sneer.

I know she's being protective, but suddenly I want to push my chair away from the table, storm off. "Marly! He was a perfect gentleman, invited me to come have drinks with him and *his girlfriend*. He wasn't trying to get in my pants." The idea is so absurd, it actually gets me to laugh.

Marly is not laughing. She drums her fingers on the table and shakes her head. "I don't like it. I don't trust him."

"You don't *know* him." This is suddenly a lot like talking to my mother.

"Well neither do you. You'd be an idiot to go anywhere with this guy. Did you tell him what you do, the healing?"

"I gave him my card, yes, but—"

"Oh just *great*, Grace—we know what he's really after. He'll take some weird pictures of you, probably ask you to get naked like the chick on his card, and then he'll plea for a free healing for him and six of his friends, and the next thing you know you'll wake up in some strange guy's bed wondering why you can't re-member the night before!" Her voice is at a shrill pitch.

"What is wrong with you?" I hear myself say. I real-ize it's a mistake a second too late.

Marly's chair makes a rude squeak as she pushes it out. Standing tall, with the first signs of her pregnancy protruding against her tight top, she's like a Greek god-dess looming with the power to curse me. "What's *wrong* with me? Oh, where do I even start, Grace! I'm a walking fucking disaster, isn't that obvious? Do what you want. Just don't come crying to me when it goes horribly wrong."

I feel slapped as she storms off, barks "be in my of-fice" at Sabrina, who stares after Marly as though she is afraid of what wrath might come her way. Sabrina smiles feebly at me, as though she'd really like to give me a hug but is afraid to leave her station. The two old men at the tables look after her hopefully as though she might be part of a show.

∞

We don't reconcile that night. I stay holed up in my room, pretending to read, though I can't focus. She doesn't knock on my door, but makes plenty of noise out in the apartment. When all is finally quiet, too qui-et even, as though I am alone, though I never heard her leave, in the silence I think about her words.

I barely remember what it feels like to have a man—boy, really—seek to get anywhere near my body. There is one kiss that I held as sacred for a long time—though the adult me, inexperienced as I am, now knows it was wrong. Marly's stepfather Bryce, twenty-eight years old when we were fifteen, with his boy band good looks and confidence to match.

Marly and I were dancing ourselves sweaty in her room upstairs, her parents gone, or so we thought. Marly made a stealthy dash to get us cokes to quench our thirst, when Bryce was suddenly standing in the doorway, wearing a white t-shirt and jeans, muscles pressed against fabric in a way that teased my teenage girl's overactive mind. "You look so alive right now, Grace," he said, stepping into the room. Wearing a purple dress of Marly's, my hair freed from its customary ponytail, I felt bold like her. I took a step forward and he put his hands on my hips. "I know this dress. It isn't yours," he said, his tone almost scolding. His eyes were the blue of beach glass. The next thing I knew, he leaned in close and sniffed my neck, perhaps a test to see if I'd pull away, but I didn't. I liked the feeling of his strong hands on my hips, of his hot breath on my throat. When he kissed me, I wasn't ready, his lips bumped my teeth, but I parted them quickly and his tongue made a dash, a hit and run before he pulled back, and not a moment too soon—Marly reappeared holding up cokes. She sneered at him. "Go have your own fun," and he grimaced at her and then left.

Other than that, Gabriel Diaz had a strong but fumbling touch—his fingers always roaming: jammed under the edges of the bra I barely needed, shoved into the elastic edge of my underpants, and then, deeper, inside me, a place so sensitive I could feel the shape of his calluses.

My own fingers find my nightgown now, lift its edges, touch a part of me where heat is still a welcome sensation. Adam's face is suddenly before me, stirring a powerful longing—and it merges with Gus's, becomes a shifting gallery of the familiar and the unfamiliar, following the loop of infinity inked on his cheek, the doves kissing Adam's crow's feet, the white of Adam's doctor's jacket impressed with symbols in bright green and red.

I cry out into the back of my own hand.

ʿƆGʕ

About a year after my father left, I woke in a pocket of gray light, indistinguishably night or early morning, with a pang of anxiety that something was wrong. I padded to my mother's bedroom, found only Beatrix, just a kitten, sleeping in a ball on Ma's pillow. Hours later, Ma called, voice groggy. "Drove myself to the hospital, damn kidney stone gave me awful fits. Didn't want to wake you."

That same suffocating emptiness fills my head now, clogs my chest as I wake. It's 2:00 a.m. I slide out of bed and check the kitchen for signs of Marly. Her bedroom door is closed and I stand outside it, fingers just brushing the smooth cool wood of it, wondering if my scarred face would frighten her in the dark. I remember the way I used to want to touch the smooth planes of her skin, free of the freckles that plagued mine—the only feature I was glad to see fire scrub away. And play with her hair, thick and lush, that we used to torture into styles, French braids and hot curlers, since all mine did was hang lank to my shoulders, barely able to sustain a rubber band.

I twist the knob and crack the door, stepping into the room, as shadowed as the rest of the apartment is white in this hour when we should all be sleeping. Her bed is empty, neatly made, with a crisp corner folded down. I turn on the side-table lamp, surprised to see that her newest sheets have tiny yellow hearts on them, a pale shock of color.

She keeps this door closed so often that I've never done more than catch a glimpse of its interior—and for all that's missing in the rest of the place I see signs of life and color here. Stuck into the cracks of her vanity mirror, at the bottom, are several photographs: The Polaroid of her mock-wedding; the entire staff of mermaids in full get-up, lounging on their outdoor "beach"; and the two of us as little girls—maybe nine or ten. It's one of the few photos of her in which she isn't smiling, her face a strange pout, skin curled in around the eyes. I can't imagine why she put that one up, but I don't want to linger on the old.

There are a handful of necklaces hanging from a white necklace tree, only silver and quartz, and a bracelet so oddly familiar stomach acid rises into my throat before I figure out why. Sterling silver chunky chain with cloisonné charms. Given to me for my tenth birthday by my father. The last time I wore it was the night of the fire, and I had always assumed that the hospital was responsible for its loss, or that it had been charred and ruined, as good as rubble at the bottom of a pile of ash in that tree house. To see it here in all its perfection, still silver, as though she wears it, polishes it—I find I can hardly breathe. It makes me wonder about that burn on Marly's wrist, the one she says I healed. The truth is, I don't remember if I had already taken the bracelet off that night in the tree house. As our world erupted into flame, it seems unlikely that the first thing she would have done was to remove it from my arm. Still, it gives me that prickly feeling of adrenaline released for a confrontation.

On her bedside table are several bottles of pills—three, to be exact. One is full, looks completely untouched, little blue and white capsules. They look a lot like the Prozac that I used to take, until we realized that the drug, not my trauma, was responsible for keeping me from sleeping, and giving my skin an itchy, crawling sensation like I'd disturbed an anthill. They finally put me on Wellbutrin, which took the harsh edge off the feelings, but I eventually got off that, too.

The other two bottles are the traditional orange prescription bottles that once littered my bedside table too, but there are no labels on them. I should not snoop; every impulse to find out what they are is wrong. I should just ask her, but I can't help it. The cool heft of my old bracelet in my hand is like justification. That she would have taken it at that moment when I lost so much—my anger is a clean steel sword on a lathe. My fingers close around the full bottle, and I see that it's just Compazine—an anti-nausea drug given to pregnant women. I hold up another of the unlabeled ones to the light. It's hard to tell their color through the orange plastic. I hate these bottles, though; they are nearly impossible for me to open without pain in my thumbs. They are red or dark orange ovals—they could be for allergies or anxiety. I don't recognize them from anything I've seen Adam hand out.

I'm still sitting on her bed, considering the pills and fingering the bracelet when I realize there's a shadow in the doorway. I feel the cold bite of guilt.

"What are you doing in here?" she asks, tone flat, as though I'm a stranger who's broken into her house.

"I woke up and felt like something was wrong," I say to her stony face. "I came in here to make sure you were okay."

"If you're looking for something to take away your pain, you won't find it in any of those."

I set the bottle down quickly. It falls to its side, but I'm suddenly afraid to set it upright, to manhandle her things any further. "I'm sorry, this was not cool of me."

Marly's exhale is so big I look up to make sure she isn't about to keel over in a faint. She stands silent for a moment, eyes moving from my face to the bracelet, then sweeping a quick survey of her room as though wondering what else I've unearthed. She finally sits down next to me. "I can't sleep. Usually I just read."

"But tonight?"

She inhales a big, steadying kind of breath, as though she has a confession. "Drew's."

"He's good to you," I say.

"He shouldn't be." She begins to gnaw at her thumb cuticle. "He should go find someone who wants what he's selling."

"I thought you cared about him." I turn the bracelet over in my fingers. It has a satisfying weight, and my fingers find the old charms as if by memory—the soft curve of the sleeping cat, the hard edge of the open book, the four poky legs of the colt. She looks at it suddenly, then at me, with the open-mouth of alarm.

"Grace, I've been meaning to give that back to you. I polished it and everything. I know I should have given it to your mom after...when I still had the chance to do it in person. I thought of mailing it, but—"

"That would have meant contact with me." No matter how hard I try to be fair, the accusation seeps up like dark mud through my voice.

She sinks into as much of a slouch as her belly will allow and suddenly this seems like the perfect opportunity to ask her about the fire, about what she remembers, those precious lost moments between spark and near-death. How she came by the bracelet. If I cried or said nothing at all, a human torch.

She must sense it too, as she turns toward me with wide-open eyes, inviting me in. The questions form in my mind, attempt to shape my mouth to speak them, but the fear is wider than I thought, and they can't make it out.

"So, you don't love Drew?" I ask instead. Her mouth twitches, her shoulders slip an inch downward, I can't tell with disappointment or relief.

"I don't know. I think that I should love him, if that makes sense. Or like, underneath all the damage, is a part that's whole enough to love him."

I sit pondering this idea of being whole enough to

love. Such an idea would never have occurred to me—I love or don't love, or so I imagine, having not really had the chance.

"I never meant to steal it." She motions toward the bracelet.

"I never meant to break into your room."

She leans into me. I'm tired, undefended, and I see this as our shoulders connect: Marly's long legs pumping, fast, furious, a race toward or against something. A sudden memory muscles through me: when Marly taught me how to make ourselves pass out when we were twelve. Head between knees; take big, deep, gulping breaths of air, whip your head up fast and hold your breath. We killed hours once (not to mention brain cells)...four hours vanished in the netherspace of fainting dreams.

"Ah Grace. I think you're the best thing to have happened to me in a long time," she says now.

And though I have a hard time seeing myself as the best thing in anyone's life, I take it. But I don't fall back to sleep at all that night. And in the very early hours of the morning, I hold her phone in my hand to call Adam—who has never steered me wrong, with his gentle frowns and his steady hands. Adam, who always seems to be touching the air around me because he can't touch my skin. Adam, whom I abandoned. It's early enough that I can still catch him at home. I dial and sit calmly through its ringing, but when he answers, "Dr. Lieb," the systems of my body go wild—sweating and prickling, like a snail under siege by salt. I want to say, "It's me, Adam, I miss you." Instead, I desperately scan the phone for the off button, which I cannot find.

"Hello? Hello?" he says. "If this is a telemarketer..." and then, to my utter surprise. "Grace?"

My finger finds the red icon, presses it down. What was I thinking?

Chapter Fifteen

Marly takes her sweet time getting ready to go to Gus's cocktail party, to which I'm urged to "bring friends"—a point I stress so Marly can drop the whole "getting in your pants" line of reasoning. I've chosen to wear the same eggplant dress I wore to the casino my first night here, minus the boots and the sweater, opting for simple black sandals—I have pretty, slender feet after all, the toes painted a nearly matching purple at Marly's hand.

The floor of Marly's room is a heap of dresses—which she tosses off with theatrical groans—before she flounces out in a kicky black dress with spaghetti straps and a high waist, entirely hiding any signs of pregnancy. Hair glossy and wild around her shoulders, just enough make-up on to look like those "natural" models in magazines—the effect is show stopping.

"For someone who doesn't want to go, you've put in quite a lot of effort." I assess the ensemble with a smile.

The ever perky left eyebrow assumes a haughty peak. "What do they call it?" she says, almost sneering. "Taking one for the team?"

I shake my head at her. "You'd think I asked you to get blood drawn."

She doesn't laugh, as I expected, but nods. "Kind of feels like that."

It will do me no good to linger on whatever is making her so unhappy, so I hope that the atmosphere of a party will shake loose some of her mood. At any rate, I've called in back-up, and it's then that he knocks on the door.

Marly seems to leap off the ground like a startled cat.

"It's just Drew." I peer through the slot and confirm this to be true.

"Shit, Grace." She puts a hand to her heart as though to still its pound. "You *know* I'm gun-shy about people just showing up. You should have told me you buzzed him in."

I'm not feeling apologetic. "Marly, you're the one who gave him the elevator passcode. I thought if Drew was with us, you'd feel more comfortable."

She frowns, but gestures at me to open the door, and takes a deep breath as I let Drew in.

Drew smells like bay rum and hair gel. The tips of his blonde hair glisten. He's wearing a short-sleeved blue shirt over crisp khakis. He gives me a quick squeeze and a kiss on my unblemished cheek, then whistles at Marly. She contorts her face into a teenaged expression of comedy that says, "who me?"

After they hug their hellos, one corner of her lip curls up and she looks appraisingly at me. "What, no wig?"

"A guy with a face full of tattoos is hardly going to be bothered by my baldness," I say, hearing the defensive edge.

"That's not what I mean..." Marly starts.

Drew holds up his hands as though we are two boxers who ignored the bell. "Let's just go and have a good time, eh?"

"Whatever," Marly mumbles, and I bite back the urge to get the last word.

༺ঙ৩༻

Gus does not, it turns out, live in town by a long shot.

"You didn't tell me this was going to be way out in the fucking desert," Marly's tone is petulant, her mood, expressed in annoyed sighs and snarky comments about anything Drew and I casually talk about, permeates so powerfully it's all I can do not to leap out of Drew's moving car. Fortunately, after nearly forty-five minutes of driving, we're there—but I'm not prepared for what I see.

Gus's house is like something out of Mad Max—a rounded dome of a dwelling that looks scavenged from the remains of other houses—no unifying paint color, just variegated patches of brown, and yet is, at the same time, strangely beautiful, almost seems a part of the land. A small group of people are mingling in a triangle that's cordoned off by ropes and tiki torches—as of yet unlit, though they give me a little shiver to see them.

I catch a flash of color like a hummingbird zipping by as Gus strides toward us. "Welcome to the earthship!" he says, arms stretched wide.

At my side, Marly sucks in air like she's shocked. "You didn't tell me this was a Heaven's Gate cult," she says loudly enough for Gus to hear. He clutches his stomach and laughs, hard, and I restrain myself from elbowing Marly in the side, if only so as not to poke her belly. Drew shoots me an "I'll take care of her" look for which I'm grateful.

Gus surveys his little domain. "Earthships are the name for these fully sustainable dwellings. 100% recycled materials, powered by the elements—sun, wind, rain."

"Oh, and do you drink your own pee, too?"

If he's put off by Marly, he doesn't show it. "Nah, we save the piss for the garden." He winks, and holds a hand out to me. "Come have a drink, Grace. Sara got called in to work—she's a psychiatrist—she may make it back before the night is through."

I can feel Marly making an "I told you so" face to my back, but refuse to look, and am impressed with my foresight to bring Drew, so I can walk away from Marly and not worry that she's alone.

Gus's fingers are light on my arm, but firm and directive, and my serpent is at once curious, sniffing out an image: *Gus and a skinny dishwater-blonde woman passed out in a crumple, needles cast to the sides of their arms.* I inhale sharp, and clear my mind, erect the mental wall that will help me not to see what I don't want to see.

Instead of taking me toward the circle of people talking, he draws me into the interior of his house, which is shockingly cool and a little bit dim—cavelike, if caves were comfortable. His furniture is surprisingly soft and there are lots of feminine touches around the odd little building—garlands of dried flowers strung at the tops of walls, soft but rich jeweled colored curtains and textiles framed on the walls, and a shelf of jagged crystals as big as my head that catch the light. Signs of the girlfriend, I presume.

"I want to show you something," he says, and he's drawing me deeper still into the house. For the first time I feel a pang of doubt about his intentions. But he isn't touching me, and there are too many people outside. Moving through his burrow to the other side, we emerge in a wide-open part of the house that fills with sunlight. There's a little pool with tiny green plants floating in it, and a tube connecting it to a skylit ceiling—though the "windows" are not made of glass, but opaque plastic.

On the walls around the circular room are more black and white photographs so bold each one feels like a punch to my solar plexus. It takes me a minute to figure out what I'm seeing: the camera has homed in so close to each framed face that at first it isn't obvious what each image is: the inside of a nostril—tiny black hairs like spores or anemones, blackheads blown up to the size of fists, skin shiny with oil; a planet of a mole sprouting two doughty hairs, like little sentinels; the slimy connective tissue between a top lip and gums.

"My proudest work," he says softly.

"It's amazing." My voice is full of awed breath. "So ugly, so beautiful."

He nods, steps a little closer to me, our shoulders touching. The water makes a gentle trickling sound and I have the oddest urge to strip myself down and step into it.

"Yes," he says. We are still shoulder to shoulder, and I'm aware that my heart has picked up its pace, that I like the feeling of his masculine body and the solid waves of energy it gives off as he stands against me. I recall with a little flush the way I touched myself thinking of his face—well his and Adam's, but still—and then I try to clutch the thought back, as though he will be able to sense it, too. Not to mention that I feel strangely, well I can't call it unfaithful, to Adam, as he's never expressed possession of me. At the same time I'm caught in my body's loop of desire, his body telegraphing that it is agreeable to mine, I so badly want Marly to be wrong about him. No matter what I feel around him, he has a girlfriend. And I rather like the idea of being an art project. Of being made important through the lens.

"Let me show you the source of these." He takes my shoulders and turns me around so that I'm facing the rounded edge of the wall behind us. He stands behind me, so close I can feel the heat of him, but just far enough that it doesn't really qualify as touching.

The photograph is of a woman's face so gorgeous, so

much more gorgeous than anyone should be allowed to be, that all my desire drains away into that pond behind us. She looks a lot like Marly—strong shoulders and slender neck, thick hair that could be blonde or red, it's hard to tell in the black and white. Beautiful Roman nose and full lips, high cheekbones.

"Sara," he says her name as a reverent whisper. The only way that I can reconcile the gorgeous woman in the photo with the distorted satellite photos on the other side of the room is by the mole that sits proudly to the side of her nose.

"Oh my," I say, and this feels like my cue to leave, to return to the heat of outside.

We stand there, pressed hip to hip, for one minute longer when the image of him lying in a heap next to an abandoned hypodermic resurrects itself then, as though my psyche is trying to do me a favor; heroin addicts don't make great partners, it says.

I step back, smile, and then let myself out to the cactus garden where Marly is at the center of the small group of people, laughing, with what looks like a coke in her hand. She watches me emerge from the house, eyes hooded so full of judgment I have a fierce and shocking urge to slap the drink right out of her hand.

Nothing happened! I want to shout. It's coming back to me, the way it was when we were girls, when she was my only friend because to try and have other friends was a constant betrayal to her. But it does look fishy, us emerging from his house alone together. I make my way to the circle, like nothing has changed at all. Drew keeps close to Marly, always in physical contact, if only a finger on her elbow, a hand on her low back. Marly seems to be giving in to it, leaning against him, and even, once, resting her head on his shoulder. I'm surprised at the feeling this produces inside me: relief.

Some hour later or so, I've allowed myself to get a little drunk on Gus's "eco-cocktails"—made with organic vodka and herbs, ginger and fennel, basil and mint, juice sweetening them. He's spinning a remarkable story about chasing down a mountain lion to photograph it, risking death when he almost leapt over a cliff, when a woman making her way toward us stops me cold.

All my life Marly has been the benchmark of beauty I studied and coveted. A natural beauty without trying—whether she was just out of bed with unwashed hair or put together like tonight. But this woman makes even Marly's head snap up, and for the first time since I've known her, it hits me: I am not the only one who envies other women. I presume the woman is Gus's girlfriend Sara, because she kisses his cheek, gives in to quick embraces and then disappears into the house not to be seen again.

Gus's friends are all artists—painters and sculptors, who have multiplied into a crowd. Before long, a tiny, beady man with a Freudian goatee and spectacles asks, "So what is it you do, Grace? Gus says you've got a secret."

The alcohol erodes my self-consciousness. "I heal people." I throw up my arms. "And it's all her fault." I point at Marly, who is shoving some food item wrapped in another food item in her mouth.

Marly swallows fast. She turns her bright smile on the crowd. "That's right, I take the blame. Silly me, had to go and get beat up!" There's strain in her voice, and Drew, frowning, swoops in to soothe her, but she throws off his arm.

"Can you demonstrate this healing ability?" Gus asks in a truly curious tone. I'm vaguely aware that around us, someone is lighting the tiki torches, as night darkens.

Marly smiles her cobra smile—the one presented to parents before lies were spouted, to Drake's Bay's bumbling police officers when we were caught doing something wrong, "What, you think she's going to slap a hand to your head and make all your tattoos disappear?"

Gus doesn't break his smile—he's probably used to worse. He makes a fatal mistake, though: he ignores Marly. "Well, Grace?"

"I don't know." I give a sloppy, alchol-laden shrug, recalling the first group healing in Drew's yard. His eyes are shiny in the torchlight.

"You really want to see a show?" Marly's voice is high and tight. "Hand her one of the torches, see how she jumps."

The entire crowd gasps as though she's slaughtered a sacred cow right before us. Drew grasps her by the shoulders and turns her forcefully away from us, then marches her off toward the desert. She tries to wriggle out of his grasp, then goes anyway.

I stand there, feeling kicked, but the crowd suddenly merges around me like a collective band-aid, murmuring their apologies for my best friend's behavior. "It's okay," I say to one woman who's muttering in Marly's direction. "Please, really, don't give her a hard time. She's pregnant, and she's been through a lot. You don't know her like I do." Even as I say the words they feel hollow; my feelings are crumpled at the edges.

In the distance she looks hunchbacked as Drew ushers her off. *Know her like I do?* More and more I find myself wondering how well I really know her at all.

They're all looking at me with genuine concern that reminds me of the nurses in the hospital who took such good care of me, the ones who stayed to tell me jokes or smuggled in food my mother brought. Reminds me of Adam's sweet gaze the first time he came to my bedside, a fumbling, earnest resident.

A bejeweled hand offers me another cocktail—it reminds me of Ma's heavily ringed fingers, rings I am aware that someday will have to be cut from her swollen body, or buried with her. I down the drink in a burning flash.

"Okay," I say, as the crowd still hovers. The torches flicker behind them, and I try not to focus on the fire. "Who's got a recent injury—something noticeable and painful?"

Heads turn, people begin to pat themselves down, and then several people shout, "Pamela!" and a willowy woman dressed in a gauzy pink dress floats toward me. Gus is suddenly there shoving a chaise lounge between us. There's a palpable hum of anticipation, as though I can hear their hearts beating in unison. Pamela sits down on the lounge and pulls up her dress to the knees. We all gasp. A huge abrasion, raw and somewhat scabbed runs the entire length of her right shin.

"Bike wipe-out," she says. "Can't ride again until this heals."

"Endorphin junkie!" Gus teases.

"Guilty." She nods, wispy hair falling into her eyes.

If I had an eyebrow, it would be crooked into a jaunty peak. I rub my hands together, just for show, and set them just above and below the injury. Alcohol makes me cloudy, thankfully obscuring whatever darker stories lurk in her body. I can feel the way the gravel and dirt ground themselves into her shin as she fell, the rough raw scrape of it, the stinging—it's a sensation not unlike burning. In fact, so similar is it, the healing feels easier than usual. The world around me disappears until my serpent and I are just a giant set of knitting needles, stitching flesh back together. Time passes and when I lift my hands off her leg the crowd literally gasps, a Greek chorus punctuating the spaces in between.

I feel myself swooning backwards, and then into a sturdy body. Between the alcohol and the healing, the world slips away from me like a pleasant anesthetic slipped into my veins.

ᎧᏩᎧ

What I'm looking at when I open my eyes are rounded brown corners, like sculpted chocolate. The air around me is cool, though I know it should be hot, given that this is the desert. Seeking the light source, I turn toward the window. In a hand carved chair sits Gus, eyes closed, chin tucked against shoulder. No matter how open I am, his is a face I might never get used to seeing in the morning. And this naturally leads me to the thought of Adam's crooked smile, how comforting it would be to see upon waking. A gentle snoring leads me to the floor, where Marly is curled up fetally around a pillow, asleep, and in the farthest corner of the room is Drew, the only one awake, unrumpled, as though he never slept.

"Good morning," I whisper to Drew. He merely nods.

The sleepers awaken: Marly yawns and stretches, while Gus simply opens his eyes, white pearls in an elaborate jeweled setting.

"Oh Grace," Gus begins before I can even push myself up to sitting. "That was like nothing I've ever witnessed in my whole life, last night. Nothing at all."

Marly rubs her eyes, shoots a hard look at Drew.

The denial is perched on my tongue—how it was nothing, how it's easiest to heal new flesh wounds, things that haven't had time to get dark, deep and latched on, when a powerful understanding ripples through me: I am *healing* people with my *hands*.

"It feels pretty amazing." I sit up now. My body doesn't ache!

Marly looks at me as though I've confessed I'm a virgin, mouth slightly open, but Gus is not done talking. "Grace, have you considered the implications of this? The scale of it? Have you ever considered working with others? You could be the power source for larger healings. You could open your own clinic!"

"Well she'd have to figure out how to stop falling asleep after every one, first." Marly pushes herself up to standing with a groan, waving off Drew who tries to help.

"I thought you were urging me to do that very thing," I say to her. "Go bigger."

Marly stretches, arching toward the sun. Her back makes small cracking noises, like a series of tiny lids being snapped open. "You know what, I'm just tired and hungry," she says, softly. "Any food in this recycled mud hut?"

I look at Gus apologetically, and he simply smiles at me. When we all emerge into the kitchen area of the house, Sara is there, hair in a messy bun, dark circles ringing her eyes. Her grimace suggests she's less than pleased to be greeted by a trio of strangers she only met in passing the night before.

"Nice to meet you," she says in a tone I might use for delivering bad news. "Sorry I wasn't social last night and I hope you'll forgive me if I don't stay. Spent half the night with a psychotic patient; the other half with insomnia trying to get him out of my head."

Gus laughs, though nothing seems funny. "Really, I was hoping you were going to cook us all breakfast." He slaps a plastic spatula against the counter. I think he's being sarcastic, but I can't tell, and the crackle of silence between them makes me anxious. It's clear, in this bright light of day, that Sara is the woman in the photographs he showed me the night before. Gus kisses her on the cheek, but she pulls away and bustles back to the room we've all just abandoned.

Not long after, over the heady scent of spitting bacon and eggs, which Gus assures us are both organic and sustainably farmed, he starts talking. For an hour he waxes on about the possibilities of my healing power. Every time I try to interrupt he says, "Bear with me, there's more," or "Consider this."

"I think the problem is that you're not finding any way to recharge yourself," he says. "You're like this huge engine—no, no, you're like something out of science fiction, some great big throbbing crystal that powers a starship or something."

"An alien?" I offer, with a smile. "I've been called worse."

"No, bear with me." He squeezes a blood orange half down onto a plastic dome, its juice dripping out thickly. "My point is that a little sleep and a nice meal are not enough. You need more. You need to be in contact with other healers, people who do what you do."

Drew starts chuckling. "Oh yeah, you mean life coaches and pseudo-shamans who offer people trips into the desert with a button of peyote?"

Gus doesn't laugh. "Just because you haven't met the real deals, man, doesn't mean they don't exist. Grace should be proof of that."

Marly has been quiet the whole time, shoveling in food, but now she drops her fork with a clatter, a sneer pinching her brows. "So, what, you string together twenty healers and build a machine that sucks the healing life force from their very bodies? I think I saw that episode of *Star Trek*." She folds her napkin carefully, then rises. "I have to get to work. Thanks for letting us stay." She sounds polite and her expression is placid, but I feel uneasy.

"It's Sunday, Marly." I take a bite of my food to make it clear that I'm not done. "You work?"

"Payroll doesn't do itself," she says.

Gus leans back in his chair, persisting in being un-ruffled. "I always love having people over. Come any-time."

"What about her?" Marly points to where Sara dis-appeared. "She looked super happy to see us all here."

Gus waves a hand in the air. "She loves it too when she's not beat."

Marly makes a dubious humming sound.

"Well, Grace, it has been a real pleasure. Thanks so much for coming into my sphere." Gus stands and holds his arms out wide, and I'm suddenly self-conscious of hugging him in front of Marly. But I can't walk away after his hospitality, either.

I step in for a polite hug. Not only does he hug me tightly, he shakes me a little and makes groaning sounds like we're lovers about to be parted. When Gus finally releases me, we exit the cool of his house and are slapped by heat. It's only 10:00 a.m. but I wouldn't last an hour in this air that's like a fuzzy hot membrane.

We slide into Drew's car, and I am all tensed up, waiting for it, for the onslaught, now that Marly has me, essentially, alone.

"I sure as hell couldn't live in a house like that," Marly presses her palm against the car window, as if reassuring herself there's a barrier. "Dirt all around you. Ugh. I'd smother in there." At least she didn't trash Gus outright.

"You can't deny it was about thirty degrees cooler in there, though." Drew tilts his face into the air vent and sighs.

They launch into a conversation about living spaces and comfort that makes me feel blissfully forgotten. Desert rewinds back to city before long, and the whole night seems like a weird dream. "Well, Marly, I have to say you were right," I tell her as Drew pulls into her parking lot. "Vegas is a place where people are less judgmental."

Marly guffaws. "Please," she says. "That was just lip service to get you to come here. People are people, Grace, no matter where you go." She turns to Drew. "Thanks for chauffeuring us." She gives Drew a little smooch on the lips. "You'd make a great getaway driver."

"I'd make great lots of things," he says meaningfully, but Marly does not acknowledge any deeper significance. I want so badly to offer Drew some sort of pithy statement, about how she's just hormonal, but I know it will come across as pitying. I squeeze his shoulder instead, and thank him for the ride.

"Sure," he says, in a voice full of sadness.

When Marly and I step into the elevator the mirrored versions of our selves look back at us—or rather, Marly looks at her feet, I look at the edges of my scars head on. Here are my shiny patches, the rough, warped circular patterns like the footprints of men on the moon. I try to see myself through Gus's lens. I suppose that you *could* call my face interesting, so long as you were seeing it all on its own, not comparing it to another's.

In the silence I wait for an apology from Marly for how she behaved. A memory comes to me instead, one of my own, of Sasha Lerner's hangdog eyes as she refused my invitation to the movies. "You probably should stop asking," she'd said. Every time I invited her along, Marly found a way to make me feel guilty for doing so.

"Do you remember Sasha Lerner?" I ask Marly.

Marly purses her lips but then nods. "I couldn't stand her," she says. "She always had to be Little Miss Know it All, the one who was always right, even when she was wrong."

This isn't how I remember Sasha at all. In my memory she was just an eager, earnest girl who lived in the wealthy part of town with one divorced parent one half of the week, and the low-budget canal with the other the remainder of it. "Why'd she stop hanging out with us?"

Marly sniffs in air and closes her eyes. "I told her that you could only have one best friend."

Chapter Sixteen

A week later

Gus and I pull up to a big hall. A banner outside announces *Healer Faire.* That extra 'e' at the end puts me in a bad mood. I can all but feel the pretension seeping out the doors in a cloud of incense and essential oils.

Gus inhales deeply. A pack of women in gauzy dresses, with fairy wings painted on their cheeks, shoots Gus wide-eyed looks, and this emboldens me to stand up straighter, with confidence. With him at my side, my face is the least surprising for a change.

Booths display the beautiful, jagged edges of enormous crystals; special water that has allegedly been touched by particles that speed up natural healing responses; herbal companies offering murky tinctures in dark glass bottles. "Oh look, there's a fortune teller," I point to a booth hung with black velvet drapes.

"I know, there's a lot of, shall we say, healing for show

here, the kind that left a bad taste in your friend Drew's mouth. We're headed back there." He points to the back of the big building where a smaller series of booths exhibit no wares or goods, just people sitting in comfortable chairs, or standing beside tables and chairs.

He brings me to a woman in a little booth with a massage table and a chair. She is big—both tall and wide, though her roasted-almond colored flesh is taut and strong, as though she is nothing but muscle. Her long black hair is glossy and in the most elaborate French braid I've ever seen, coils of it weaving in and out like an M.C. Escher drawing.

"Sasheen—this is Grace."

Sasheen eyeballs me, smiles slightly, and nods. She takes my hands and pulls me toward her as though directing me onto her lap. Her grip is forceful, strong enough that even a month ago I would have cried out in several levels of pain. I feel commanded by her powerful energy, which speaks to me louder than any words—though she hasn't spoken any. She motions to the massage table. "Sit," she says.

There's no way I'll make it up on the tall table by myself. "Do you have a stool?"

Her eyebrows form a funny little peak, and then she laughs. "No," she says. "Just get up there."

The defense is prepared in my head: how my bad right leg and my scarred underarms make these kinds of actions difficult, but under her unwavering gaze I feel afraid to say no. Somehow, with a great heave and inhale, my butt meets table.

She scoots a rolling chair toward me, presses her fingers into her eyes as though they hurt, sniffs, then looks at me. "Like you, I don't use any props. It's just this vessel of mine, and that's all. Unlike you, however, I know where it comes from, and what I want to do with it."

"You don't know what..." I begin to say, but the words falter. I don't even know what it is I'm about to accuse her of.

She doesn't even stop to acknowledge I've spoken. "You can call it whatever you like: Gaia, Jesus, the Great Spirit, the Archangel Michael, Beelzebub, the Ghost of Christmas Past—until you connect with it, you're always going to run out of energy. You can't run a vehicle on water—well, you can, but you'll get shot for trying—" she breaks off into peals of laughter, slapping her own knee. "What I'm saying, Grace, is that you're running yourself dry. And what's gonna happen, if you don't plug into that bigger source, is you're going to start stealing it from your own body."

"I already hurt." As if on cue, my hands start to throb. "My body aches every time I..." In her presence—she's like a mighty oil field compared to my tiny backyard trickle—I find I don't even want to say the word "heal."

"Lie on down," she says, and though I really don't want to, I do.

Sasheen puts hands on me that are as warm as the red rock when the sun hits. They feel like irons, smoothing me out, then she begins to knead me, a welcome and also somewhat unfamiliar sensation; it's been so long since anyone could touch me without consequence. At first she avoids all those places where I'm a fusion of my own self and skin grown in labs. But it isn't long before her hands seem to pry apart frozen places in me: she goes for the taut skin beneath my arms; she is unafraid of my bad right leg. I can't even cry out, the pain is so sharp and startling, so different from burning, itching—this pain is all sharp, clear and transparent. I pant like a dog in the sun.

When she's done, we are both sweating, and tears are pouring down the sides of my face as though she uncapped a bottle that has long been overly full.

She sits by my side with absolutely calm and quiet. Her solid presence beside me as I lie there, crying, reminds me of the last time my mother left the house with ease to come to me, when I was scraps of ruined flesh in a hospital bed. I can vaguely make out the memory of my father behind her but that drifts into smoke.

She leans in close to my ear. "If you don't let them go, you carry them in your body. They corrode your heart and spirit next."

When she's done with me I feel slightly bruised in some of the places she massaged deeply, but also lighter. I'm achingly thirsty and down 32 ounces of water in one sitting. Gus takes me to lunch at an outdoor café.

"One of several times when I was trying to get clean, I went through a natural healing route. Even did something they call a 'shamanic healing'—" He chuckles and nearly chokes on his falafel. "It started with primal screaming and ended with an enema!"

Laughter rises up in me in such an effortless way that it feels therapeutic, as though whatever Sasheen broke free can now dissipate and leave me.

"Did it help you get off drugs?"

"For about a week." He smiles. "Turns out that the si-ren call of heroin is more powerful than any shaman. Or, I should say, any false shaman. Never worked up the nerve to see the real deal—a friend went to one down in Brazil. I wanted to, but I was terrified. Heroin is like this big Tony Robbins salesman with perfect teeth who makes you believe that you can do anything...as soon as you drag your unshowered ass off the couch, empty the weeks' worth of garbage, and burn the clothes you've been living in. At least for awhile. And then you're just hoping to score so you don't go into withdrawals, where you feel like your skeleton is being ripped out through your teeth."

I try to imagine being in the grips of something that powerful. There was a time when we were girls when I felt that life without Marly was unthinkable. Weekends where she was grounded or I was warned to take a break, that our separation was so painful I thought I might actually die.

"So what did finally get you off the heroin?" I can still see the vague echo of him and a woman crumpled into lifeless curls on a dark floor somewhere.

For the first time I can suddenly see the "real" face inside Gus's inked one—an ordinary, dark-eyed man, probably the kind you'd barely notice passing you by.

His eyes go shiny. "My daughter died."

It's like all the organs in my body are momentarily squished flat, no room for breath.

"Oh," I whisper. "I didn't know."

"That's when I tattooed my face," he says. "I didn't

tell you when we met—I don't often, because how do you just, in casual conversation with a stranger, say all this. I checked myself into a rehab clinic. A lot of people in my shoes would have just let the heroin kill 'em at that point. All I know is that I *wanted* to feel pain. I wanted to feel the death of the addiction, my every endorphin center in my own brain completely shot. And I did. I died a few times over myself in that fucking hell hole. And when I was finally clean and sober, then I kept on dying for a good long time after in my grief."

It isn't necessary to touch him to feel the edges of his pain—like something jagged and bright moving through me, chopping and tearing as it moves.

"What happened to your daughter?"

Gus looks at the table, his fingers drawing circles upon circles there. "My girlfriend, Maya's mother, she was sick, too, I mean with the heroin. She made a dark choice, thinking we'd never get free."

I'm struggling to figure out what he's hinting at when he finally says, "She took Maya with her."

The weight of this truth, that he doesn't mean she kidnapped her child, is so heavy I have the urge to lie down on the ground, sink into the heft of the sorrow.

But Gus shakes his head. "This—" he points to his face, "is an amalgam of pictures Maya drew for me over the years. Best way I could think to honor her, after quitting dope, that is."

He frowns at his food like he's no longer hungry. My own appetite has also fled.

"I just ask you one thing, Grace, now that you know more of my story."

Looking at him now, at the red and green rendering of a young girl's hand, the doves, the symbols now tell me a different story.

"Don't relate to me in pity. Don't feel sorry for me. I'm as responsible for her death as her mother. And I make my peace by living my life, by doing what she would have wanted."

He's left me speechless. I want to touch him, console him, but I simply hold his gaze as long as he'll let me.

ᘁᗧᘁ

Before he drops me off at Marly's, he puts his hand on mine. "Grace, I want you to know you can use the earthship anytime if you need a place of your own to heal. I know it's not super convenient, but it's quiet and peaceful...and cool."

"What about Sara?" I am keenly aware of both her presence and her absence in our latest interactions.

He tilts his head back slightly. "She works all the time, Grace. And when it comes down to it, it's my place. I'm extending the invitation."

ᘁᗧᘁ

When I let myself back into the apartment, I am both lighter and heavier than before I went out for the day. But I'm left with one powerful certainty: I can't keep healing people at random. I need to choose, focus this force, whatever it is, in a direction that makes the most sense for me.

Marly comes out of her bedroom clutching a book. "How was the hippie faire?"

"Profound." I do my best to ignore her tone. "But I didn't meet any hippies. I did meet a woman who does healing work...not quite like me, but I feel amazing. "And," I toss my purse onto the couch before heaving myself after it, sinking into the pleasantness of allowing my body to relax. "Gus offered me use of his house, or earthship, whatever they call it, for future healings, too."

Marly's lips are pressed together tightly, as though she's working on another insult, then she says, "I bet he did."

I feel the bait but refuse to take it. "Marly," I say softly, "I'm not going to stop being your friend, you know, just because I've made a couple new ones."

Marly's body goes very still, like a doe the human hikers can't see. She looks away, out the kitchen window, then slides one hand to her belly. "You worry about the weirdest shit, sometimes, Grace," she says, then turns away and walks with heavy footsteps back to her room.

Shame rushes hot to my face. I'd make a perfect figure for Gus's portraits right now. If she isn't feeling threatened, then why is she acting this way?

Chapter Seventeen

Marly's flipping tiny pancakes on her griddle when the buzzer rings. "Shit," she cries out, as though she's still expecting something terrible to turn up on the other end. As she stands there considering the buzzer, the acrid smell of burnt food clouds the room. Marly jabs the button to let the person talk.

"Marly? It's your mother." The words are matter of fact and crisp, like an order. Marly stares at the intercom. "What the hell does she want?"

"I don't know, why don't you ask her?"

"Easy for you to say, Grace." For a moment she looks at the buzzer as though it is responsible for summoning her mother, but then presses it.

Several minutes later, there's an insistent rapping, symmetrical in its sound. Marly opens the door with the same sluggish effort of a teenager letting a parent in her room. "Sonya," she says to the woman standing there.

"I hate when you call me that."

Marly's mother is shorter, denser and more wiry than Marly. Her hair is platinum blonde and her skin is taut, as though someone were holding it behind her head. Her make-up is clean and simple, and she's dressed in a beige, conservative skirt and blouse. With pearls.

"It's your name," Marly says, and her index and thumb fingers twitch together, as though they'd love nothing more than to grip a cigarette.

Sonya walks into the apartment with the all-business stride and gaze of a real estate agent. "No art? Marly—it's so empty."

Marly folds her arms and nods. "Next insult?"

"It's not an in—" Sonya's eyes land on me, and in their gaze I expect to see typical shock, or years of regret. But I see nothing, she looks away so fast. Not even a hello.

"Why are you here?" Marly asks, folding her arms in such a way that she draws attention to the mound of her belly, which is still small, but Sonya can't take her eyes off it.

Sonya speaks, head tilted down, as though to her fetal grandchild. "I'm separating from Bryce, I have inheritance money to burn, and I miss my daughter."

Her eyes are still at belly level but she doesn't ask. Marly snorts. "You're not even divorcing him? Just separating? La-dee-fucking-da."

"You should be happy," Sonya says, as though words can will Marly to change her mind.

Anger pinches in Marly's features, hardens up her

softness like plaster of paris. "I would have been happy if you'd never married him."

Sonya plunks down on the couch in such a similar limbs-akimbo way to Marly that I almost laugh. "You've always had an irrational grudge against him. He could never replace your father, whom you can't even remember."

"I remember him," Marly says simply. "He smelled like mint, which I think he grew in a little box on the window-sill. He ate weird food that you complained about, stuff without oils and no meat. He jogged every day."

For a moment Sonya's eyes widen as though with surprise, then she coils that smile back into place. Her cheeks don't budge. "You don't remember those things. I told them to you."

Oh how I wish I could creep out of the room unseen.

"Well I remember that I felt loved once, and after he dropped dead, never again." Marly extends an arm out and bangs it accidentally into a lamp, then clutches it back to her chest.

"Your grandmother left me a sum of money," Sonya says, announcing the end of the subject in such a famil-iar way that I know where Marly learned the strategy from. "I thought I'd come and try to celebrate. See my girl. Treat you to something you want."

"I have everything I want." Marly turns and looks at me. "Grace and I are happy."

$\wp\odot\wp$

The restaurant is my nightmare. Bright lighting, a sin-gle floor of tables pressed close together so that we're in hearing distance of one another's conversations and poking distance with our forks. The waiter, tall, thin and early balding, looks only at Sonya and Marly. I would need a collar and a leash to rise in his estimation. Even though I didn't want to go with them, Marly insisted, whisking me off out of earshot to cajole me. "Please don't leave me alone with that woman. I don't know what I might say."

After we've been served drinks and sipped through an ungainly silence, Marly asks her mother in a tone that almost sounds concerned, "So what will you do now?"

Sonya sighs and pulls her napkin onto her lap as though it can protect her, then shakes her head. And for a moment I feel sorry for her. "The father," she says then, abruptly. "Is he the one in the wedding polaroid? I don't see a ring."

Behind Marly, an elderly woman with her hair in an elegant bun and a pearl necklace that puts Sonya's to shame, stares at me. It takes me a moment to realize her gaze contains none of the pity or fear I'm accustomed to seeing; she's actually glaring at me, as though I've injured or insulted her.

The only thing to do is to focus back in on the tension between mother and daughter.

"Don't know who the father is. Could be one of so many," Marly says.

Sonya closes her eyes just briefly, as if she wants to weep but won't allow it. "So you got the wedding annulled, I hope."

Marly shrugs. "Might keep him, for the tax deduction."

"Why is it so hard for us?" Sonya tosses down her

napkin. "Just a simple conversation."

Marly throws back the remains of her Perrier like it's a shot of vodka. "Are any of our conversations really simple, Mother? You don't mind all the elephants crapping right in the middle of the room, I guess. I, on the other hand, can't stand the stench."

"Keep your voice down," Sonya says. "Are you taking medication?"

Marly just about slams her glass onto the table. "Oh yes, you broke it, now get medical science to fix it!" Her voice is shrill.

Sonya frowns into her chest as though she regrets coming, too. "You are just like your grandmother."

"Shame you didn't let me stay with her when you moved away, where at least I would have not been so miserable." Marly chances a quick glance at me, but it's more like she's using her eyes as pointers. Her mother smiles tightly at me, and asks me one question:

"How are your parents?"

I open my mouth wondering how in hell to explain, but Marly does it for me, "Don't ask if you don't really care about the answer," she seethes at Sonya.

Our waiter returns and takes our order. Before returning to the kitchen, he harks to the crooked finger of the elderly woman behind us. He bends in close to her, then pulls back as though she has bad breath. He nods, then trundles off purposefully. I prefer focusing on this little play rather than what's happening at our table.

"Bryce and I are splitting up. Why doesn't that make you happy?" Sonya says.

"What's her name?"

"Oh just stop with that."

Marly looks away. An older manager type now pauses at the gray-haired woman's table, and I realize that she's red in the face. I can hear her voice, not what she's saying. But in the moment before the manager turns away from her, I feel it. By the time he approaches our table, I'm already pushing out my chair.

"Madam," he says softly to Sonya. "I wonder if you would mind us moving your table to one over there—" He points to one that, while it couldn't be called hidden, is well out of eyeshot of the woman who was glaring at me.

"Excuse me?" Marly says.

"It's just that we have such a full house and need to reapportion our stations to make it easier on the waiters," he says tersely, not looking at me.

"It's okay, Marly." I put my napkin back onto the table. Frankly I'd like nothing more than to leave right now.

"Really, it's just a little move," Sonya says, somewhere between placating and pleading.

Marly whirls on her. "They want us to move because that little biddy doesn't want to look at Grace. You know it and I know it. I don't pretend that things aren't happening right in front of my fucking eyes!" Marly says, shrilly.

"Oh no." The manager holds up his arms in protest. His cheeks have gone red.

"Don't bullshit me." Marly takes my arm just as the waiter delivers our food.

"Marly," Sonya warns in a low tone. "Our food is here. It's a little move, what does it matter?"

Marly's hand twitches as though she is about to slap

someone, and her energy has the momentum of a train rumbling down a track. *Marly slumped on the floor, blood from cuts that went too deep turning the edge of her yellow dress sunset orange. "They want to send me away, Grace. They think I'm uncontrolled."*

"It matters because Grace is my friend. And I won't eat at an establishment that would ask her to move to satisfy one OLD BITCH." Marly lifts her voice on the last two words and the offending woman looks away.

"You're being childish." Sonya's voice is like a blade.

"That may be, Mom, but now you can't send me away because you don't like it when I tell the truth!"

Sonya is mid-protest when Marly steers me out of the restaurant. When we're enough distance away to satisfy, she pulls out her cell and calls a cab company, but keeps walking.

"You're really just going to leave her there?" I ask, when she hangs up.

Her hair crackles out around her face when she turns back to me, adding to the bulk of her stomach, and she seems bigger than life. "You're not pissed about what just happened?" she counters.

In moments like those I am a steel container. "Marly, frankly I'm surprised by how *rarely* something like that happens." I keep my pain and shame so far inside me I'd need a key and a code to unlock them. "Thirteen, even ten years ago it hurt a lot. I spent nights crying myself to sleep after running into people like that old lady. But I've lived with it, every day, okay?"

Before I can get a read on how she's feeling, she bursts into tears.

"What did I say?"

She's crying too hard to answer me, messy tears that make her nose run, her make-up washing off in big streaks. I fumble in my little purse for a tissue and hand her a crumpled one. I wait for it to subside, but it doesn't, even by the time the cab pulls up. A line of women in sparkly silver leotards and fishnets emerge from across the street, though we are not on The Strip, and I have that fractured feeling of a dream where the meaning is trapped inside a density of symbols. I shove her into the backseat of the cab.

"Everything okay?" the driver asks, as Marly moves on to the hiccupping stage of crying.

"As good as it's gonna get," I say, and give him her address.

"No, stop and get burgers." She chews her lower lip. "I'm fucking starved."

She cries all the way to the In and Out Burger, stopping only long enough to eat. My appetite is gone; I can barely manage my chocolate milkshake. The crying picks back up on the way to the apartment, and she wipes her face with flimsy napkins from the takeout bag. When we reach the apartment she looks almost as bad as the night she was beaten, puffy and dark-eyed, make-up half-smeared around her face. Sonya is waiting outside the building, smoking a cigarette and pacing. I give her credit for coming back.

Marly takes one look at her mother and breaks into further sobs. "No," she shakes her head at her mother, then turns her back. "I can't. I just can't do this with you."

Chapter Eighteen

A tumbling, clanking sound like raccoons tripping through the neighbors' recycling wakes me an hour earlier than I'd planned to rise. Every drawer and cupboard in Marly's kitchen is open, half of their contents sprawled on the floor in little piles—bowls and silverware and glasses on one side, boxes of cereal and cans of soup and spices on another. She is on her knees, head jammed in the oven, body quivering. It takes me a second, body twitching but dull with sleep, to realize that she is in there cleaning, not trying to off herself.

The scent of cleaning chemicals rises in a plume behind her.

I clear my throat, so as not to scare her. She doesn't seem to hear.

"Marly," I whisper, and she bangs her head into the top of the stove with a moan of pain.

"Oh, Grace!" She pulls back and sees me. "I'm sorry, didn't mean to wake you. I just realized how dirty this kitchen is." It's a kitchen that never so much as acquires a sticky countertop because she wipes it down several times a day.

"I don't think those cleaning chemicals are good for you," I say, trying not to sound scolding. I reach forward and brush off tiny black particles floating on her scalp.

"Ha!" Her words whip through the air. "Chemicals—they're either keeping us alive or they're killing us, right? Multi-billion dollar industries trying to convince us of one thing or the other." Her eyes are bright and wide, and she's tapping her fingertips together, some weird version of sign language.

"Have you had coffee?" I'm slightly alarmed at the speed of her words.

"Not yet. Let's go get some. I don't have to be at work until ten, but you, young lady—" She wags a finger at me in an uncharacteristically silly way, "—have a healing today. I'll drop you."

"Let me at least get dressed."

Marly looks down at her own white cotton nightgown with surprise, as though she forgot she was wearing it. "Oh," is all she says, but nods and begins to move toward her room.

"Can I put all this away for you?" I call after her.

"No need," she calls back. "I'm going to label the shelves, reorganize, reclaim!"

I stand in the kitchen, feeling comfortable in its clutter, with an urge to empty the remaining cabinets, pull the boxes and mugs and jars of sauce around me like a cocoon.

༼ଓଡ଼༽

"Marly, could you slow down just a little?" I plead.

She swerves into the right hand lane, cutting off a driver in a big black suburban who honks. She flips him the bird and I bite the inside of my cheek tasting blood and half-expecting him to chase us down and threaten a fight.

Somehow we make it to a restaurant—my eyes are closed half the drive—sliding into a parking spot like TV vigilantes.

Marly tosses her hair out of her face as she gets out of the car. "Ever have a morning where you just wake up and you think: 'Life is short, and I'm not going to squander it'?"

Do I? "A few months ago, I'd have said no."

Her bright eyes are on me. "But now it's better, right? Everything's better since you came."

Her smile is infectious—my own lips curl up. "Yes, now I feel like I'm not just squandering my life."

She nods, then turns and begins walking toward the restaurant, Amici's.

I realize she's not waiting for me only after she's halfway there, and hobble after her to catch up. I've put on my going-out-in-public wig, with the soft red waves, where the hair drapes nicely over my bad side.

It's only 9:00 a.m., but we've stumbled into some sort of hybrid bar/café/casino. Faux Italy appears to be the theme—fake olive trees, Italian flags and posters of Sophia Loren tacked all over the walls. Red plastic booths that sigh and stick beneath our thighs. There's a bar with a TV playing a black and white movie, where four men sit like movie extras, each with a near empty drink already, one also with a cup of coffee.

In the far back of the restaurant there's a mini-casino—poker tables, roulette wheels and a small bank of the old-fashioned slot machines with the pull-down handles. Patrons are there already, too.

"I was expecting Starbucks," I say.

An unexpected waft of cinnamon hits my nose. Marly inhales theatrically, shoulders rising to her ears. "Oh god, they make the country's, no, *the planet's* best waffles here." She slaps the table for emphasis. "Loser used to work here. I think he had them put a love potion in the waffles to woo me."

Usually Marly eats rabbity salads and tiny chunks of cheese, so I didn't figure her for a waffles girl.

A jukebox near the entrance clicks over and begins to play "That's Amore."

"God, Grace, we should take you on the road—the traveling transcendental healer. Can't you see it? I bet those Midwestern towns where everyone's bred on milk hormones and dies young of cancer would pay big buck for your skills." She's sitting up straight and looking past me, as though she can already see it.

"I'm happy here." I smooth the unwrinkled folds of my skirt just to have something to do with my hands.

She nods vigorously, her unkempt hair sliding into her face. "Of course, but what about New York? Grace, don't you see how we can parlay this into something bigger? Where do you want to go? Have you ever thought about the places you'd like to see? Paris?

Rome? The white sand beaches of Monte Carlo?"

"Alaska." *Wide, white expanses of snow, cool mist, air so crisp it needs moisturizer.*

She cocks her head and frowns. "Really, Alaska, that's it? I think the Eskimos have their own natural form of healing."

"I've never seen snow," I say. "Not in person. Never went sledding, never skied or even got to make a snowman. My mom hated the cold and my dad...went along with her."

Marly frowns.

"Or even just Glacier National Park, Montana. I want to see those big, hulking cliffs of ice—there's something so vast and beautiful about ice."

Marly clutches herself, shivers, as though I've invoked the cold.

"I'd have thought with your penchant for all things white you'd like snow."

"Ice is lonely, Grace. Nothing grows in snow. It's death in white. Your heart beats slower, your body doesn't want to move. No, give me fire any day!" She looks at me as though she's challenging me to say something. "Campfires, firewalkers, fake fireplaces," she amends, suddenly throwing her arms around me. Unprepared, a vision: *pulse and pound, music moving us.* She releases me and it's gone, though I can feel it still rippling inside me.

We order waffles that come heaped in fresh whipped cream and strawberries. Strong coffee. We eat until we are gorged, until my belly feels it will rival Marly's.

With a twinge of panic I note the time: 10:00 a.m. "Don't you have to be at work?"

Marly shrugs. The jukebox clicks over to Madonna's "Like a Virgin." Marly squeals, pushes out of the booth and jumps to the floor. There's a small square of dull wood obviously reserved for dancing. Marly—dressed for work in a sexy, shimmery green tank over a long flowing skirt—begins to do just that. Despite being nearly six months pregnant, or perhaps because of it, she's radiant—breasts pressing out of her tank, belly obscured by the skirt. She looks like a free-spirited hippie girl.

Now the guys at the bar are whistling and clapping. One of them is youngish, in a way that makes me nervous—he looks like he never went to bed last night, dressed in an expensively crisp silky shirt and rumpled pin-stripe slacks. I slap down cash for our breakfast and make my way to her on the floor, with every intention of getting her out of there.

Before I reach her, a waiter approaches her with a shot glass, pointing back to the bar when the young guy raises his own shot glass.

Marly's hand closes around the glass. She smiles at it as though it just magically appeared in her hand, then frowns at it like it's poison. I'm close enough now to take it from her, grab her elbow and slide her out of this place I hope never to return to, when she does it: knocks back the shot in one tilt.

I grasp her arm, aware that I'm squeezing too hard. The music seems louder suddenly. I'm tired and afraid and the memory vision is so strong that I am powerless to the weight of it, the last time we ever got to go out together, thirteen years ago.

The club was all pulse and pound, music so loud we couldn't hear ourselves talk, lights just dim enough to blur the edges—a sea of gyrating silhouettes. It made me think of the Roman orgies I was not supposed to have read about in a book my mother didn't know I had, tucked far back in my closet. Our mostly bare legs in high heels were enough to get us in despite our age. Inside, I was lost in a sea of bodies, terrified that I'd lose Marly.

Beside her I felt like the tin man, barely able to bend my joints, but I didn't care. Marly pulled me to her, danced against me as though we were lovers, then flipped behind me, slipping her body down mine in a wriggle. Men watched appreciatively, and I felt as though in some way, I belonged to her—we were for each other.

The night whittled down to a blur, and then we were stumbling outside into the chill whip of Bay air with two guys—both dark haired and moist eyed, complimenting us, cajoling us to come back to their place.

I fell asleep on the drive, awakened by Marly's insistent grip on my fingers, pulling me out, up a staircase that overlooked the water of Sausalito. Men with money, my mind vaguely registered. A clean, spacious, well-decorated apartment. Two big leather couches, and the guy with Marly—Rick—pulling her down onto it, her on his lap. Mine—Brady—excused himself to use the bathroom. I stood, transfixed at what unfolded before me. Marly tossing off her silky black tank as though it was an old skin, not at all disturbed that I stood there watching her. Rick's face pressed into her breasts, hands unfastening her bra, and then, hot tongue encircling her nipples. She gasped, I gasped, as though I was her, as though he was touching me.

An unbuckling of pants. I wanted to call out to her: wait!

Brady returned, his hands at my waist, his mouth on my neck. He pressed, hard as steel against me.

Rick's pants were still on, I was relieved to see, Marly grinding upon his lap, both of them locked at the lips. I wanted suddenly to wrench her off, to push Brady away and run. There was an essential wrongness to this.

Brady nuzzled in, spun me around and jammed a hand between my legs, a finger finding its way where none had before. "Ow!" I said. "Too fast."

"Hey, just relax," he said. "It's ok. I'll go slow."

The alcohol haze was wearing thin. Suddenly I felt a clean, cold sobriety snake over me. We had made a terrible mistake.

I had.

Brady gently pushed me into the leather recliner at our side, leaned into me, breathing heavy, eyes glazed. I shook my head. "No, no, I'm not ready," I said. "Please."

"It's ok, I'm a nice guy," he said, hands continuing their trek.

"I don't want to," I said.

"Hey!" Marly suddenly snapped free of Rick, pulled her tank down over her unsnapped bra. "Did you hear her?"

"You a couple of fucking teases?" Brady asked. "Or do I get sloppy seconds from you?"

The look in Marly's eyes was cold and terrifying, reptilian. She was up in an instant, yanking Brady off of me with surprising strength, so that he tumbled to the floor, where he remained. Rick looked on with an amused smile. I realized in that moment how drunk these guys really were, and how lucky that we'd made it to their house in one piece.

"You think that's funny, asshole?" she said.

It happened in a flash. She suddenly had in her hands a long brass fireplace poker. Brady laughed, and I knew before she even moved that he had sealed his fate. The poker came down on his left knee with a sickening sound, and he began to howl and curse and for one terrifying moment she pointed it at his face, as though she might ram it right through his skull. Rick's eyes went wide, but Marly tossed the poker with a clank, grabbed my arm and pulled me out of the apartment. I was barefoot, having left the pumps, stolen out of the back of Ma's closet, behind.

"Fuck!" Marly shouted. "Fuck fuck fuck."

"Why did you do that, Marly?" I shouted, panting. "Where are we? I don't even know where we are. How are we going to get home?"

"Well we can't call my parents!" she cried.

"We're in Sausalito, Marly—we have no money, and I'm sorry, but I'm not hitchhiking back home again. It's late. All the serial killers are probably out now."

It began to dawn on me as we walked further from the scene of the crime what would have to happen. "We'll have to call my parents," I said.

"No!" She stopped, turned to me and grabbed me by

the shoulders. "They'll tell mine," she said. "Don't you get it, Grace—there is NO way my parents can know where we've been, what we've done."

"What about your grandma?"

She stopped, nodding up at the sky, then turned around and pulled me to her. "You're brilliant, Grace!" I was keenly aware of the curves of her body against mine, the smell of her, musk and sweat and alcohol mingled. I wished in that moment I could be her—bold the way she was bold, forward without fear of being rejected, powerful in her physical body, desired.

We had barely reached the Safeway, and the payphone, when a highway patrol car pulled up beside us. "You ladies look a bit young to be out so late," said the officer, who was himself young and handsome, and made no secret of ogling Marly.

"We're just headed home, officer," Marly said.

"Where'd you come from?"

Marly's charm hardened into steel edges. "Just taking a walk."

"A walk from a condo complex near here? Where a man says a girl took a fire-poker to his knee cap?"

I saw in her face the urge, the intent, to run, but I grabbed her arm. That would make it so much worse.

Now, the memory freed from my body, I return to the present. The waiter carrying a tray with three more shots our way breaks my reverie. "Hey, she's pregnant!" I shout, loud enough to be heard over the music. The guy at the bar frowns in surprise, but Marly turns to glare at me. She slips out of my arm and chases after the waiter calling out "Yoo hoo!" in a silly tone.

I'm going to need help getting her out of here. I dig into her purse for her cell-phone, where I find Drew's number programmed. It takes a lot of fine concentration to work the damn thing with my bulky thumbs, but soon it's ringing, and I pray that Drew can get away.

He answers.

"Hey, it's Grace calling," I say, talking loudly over the music. I don't dare go outside and leave Marly.

"Grace, is everything ok? You sound like you're shouting in a wind tunnel."

"I need your help. Marly's...not herself and I can't control her. Can you come get us?"

"Ohhh," he heaves a sigh. "Give me the address. I'll be right there."

All I can do for the fifteen minutes before Drew arrives is stand sentinel to keep any more drinks from making their way into this crazy dancing Marly. I don't know what's wrong with her.

Drew arrives in his work clothes: black suit and bright blue tie. I'm grateful for both his height and strength, a bulwark against these forces suddenly out of my control. When Marly sees him, she pouts. "Oh no, I'm being bad again, a bad little baby in need of a beating."

"Come on." He picks her up as effortlessly as if she is, in fact, a baby.

She pounds on his back lightly with her fists. "But I'm having so much fun."

"Well I think you're the only one, sweetheart." He slides her into the backseat of his car and buckles her in. "How much did she drink?" he asks

I take the passenger seat. "Only one shot."

Marly mutters and swears under her breath.

"You know better than that," Drew says over his shoulder, getting into the car himself.

"You better, you better you bet," she sings.

"What's wrong with her?"

Drew shakes his head as though it's nothing. "She just gets worked up from time to time. Overly-emotional. That prick didn't contact you again, did he?"

"Prick, ha!" she starts laughing. "This'll only prick a bit."

"I'd say this is more than emotional," I point out. "She's acting insane."

"Pregnancy hormones," he shrugs. "They do different things to different people. This is Marly's version."

"This is your brain on drugs," she says in the backseat, then cackles. "Or two shots."

I crane back to look at her. "You only had one."

"Double shot!" she crows, as though proud of herself.

Once at her apartment, Drew gets her upstairs, though she refuses to get into bed. I get the task of calling Sabrina to tell her that Marly won't be in to work.

"Is she ok? It's just pregnancy stuff?" she asks.

Her tone is so worried, it prompts me to ask, "As opposed to other kinds of stuff?"

"Well, you know, like when she doesn't want to take her medications?"

"She's fine." I'm unwilling to admit there's yet another thing about my best friend that I don't know. Marly begins to put her kitchen back in order, singing to herself as though Drew and I are not here. He sits, slumped in her soft couch, hand on his forehead. "What do you know about her medications?" I ask softly, so she won't hear.

"Run of the mill anti-depressants, anti-anxiety stuff. Isn't everyone taking that shit now?"

I think of the bottles in her room, the weight of the unknown pills like a bad taste in my mouth. "Is she supposed to be taking that stuff while pregnant?"

Drew sighs heavily, "Grace, I'm not her doctor. In fact, I'm not even officially her boyfriend. I helped her refill her 'scripts when her insurance was cancelled. As for the rest, you're just going to have to ask her."

A rush of shock. "When did her insurance get cancelled?"

He runs his hands through the stiff landscape of his hair. "Months, a long time—look, I'm going to get major shit for taking my break early, and twice as long, so I'm on my way." He stands, smoothing out the creases in his pants, but those in his forehead deepen. "Be good, Marly," he calls to her.

She raises her head from the refrigerator, where she's pulling out food and setting it on the floor behind her. "As if." She waves at him.

While she's busy putting the kitchen back in order, or pulling the rest of it apart (I can't tell) I walk past her room and peer in. At her bedside, where she caught me snooping in her pills, the side table is clear and empty. I want desperately to leaf through drawers, even her purse. I bet Adam would know what she's taking. Maybe he could even help.

Chapter Nineteen

I wake to the feeling of my bed sinking down beneath the weight of a body the next morning. I peel my eyes open to see Marly sitting there.

"I'm not...I'm not an alcoholic, Grace," she says in a quivering voice. "And I know I shouldn't drink, but it's just like...it's like the perfect medication."

"What is the deal, exactly, with your actual medication?"

What am I waiting for? A big confession, a diagnosis that will help me make sense of what happened? She twists her fingers together over and over—so fast and hard it looks as though she's chafing them.

"When I decided to...stay pregnant, my doctor had me switch anti-depressants because it's safer for the baby. This medication is...different. That and the hormones. And my mother. Marvelous, manipulative mother."

"I wondered if it had anything to do with your mother."

"I wish I had nothing to do with my mother. I wish I could become un-related to her. Ditch the DNA that comes from her."

As I sit up, my body complains in its language of stiffness. My muscles feel tighter, denser, than usual. I think about Sasheen's saying I should recharge myself—I'll go see her again. "I remember how uptight your mother was when we were kids."

Marly sniffs and shrugs. "I know I should ease up on her. I tell myself I will, and then I see her and I just go crazy, coo-coo!"

"You want to talk about it?"

Marly shakes her head subtly, and I'm tempted to press it. But she stands up quickly in a way that makes me wonder if my thoughts are somehow translated plainly into my face.

"I'd like to take you somewhere," she says. "So up and at 'em, rise and shine!"

಄

When we pull up to Drew's house I feel a little hitch in my guts.

"Marly, I don't feel all that social today."

Marly bolts out of the car—still full of the springy energy that started at the diner. When we approach that jarring turquoise of Drew's front door, Marly lets us in.

"Shouldn't we knock or announce ourselves?" I hesitate just in the entry. "I don't want to barge in."

Marly rolls her eyes at me, and pulls me through the

house then out the sliding glass door to the backyard where I healed the man named Ray. She does a Vanna White swoop of the arms in front of a big shed. It's painted a soft green, and baskets of philodendrons drip from its eaves.

"Go on, open it," Marly says. "Open sesame!"

With a deep breath I turn the brass handle, cold beneath my palm, and open the door.

Drew lies on a burgundy leather analyst's couch reading *Fish & Game*, of all things. The legs of the couch are buried in yellow shag carpet so deep it looks capable of housing mammalian life. A sheer curtain covers the one small window, a slightly crisp ficus tree tilts slightly to one side in a floral pot. The real capper, however, are two large velvet paintings of Elvis, one of him rocking out with his guitar, and the other, a close-up of his crooning mug.

"Love shack?" I ask.

Drew and Marly both laugh, their voices joining in a nervous symphony.

Marly takes my hand. "I wanted you to have a place all your own, a quiet place where you can heal, one-on-one, intimately. A little temple."

It all comes clear to me. She doesn't want me going off to Gus's to do my healings. She wants to keep me close. This is Marly's version of staking a claim. Or, says the more generous part of me, maybe it's her way of apologizing.

Frankly, it's the sorriest excuse for a temple I've ever seen, but the look in Marly's eyes is edgy and unreadable. I know what I have to say: "I love it."

"You do?"

"Yeah. The Elvises are a nice touch."

"I put those up as a joke," Drew says, toeing something on the floor, not making eye contact with me. "Sort of tacky chic. Sorry, I didn't have a lot of time to get it ready." He shoots Marly a quick look but Marly is a blur of movement, hands whirling and mouth spinning.

"You could put shelves here, hang something from the window here—shiny things, you know—a little mesmerizing." She goes on about further decorating options while Drew does a poor job of pretending to smile.

"Those are great ideas, Marly." I hope I don't sound patronizing. "But are you sure? I'm fine going to people's houses and things."

Drew opens his mouth but Marly intervenes: "No, that's beneath you. Maybe if you do a group thing, but people should be coming to you, and Drew's got the perfect yard. The ambiance is right, charming, peaceful."

Her fervor makes me feel I'm being sold a piece of real estate I'm not sure I can afford.

Drew clears his throat after a heavy glance from Marly. "If it's okay with you, Grace, you could do trades on friends of mine—not that many—every month instead of paying rent."

"Won't this inconvenience you, Drew?" I want to give him an out. "To have people traipsing through your yard?"

Another glance from Marly and I start to feel awkward. There's reluctance in Drew's every gesture and expression.

He shakes his head. "Oh no, you can let yourselves in around the back. Besides, it means I'll get to see more of you lovely ladies." He looks at Marly when he says this, but his eyes are hard.

Her eyes, in contrast, are moist, and she takes my hand for only a second. "I know I've put you through a lot, Grace. I just want you to know that it a privilege for me to get to watch you do what you do. I am so lucky to have you as my friend. And with you in my life, I know that I can do things the right way."

Drew smiles perfunctorily and claps his hands together. "Well, there you go," he says.

"This is more than I could ask for," I say, for Marly's benefit. "I'm touched."

ᛡᚷᚷ

Since Marly's attack, it's not uncommon for Marly to glare at some poor resident in the parking garage that she doesn't recognize, clenching her keys like little daggers between her fingers. So I am not the slightest bit surprised when she shouts, "What do you want?" to a man who's gotten off the elevator and is walking our way.

"Adam?" I say. I don't quite believe it's him. He holds a gray sweater folded over his arms, and a small backpack on his left shoulder. He's wearing a jersey-knit cobalt blue shirt that is so different from his doctor's coat.

"You didn't tell me you invited the good doctor." Marly elbows me suggestively in the ribs.

"She didn't." He gives her an assessing glance, as though she's an ailing patient. She returns it, and I feel like joking that we need pistols so they can have an old-fashioned duel.

"Well, I'll give you two some time." Marly winks at me before heading to the elevators.

When the elevator doors close on her, Adam moves closer to me but stops just shy of touching me. He is gazing down at me with such obvious and familiar tenderness, I wonder how I ever missed it in his eyes before. I relish the gasp he makes when I grab him in the kind of hug the pain made impossible for years. I never knew that he smelled like cinnamon and earth after a rain. His heart is beating almost as hard as my own.

"It doesn't hurt, to touch?" he asks.

"Not with you," I whisper into his neck. The larger truth, that learning to heal has channeled the pain, I keep to myself.

"Is it weird that I came?" he says into my shoulder.

"No, I'm just so surprised." I am overcome by the density of Adam in my arms. But as we hold each other, I feel a ripple of sorrow, and an image starts to form and I start to pull back. Before I can organize my thoughts, he kisses me. It's not exactly lustful, yet definitely not the kind of kiss you give a friend.

"Come up to the apartment," I say, flustered.

When we make our way inside, Adam regards Marly's apartment with wide-eyed awe. "Is she color blind?" he whispers.

"No, she says it keeps her head uncrowded." For the first time I realize how odd this sounds.

Adam raises an eyebrow but says nothing.

Marly appears to have hidden herself in her room, and I am grateful. But now that we're alone, I'm afraid of what he'll say to me.

"I know you called. So I thought I'd reply in person. Make a statement."

I look down at my hands, my thumbs sitting like disobedient animals in my lap. "I'm sorry I took the cowardly way out. I didn't know how to tell you I was going to stay after everything you've done for me."

"I'm not mad at you; you inspire me, Grace."

Now I look at him, surprise flapping wide wings inside me. "That's not what I thought you were going to say."

"Coming to Vegas, finding out what Marly has to offer—I know that was guts at work. I was afraid I might not see you again, and then, I realized hey, I'm a grown man, I can go visit. What have you been up to?"

His words light a sun in my heart. Then it's eclipsed. What have I been doing all these months? Do I tell a man who's gone through medical school, a man who patently disapproved of "energy healing" that I'm flinging my hands at illness all over Vegas? *Don't tell him*, says Marly's voice in my head.

I lean to kiss him, and he kisses me back willingly, but then pulls himself away. "I didn't come here with any expectations, Grace. Don't feel like you have to—"

There's no way I'm going to let him finish that sentence; I press myself to him, surprised at how well our bodies match in size. My breath is quick and unbidden. Then, without any warning *I* enter *him*—or so it feels.

My serpent is drawn directly into the center of his chest, just beyond his heart. I gasp. This place inside Adam I've found is icy, literally; my whole body is chilled and numb as though I've been dumped into ice water. I see her so clearly for a moment that I almost wrench myself out of his arms. She died, drowned in a near-frozen lake. She was older, and everything to him, more mother than sister. Her brown hair fans out like a mermaid's as she floats face down. Waves of tender feelings tell me she protected him and nurtured him.

"Grace, look at me," Adam says. It takes everything I have to find his eyes, to leave behind the blank gaze of the dead girl, and the spiky waves of pain in him.

I look at him, and he looks at me—monster and maiden both—as if I am beautiful.

My serpent catches another scent and flicks back to the center of Adam, alerting me to small injuries along the way: a barely healed broken clavicle from a bicycle accident; a tiny bee-bee gun pellet still embedded deep in his left shoulder; a gall stone small and unnoticeable sitting at the throat of his gall bladder. He gasps as though I have poked him, and though I try to fight it, my serpent curls its tail around these damages and fixes those it can. Once it has satisfied itself with the physical ailments, it dives near his heart again, into a deep ache, not quite grief, not quite sorrow at the sight of a patient groaning for relief in her hospital bed, thumbs sewn deep into her abdomen in order to heal them. "Smother me," she says. "No one will know you did it."

Me. Thirteen years ago.

"In order to save your thumbs, we have to do a special

surgery," the resident tells me casually, like we are discussing the hospital menu. My thumbs burned badly. I'd reached toward my face to protect my eyes, plunging them into the corona of fire fueled by my hair-spray and the polyester boa wrapped several times around my neck. "I won't lie to you, Grace," he says, pursing his lips. "It will be difficult. You will need lots of support." I barely had eyelids and couldn't smile. I had not been to the bathroom by myself in one-hundred days.

"More help than this? What's the difference?"

He sat in the uncomfortable plastic chair by my bedside and took my hand, squeezing the wrist lightly. "We'll make an incision on the lateral side of your abdomen. There are lots of blood vessels there, with rich blood supply. We'll insert your thumb and sew it loosely into the incision so that your thumb gets this much needed blood flow to save the damaged arteries. This way, you won't have to lose your thumbs. The thing is, you can either do them one at a time, or both at once."

"How long?" I asked, as if time meant much anymore.

"Each side will take about three months."

"Both." I decided. "Do them both at once."

"You're sure? You'll need someone to do everything for you, Grace. Absolutely everything. You might feel...trapped."

"I already feel trapped."

I thought I was making the right choice, but within the first hour after I swam through the haze of anesthesia to feel myself pinned, I realized I'd underestimated what it would be like to lose the use of both my arms and appre-

ciated that there were conditions worse than being burned alive. The only thing that kept me from rolling into a position where I could smother myself—which I thought about at least once a day—was Adam's kindness.

"Grace, you're crying," Adam-of-the-Present says.

I push him away. It's the only way I can break the cord, pull the serpent back from its descent into parts of Adam even I can't bear to go.

"I'm sorry."

He looks stricken and I know it's only partly due to my confusing messages; in touching upon these pains, I've awakened them inside him. Is this truly my lot? He murmurs, "It's okay" several times into my ear. I've never felt less sure of that.

Marly's trilling entry jars us both. "Hello love birds! Grace you have a healing—"

Fortunately she catches the warning in my widened eyes and the slight tilt of my head.

She starts again. "A healing day at the spa scheduled."

Adam looks between us. If he has registered anything odd in her words, he doesn't reveal it. He plants his hands on his pressed khaki thighs and rises, face remade in his well-meaning-doctor expression of general cheer. "Well I'll leave you to it, then."

"Adam, I—" But I don't know what.

Adam kisses the top of my head, and murmurs into my ear, "I'm staying at the Best Western about twenty minutes from here. He smiles politely at Marly. "It was nice to meet you," he says, and then he pushes past her and at the sound of the apartment door clicking shut, my stomach lurches.

Marly turns and stares in the direction he's gone, then back to me.

"I can't tell him, Marly. And if I can't tell him about the healings, then I can't be with him, can I?"

"Why can't you tell him?"

"I can't believe you'd ask that! He's a *doctor*."

Marly's expression is on the verge of offended, but she shrugs. "Kind of came a long way to see you, didn't he?" She strokes her belly. "But you do need to get ready. It's your last group healing."

Chapter Twenty

My mother's words travel with me: *You have to be-lieve in something bigger than you.* Today I am healing in a church—one that has been converted into a meeting hall, but which still bears the pews, altar and stained glass panels of the story of Jesus's crucifixion. I stare at myself in a mirror, and recoil from what I see. Perhaps it's the sallow fluorescents, but my skin looks shinier, puckered at the edges of my scars worse than usual. Or have I become too much a stranger to this face? Sometimes, more than anything else, I miss my hair. I hated it, back then—frizzy and flyaway at worst, and I could never go more than a day without washing it. But now? To run my fingers through it, to smooth its softness against my skin instead of these competent wigs, oh! Several weeks back I'd whipped off my wig in the middle of a healing just for relief from the heat without even knowing it. The audience had cried out with a kind of wild joy.

"They want to see the whole you stripped down to nothing," Marly'd said. So we adopted the "removal of the wig" as part of the event. I come out, say a few words, meet people, and then before I begin, I pull off the wig. It felt a little showy at first, but I liked the symbolism of it—and now I don't have to worry about over-heating.

Marly is out front gathering money and chatting people up, taking their names and ailments down on little slips of paper, which I will draw from once I get out there.

I scratch a suddenly very itchy patch of skin at the back of my neck, and Marly is at the door to the little room "You okay?" she asks. "Grace, I think there're a hundred people out there!"

I've seen crowds of thirty, but never one hundred. I can work on maybe eight people in a sitting before the heaviness forces me into a blackout sleep. "I'm tired today. I feel funny." I must sound like a diva.

She frowns and taps her fingers on the door jamb. "What can I do to help you feel better?" Marly comes over and gently strokes my shoulders. "Only do a few healings out there." She nods toward the door. "I don't think anyone's going to be disappointed."

I feel like a reluctant toddler as Marly escorts me out to the stage.

From the cup I select the first name and ailment, call out "JoAnne Templeton," and a middle-aged woman in a pale blue pants suit limps up to the dais upon which Marly's dragged a chaise lounge from who-knows-where. I instruct JoAnne to rest into the chaise lounge, put pillows behind her neck and under her knees. She has skinny legs and arms, but an enormous belly. The little piece of paper reads: *Uterine cancer.* The swelling is bloating, I know. Cancer patients seem to take on water like leaky ships, as if to buffer the healthy cells from the sick.

My hands ache as I hold them over her. When I rest them upon her, I feel as though someone has opened a window and let in a humid and cloying draft of air. She groans slightly and shifts, and my serpent and I make our way into the wet and sticky interiors of her illness. It's like diving from a high ledge into a stagnant pond, thick with debris and sludge. I feel momentarily nauseous as we burrow into the sickness until my serpent's light begins to cut through it, pull it apart like taffy, dissolve its darkness...*Can't get comfortable. It hurts. Not just change-of-life.* I hear these words in my head, which is not uncommon, but my serpent suddenly moves away from the woman beneath us, pulling me as though beyond the door. Much farther away than that. My client shifts uncomfortably. *Damn doctors will just try to make me pay for expensive treatments.* I will my serpent back to my client's body, but the words just keep coming. *Nothing anyone can do anyway. Grace doesn't need to know. She can't heal me.*

"Ma?" My hands pop off my client and I sit up, staring straight ahead but not really seeing the crowd. "Oh my God! Ma." Though I am vaguely aware that the woman on the chaise lounge has had an incomplete healing, I can't stop myself. I've picked up on Ma's thoughts. Ma is sick, and she has no plans to tell me about it. I ease down off the stage, which cramps my right leg, and stumble down the center of the aisle. People stare at me and murmur to each other.

Time slows not unlike dreams, in which I can run but not get anywhere. I walk fast, panting, several blocks away from the building and find myself standing on a corner populated by fast food restaurants. It's a few minutes before all the swirling energy of urgency settles long enough to let me think clearly. I must look a strange sight standing on the corner, my hand shading my eyes from the lights, dazed, like I've just been thrust out of a moving vehicle. The cell phone I keep on me is tucked into my skirt pocket, and I withdraw it. It takes my ungainly fingers a long minute to dial my own phone number.

To my great surprise, without more than a couple of rings, Ma's croaky voice answers, "Yeah?" The phone makes her sound tinny, distant.

"Ma, God damn it, why didn't you tell me you were sick!"

Ma clears her throat several times. "Gracie, my little heathen," she says, though her tone is tender, not irritated. "How in Heaven's name did you know that?"

"I felt it—or heard it, I guess—your thoughts, while I was doing a healing on another woman with uterine cancer. That's what you have, isn't it?"

Ma makes a whistling sound. "I prayed for miracles, Gracie, but I have to say, I never saw this coming."

"If you're not going to let the doctors help you, then

you need to let me come home and do it. You know I can heal you."

Ma snorts. "No, Gracie. Of course I'm seeing the doctors."

"But I heard your thoughts about how there was nothing they could do for you."

"I will admit I'm amazed that you know this, Gracie, but don't you think it's more likely you picked up on the thoughts of the woman you were...healing?"

"It was your voice. I heard it clearly."

"Well, sorry to disappoint, Gracie, but I'm under treatment, and it's not so bad. It was a little tumor. A tiny dose of chemo, and one small surgery for now. If they want me to have the whole kit and kaboodle taken out, that's what I'll do. Nothing to worry about, I promise you."

"Ma, I could fly or drive home in a day and heal you, and you wouldn't even have to bother with surgery or chemotherapy."

"Grace, live your life. I will be fine." Her voice is sure and strong and there is no arguing with her. "You're good, I hope?" she asks, "Marly too?"

I can barely believe my ears. She's asking after Marly? "Yes, we're all good," I say, because what more can I say? "Are you getting out?" It's hard not to imagine the house as having cancer along with her, its stacks and piles like polyps, tearing the place down slowly by its seams.

"Gracie. Don't worry. Just keep doing what you're doing. I'm serious."

There's no point in fighting her over the phone. "Okay, Ma. I love you."

"I love you too."

I still have the phone held up to my ear, though Ma has hung up, when Marly finds me, red in the face and out of breath. She must have run after me—and I must have gone further than I realized. "I started picking up on Ma's thoughts." I'm quick to my own defense. "She's sick."

Marly takes a deep breath and looks at me as if I'm crazy. "You just, picked up on her thoughts from all this way away?"

"She has uterine cancer, too. I think that's why. I was already on that frequency; does that makes sense?"

Marly looks at me and I want to look away because there's pity in her eyes. "Grace," she says, in a voice so soft it looks as though she's mouthing the words. "I'm so sorry."

I nod, then tuck my chin toward my chest. I have to go home. I can heal her. She can't deny me if I go there in person. "Come back to Drake's Bay with me," I state plainly.

Marly takes a step away from me. "No." She sounds surprised at herself. "I understand if you need to go. I won't make you stay here, but I...can't go back there."

I can't decide if she's playing the martyr or being sincere. "I'm not going back there *to live*. I have a bad feeling about Ma. If I can heal her, then I can stop worrying and wondering."

Marly's face becomes entirely blank then, as though her soul has ducked out for a smoke. "How do you know you can heal her?" Her voice is sharp.

"Excuse me? What is it I do all day every day?" I say.

I am unpleasantly reminded of many occasions when I came to her house just in time to stop her from throwing back a bottle of pills or pressing an X-Acto knife into her wrists when we were girls. "You could have helped *me* more."

I don't know if she means back then, or now, but her face crimps into a hard, unattractive grimace.

"I can't make you do anything!" I shout. "My mother may be *dying* of uterine cancer and all you can think about is yourself?"

"I have given you a life! If not for me, you would still be living with your mother," she says in a low voice. "It's like you're trying to sabotage that. Like you're back where I found you in Drake's Bay."

A vent of accusations wants to burst out. "If I remember correctly, I 'found' you. Because you didn't have the courage to face me." The words come out flat, pressed between plates of outrage. I stand up as straight as I can. "I didn't know you could be this selfish."

Chapter Twenty-One

Behind the cereal in Marly's cabinet, fumbling with the feeling of doing something I shouldn't, I find what I am seeking: a half-empty bottle of pale amber tequila, and that cool bottle of vodka she'd set out like a taboo prize some months back. What I want is to drink just enough to swoon my serpent into a dazed state, to make it lazy and ineffective. Adam has been here all day, alone, in a hotel room, and I want to go to him. I need to go to him. There may be no one else who understands as deeply as I do what it means that my mother has cancer. And there is, of course, the other reason, which still feels like a joke played by some reality television show; I want to catch him before he realizes that there is nothing to love in one so damaged as me.

I fill a small glass, drink, and sit, waiting on the couch to feel that sensation that is like swimming without making any effort. When it hits, I call a cab.

Of all the fancy hotels in Vegas that Adam could treat himself to, he has chosen the Best Western. A step up from a Motel 6. He is frugal to a fault; I've been in his house enough times to know that it could benefit from fresh paint, new furniture—he lives surrounded by his father's old belongings as though he inherited the Senior Lieb's persona, not just his practice, after he died.

By the time I'm standing at his hotel door, knocking, my mind feels like a raft that's been pushed away from the shore of my body. It's a pleasantly freeing sensation and makes me wonder why I've spent so many years avoiding the very substances that could give me this lightness of being.

Adam pulls the door open with one hand, his laptop balanced in the other hand, a pen clutched between his teeth. He's wearing thin cotton plaid pajama pants, a plain white T-shirt. I've never seen him so stripped down and I feel almost embarrassed, as though I shouldn't look.

"Grace!" He almost drops the laptop. It teeters precariously as he maneuvers it to the bed and plops it down, the pen falling from his teeth, forgotten.

"I'm sorry for chasing you away earlier." I step into the room with a potent sense of crossing a kind of threshold. "I'm in a very strange place," I mean emotionally, but I suppose I mean geographically too.

He nods, but doesn't smile, his bangs sliding across his forehead.

My body feels like a blur beneath my head. Why am

I here? I move into him, fold my head against his chest. It feels so right, and yet, like I'll get into trouble for being with him.

"You're crying." He alerts me to the fact before I even realize it. "What's wrong?"

"My mother has cancer." *I don't know what's happening to me.*

His shoulders slump and his gaze softens on me. "Oh God, no. I'm sorry."

I nod. "It's not right, not fair."

He leans into the wall behind him and cradles me. "I said that a lot in my residency—it's not fair. I kept telling my father I was going to give up on medical school, join the Peace Corps. He pushed me, said there's always suffering in life, so why not be one of the few who can actually do something about it."

I smile, thinking that maybe what I do qualifies in this category, too. Only I can't tell Adam this.

"I'm going home, to help her." I look up at him, seeking validation. "She needs me."

He pulls slightly away, frowns. "You seem happy here." I can't read his tone. Does he not want me to come back to Drake's Bay?

"But I can help her!"

He shakes his head. "How? By doing what you've always done all these years, Grace? I think you seem happier now than I've ever seen you."

I want to throw myself at him, part rage, part desire to be comforted. *You have no idea what I can do, because I can't tell you—you'll laugh at me, tell me I'm crazy.*

Instead, I do the bidding of the alcohol that's strumming my veins like a rare instrument...I step out of the easy-release dress I put on. In a moment, I'm standing there in my bra and underwear—the only set I own that contains lace: red. I'm hoping its frills will distract from the patchwork squares of dark and light skin that criss-cross my chest, that it will call Adam's attention directly to my breasts, what little I have. From below, with the exception of my butchered right leg, I am smooth skin, slender tummy, hips that swell into womanhood.

I grasp Adam's hands and slide them to my hips, hook his thumbs into my underpants and push downward. He groans and his hands slide to the firm soft skin of my buttocks, knead it with his strong fingers, push my underwear to my ankles, and then, using his foot, slides them off me completely. He drops to his knees and kisses my stomach in slow, soft circles, presses his face into my downy hair and breathes me in. Visions waver in and out of my mind—but I don't allow myself to linger on them—the alcohol makes that so much easier.

His mouth rises up my stomach, teases my belly-button, then his fingers are unhooking my bra and his mouth is—glorious, hot—a shock of surprise against one nipple, then the other, until his mouth is finally on mine, light and gentle.

"You won't hurt me," I say, but he pulls back sharply.

"You've been drinking," he says, his expression pinched, as though I've hurt him somehow.

"Just a little," I say. "I was nervous."

He sighs and steps away from me, averts his gaze from my body that is pulsing with need for him.

"Not like this, Grace."

He can't be serious. "What? Why? I'm an adult, I'm here by choice."

"If you needed to drink first, that doesn't feel like a confident choice."

I want to stomp my feet, throw a tantrum. But that which would explain my behavior is only going to make me sound insane.

With the urge to bolt, I quickly pull my crumpled dress from the floor and hold it against my body, to cover me.

"Please don't go." He frowns at me, voice soft, and holds out his hand. "I want to, Grace. I just don't want to be something you regret. Stay the whole night. Stay with me."

I'm rigid with indecision, fear that too much time alone will lead to me revealing my secrets and driving him permanently away. But he did come all this way to see me. I exhale, then sit down beside him on the bed's edge.

"Do you remember when you started working for me, how you wanted to become a nurse? Do you still ever think about it?" he asks.

I remember the way the slightly musty smell of his office used to excite me—it was a place where I was use-ful, where I did not have to navigate piles and stacks and rotting things with my every step. I remember holding up the medical instruments, high with the idea that I could do for others what was done for me in the hospital. "Maybe that was just my way of having hope,"

I say. "That I could have a normal life."

He laughs. "Why is everyone so preoccupied with normal," he loops his arm around my shoulder. "I think we'd work really well together." He clutches me closer. "That's all. I know you'd be great with patients—you have so much empathy for the suffering of others."

I feel myself tense beneath his arm. *I didn't choose that suffering. It's not like my empathy is some sort of noble event in my life.*

I don't like the parental tone in his voice, like he disapproves of what I'm doing, which probably looks like a lot of nothing. "I just don't know what I think. Don't you get bored in general practice? Do you ever think of specializing? Picking a focus?"

He leans back onto the bed and I want to slide my hand up his shirt, tease the pale brown tufts of hair there. "All the time," he says. "There are days I'd like to give up my practice altogether, go volunteer my time with victims of war and other such saintly enterprises."

"You don't have to give up your practice to do that."

"I know. But it's really easy when all you have going on is work, like being on auto-pilot."

"Is that guilt?" I press my face into his chest. With closed eyes the world tilts slightly behind my eye, as though I'm on a boat that's hit rough water.

"Maybe," he says. "But I'm not interested in being the guy that guilted you into coming home to the job of caretaker when you just got away."

"Most people figure this stuff out when they're like eighteen, not twenty-eight," I say into his shirt. "I'm a really, really late bloomer."

"That's not your fault, Grace," Adam says quietly. I sit with that a moment. In an instant, I can see flames behind my eyes, can smell the singed sweet smell of burnt flesh. Young Adam, the shy, awkward resident of thirteen years ago, rises before my eyes giving me an apologetic smile. *"You're going to be ok,"* he's saying. *"Until then, I can always tell you really stupid jokes."*

The alcohol is making me heavy, sleepy. I crawl up onto the bed and lay my head on the pillow. Next thing I know, I'm peeling my eyes open in the dark, the only light an incandescence from the street seeping in the curtains. The digital clock says it's 4:00 a.m. I'd been dreaming of thick fogs, dense muddy pits into which I kept falling, unable to pull myself free. My dress has come off; most likely I shucked it off in a fit of night heat, which happens to me often. The sheets are almost painfully stiff beneath my naked body, next to Adam, who is still clothed. He senses my movement and reaches for me, hands pulling me at the waist back toward him, so that we are spooned, cupped, a fit so sweet I'm surprised it's only the first time our bodies have done this. He's firm against me, and I'm nearly breathless with desire.

"The alcohol has worn off," I whisper.

"What about...?"

"I take birth control pills for my hormones," I say softly.

"Turn on that lamp," he says.

"No..."

"I want to see you."

He doesn't wait for me, but leans across me and does it himself.

"I don't want you to have any doubt." He leans down to kiss my ruined mouth, then my neck, tracing the scars and grafts.

But I can't have it sweet and slow—that will only give my serpent further chances to investigate Adam, disgorge his memories or feelings in ways I may not be ready for. I pull him to me like he's a raft I'm clinging to, open myself, cajoling him, though I can feel how he'd like to take his time.

I dispense with caressing and instead, press him against me, as though I can imprint him on my body, scar myself with him. It's a moment's pain, a rush of sweetness that persists, the smell of charred skin and burnt hair alive in my senses again exploding outward into sparks that fill my whole body, and then we're both lying there in a sweaty daze as though we've survived an earthquake.

"Grace, you..."

"I'm sorry," I whisper. Is this how it will be for us? Me, never able to look at him, let this joining unfold slowly?

I sit up. "I should go," I say.

"It's five in the morning!" he says. "Was it so awful?"

I stroke his chin. "Not awful at all." Then I bend down and kiss him. "I have a lot to figure out."

I rise and dress quickly, because if I stay he will want to talk, demand answers I don't want to give.

Chapter Twenty-Two

Two days later

Gus leans in close, fingers soft and masculine smelling. "Can I?" he whispers.

Can he? How else can we do this if he does not? My breath is a stone skipping a lake as I nod. His fingers make contact and I am embarrassed by the gasp that escapes me.

"Do you feel my touch there?" he asks.

"Some of it. There are places with no sensation."

"Show me where you feel me."

I inhale deeply, then reach up, guide his fingers with the lightest touch to my cheek. "At the center of the scars is a nerve bundle that somehow escaped the flame and the scalpel."

His finger lingers there, lightly, yet I feel nothing that is not centered in my own body—cells lifting themselves toward his touch, heat passing between pores. I close my eyes, not because he is hard to look at—though he is at this proximity, as I must be—but because it is too raw to be so close, like the doctors who stared past my humanity, seeing only my wounds. I'm wearing a simple white shawl over my bra, draped around my shoulders. He removes his finger and I feel a rush of...something, disappointment? Guilt? I'm not sure. And then he is all business behind his camera. Turning me, propping me, posing me—with and without my shoulder length red wig, the one most like the hair I actually had. Hair Marly used to twist into silky little braids that would not hold unless we secured their ends with tight rubber bands that ripped when they came off.

I don't know how long he snaps, his digital camera something my father would likely scoff at—or maybe not, what do I know, having no contact with him; perhaps he's made the switch from the art form he loved so much when I was a child. My neck aches after awhile, and Gus sees my fatigue, setting the camera down. He comes to me and rubs my neck, strong thumbs kneading the base. I don't want to relax into him, because it's wrong; not twenty-four hours ago I was in bed with Adam, and Gus has a girlfriend, and worse, whatever desire is passing from him to me is purely fetishistic. I am an object of his lens, a woman of strange power. *You called yourself a woman,* says a voice that matches Ma's in my mind.

I ache to be one again, the way I was with Adam.

The tips of his fingers are kneading away tension, lighting nerves awake, sending signals to the southern hemisphere of me, when a voice rents the moment and has me ready to cower. "Why didn't you say you were working," says Sara, who is suddenly in the doorway. In person she is never as luminous as the photograph of her on his back wall. Today her face needs sleep and lots of water to plump up to its rightful beauty.

"Because I didn't expect you," he says, with no tone of defense, which surprises me. Maybe I'm making it all up in my mind, this fleeting desire his body language suggests. I'm crazy to think he could find me attractive.

"Mmmm," she says, arms crossed. "My shawl?"

Gus sighs and if I were wearing a shirt I'd happily toss the fabric back to her. She turns then to look at me. "You look very natural in that wig," she says kindly. "You had straight hair, didn't you?"

"Uh, yeah." My heart jogs the way my legs want to. She smiles wearily at me. "I can tell." Then she turns and walks off to some other part of the house.

"I really should go," I say, reaching for my clothes.

Gus shakes his head. "Wait, not yet, I want to make you a print. There's a shot in here, I can feel it, a really good shot."

Though my own shirt is thin cotton, it feels as protective as a big downy jacket right now. Gus plugs in his camera to his computer. "Sit, go ask Sara to make some tea," he says.

The idea horrifies me. "I'm not going to bother her."

His computer makes little beeping noises. "Grace, she's not upset. She's not jealous. If that's what you were thinking."

I shake my head, embarrassment prickling at me. "I didn't, I don't...."

"Art is an intimate process—it can seem to butt up against other libidinous aspects...but I'm not some womanizer, if you're worried."

"I know you don't find me attractive," I say, crossing my arms across my breasts, feeling rejected though I know it's foolish. "It's something about me, what I represent, how I help you make your art, or the healing thing."

"Aha," he says to the camera screen, as though he hasn't heard anything I've said. He hits more buttons and then a printer beside the computer disgorges an image. It's 5 by 7, and as it grinds out the pixels of my own face, a tremendous anxiety builds in me.

"I don't think I want to see." I rise looking around for my bag. But it's too late, he's pulling it off the printer shelf, blowing on it and then thrusting it in front of me.

"That's who I see," he says.

There's a woman in the photograph, turned to the right, where the vast majority of my face is the least blemished, a solid semblance of lips. The side of me that took the least heat—literally. The wig is balanced in such a way that it follows the curve of my jaw, exposes a delicate ear, a suspicious but not unlovely eye.

It all suddenly makes sense to me. "I'm the ugly, made beautiful. Sara's the beautiful, made ugly." I feel tears burning my voice. "It makes for good juxtaposition, right?"

Gus opens his mouth as though to protest this truth, but then closes it. "Not in those exact words, Grace. I was hoping you'd agree," he says.

"I guess I sort of thought...you were my friend,

first." I push the paper image away.

He frowns, a red and a green stripe meeting across his brow. "I am, Grace. The two things aren't mutually exclusive."

"But maybe they are." An embarrassing trickle emerges from my nose, forcing me to sniff it up. "For me."

He stands there, staring at me as though I'm speaking another language.

Sara's suddenly in the doorway again, hair down, looking a bit more relaxed. "I told him you'd feel this way," she tilts her head in a friendly way. "Exploited. Objectified." She's holding a drink, something amber colored, fat square ice cubes suspended in it. "For a guy who's been through so much, sometimes he lacks basic empathy. I'll drive you home, if you like."

"Come on," Gus shoots Sara a side-eyed sort of glare, "you're beautiful, Grace."

"I'm beautiful when you prop and pose and light and wig me, you mean," I say.

He snorts. "Isn't that what women feel they have to do? Aren't they always ripping out their body hair and applying make-up and paying hundreds of dollars to have their hair color changed? Who the fuck cares! We see what we want to see anyway, Grace, and I'm not talking about vanity."

"I wouldn't know," I say, even though I know I sound petulant.

Sara takes a sip of her drink. "Come on, Grace, let's talk in the other room while the artiste has his tantrum."

I shake my head at the way they can speak so openly, if not a little unkindly, about each other in front of each other. My parents always spoke in barbed hints and laced statements that could easily be denied when accused.

She leads me to what is like a living room, though it resembles more of a fancy wine-cave, with a skylight made out of plastic bottles full of water that pull in light and look vaguely like lit bulbs.

"Normally I'd be the first one to tell you to tell him to go fuck himself," she says cheerily, as if we're talking about picnics and puppies. "But here's the thing," now she drops her voice to a whisper. "He's sick. I think serious sick, though he's trying to keep it from me. It's hard to tell under all that ink, but he's not looking well. I think it's something he got when he was using."

I'm struck dumb by the knowledge that he's sick but hasn't once asked me for a healing.

"He's not going to ask." She anticipates me, then finishes her drink. "And I don't want to beg."

"Of course I'll help him."

"Then let him use your photos in the show."

Confusion thunks down, a heavy curtain between us. "Don't you want me to *heal* him?"

She frowns. "He's been looking a long time to finish this project, Grace. I'm not sure he's got a lot of give left in him after this." Sara tucks a hank of blond hair behind her perfect ear.

"You're saying he doesn't want to be healed?"

As if he can hear us, which seems unlikely, Gus makes a frustrated groan from the other room, then there's a sound of something crumpling and being smashed, as though with a fist.

"I'm saying I don't think he *can* be healed."

I realize she's not talking about some needle-borne virus, but about Maya, his lost child.

I feel the imperfect edges of coercion and pity scraping against one another inside me. "Okay, I guess." My voice sounds thin, unconvinced.

"Good enough." She sets her drink on the table. "I'll tell him, and if you like, I'll drive you home."

ဢၐ

As we're nearing Marly's apartment, Sara says, "It would be really cool if you'd consider doing a healing as part of the opening of the show. That way, you get something out of it, too."

Chapter Twenty-Three

I come by myself, by cab. I've told Marly only a little bit about the show. The gallery, set in an old warehouse, is much bigger than I imagined, big enough for a sports game with fans. Big enough for a faith healing. But if you don't know where you are, you could easily miss it, thinking it's a place to buy lumber or rock for a back yard.

The show is only announced once you're standing at the door, written in light.

I look but can't find the projection source. The entrance is a curtained tunnel—I walk in shadow, with a seepage of blue light beckoning me from up ahead. There is a slight hum of music and chatter, though I'm early, as Gus asked me to be.

Halfway up the tunnel little lighted images appear, as though I've tripped a wire, projected onto the cloth: models, women made perfect by fasting and photoshop, with sleek limbs and lips that plump forward of their own accord. I've seen them all my life—their flattened bodies are stacked to the ceiling in some of Ma's corners, sating her need for filling emptiness—her body, her house, her mental chambers. And I get it, as I walk: there is something so satisfying in symmetry, an ease that allows the mind to feel safe.

I startle as the projections stop, and a well of panic hits me in the dark tunnel—a feeling of suffocation coupled with fear of what Gus has planned for the second half of the projections. Maimed and crippled bodies in hospitals? Other burn survivors who've suffered worse than I have?

The new projections begin: close-ups of the natural world: spirals worked into fossils, the up-close magnifications of crystals and amoebas, a different kind of symmetry.

Bolstered by this, I move ahead, up to the edge of the curtains, and push my way through.

A tiny section of the huge warehouse has been cordoned off, fit into a neat square that houses the photographs, a huge throne-like chair at the center on a tiny raised dais.

The overhead lights are low and blue. Each photograph is lit by its own small team of bulbs, but you have to stand before one, or a triptych of several, to get the full effect.

And there, a light sculpture hanging at the start of the show reads "Symmetry."

Gus rushes toward me, dressed in a dark grey suit that shines even in the dim light. Sara is talking softly to a server in a tux. She, like me, is also wearing black—a long dress that brushes the tips of her black pumps, but her hair is up high on her head. I'm wearing the long straight wig, the one in the photographs, and my dress only falls to my knees, one I spent two painful hours shopping for, trying not to take it personally when the salesgirl—she couldn't have been more than 17—never once offered me help.

I'm afraid to look at the photographs. Out of the corner of my eye I see them but I don't want to look at them fully. Perhaps I can make it through the whole night without doing so.

"Thanks for coming early," Gus says. "Do you want me to walk you through the show once, before people arrive?"

I shake my head. "I don't think I'm ready."

He nods. "I get ya. Later, then. I hope you like what I've done."

I can't even look at him because there's a photograph of me in the distance behind his head, the one in the wig where I look most like my undamaged self, a tease of symmetry I'll never have again.

I know Marly would hate this whole thing. And maybe I should, too. Nerves are beginning to eat at my stomach. I should never have agreed to do a healing under these circumstances—it's ridiculous. What if I can't perform?

Sara offers me something delicately arranged on a cracker, so pink and shiny, it looks almost fetal, and my stomach lurches. I wave her away but accept a champagne cocktail and go to admire the pieces of Sara, for that half of the show is safe to me.

Alcohol molecules swim in my blood like tiny mermaids and then suddenly Gus is speaking in an excited tone, and urging Sara and me to stand at specific spots. I'm on the right, toward my half of the show, and Sara is to the left. We are Isis and Osiris, which makes Gus the gatekeeper to the underworld.

The size of the crowd stuns me: it seems impossible that any one person could know so many other people; Gus is a bigger artist than I realized. The rushing murmur of voices is morphing into a kind of primal song, a staticky buzz like bees in a swarm.

I don't drink more than one glass of champagne. I must keep up the protective walls tonight, so that every person who steps up to me and puts a hand on my arm or shoulder, murmuring their awe at my photographed face, doesn't deliver an injection of their own pain, too.

My cheeks hurt from smiling, especially my left side—ironically the side with fewer nerves. Every blonde head, every passionate exclamation, makes me look for Marly. We haven't been on friendly terms since I shouted at her after the church healing. Every time we're in the same room together, there's a charged feeling, like a lightning storm on the horizon. I'm hurt, though not surprised, that she isn't here. And the longer I stand with my faux-smile, alone, the less sure I am this was a good idea. I've allowed myself to be objectified, taken apart, sliced for the camera—my wounds made into a novelty that someone can hang on their wall.

The blue lights flicker for a moment and then flip through an array of pink, green, then yellow. This causes the room to quiet, and then Gus steps up to the big throne-chair and smiles. "Thanks all of you for coming to Symmetry. I'm really proud of this one. A big thanks to Sara and Grace, who made it possible, of course."

Hands clap, loud, like a flock of pigeons rising. He goes on to talk about the show, but I've stopped listening: Marly has just popped out of the birth canal-like curtains into the room. She sees me and nods just slightly. Rather than join the crowd gathered around me, Gus and Sara, however, she walks past us all. She's surprisingly dressed down—black capris, a white cotton blouse that shows her obvious pregnancy, hair in a ponytail, no make-up. The plainness makes her seem sad. I have the feeling that she's done this for me, made herself smaller, less pretty, and it makes me want to rush over and tell her that I love the big boldness of her.

I turn my head slightly to watch her enter the show with a bubble of anxiety. It wouldn't surprise me if she felt the need to make a public denouncement of Gus's work.

Gus just keeps talking about his inspiration. I know that Marly is looking, and now, suddenly, I wish I'd been braver and looked at the photographs myself, first.

In a lull of Gus's words, behind us Marly gasps, "Wow!" And I can't tell if this is a pre-explosive "wow" or one of awe. I turn.

And really see what Gus has done with my face.

At first I feel not shock, not disgust, not happiness or pride, just: nothing.

It's as though I'm looking at a series of Hubble telescope pictures, returning proof of life on other planets. My scars up close, blown up to the size they are, in black and white, are otherworldly, all texture and pattern. Not any more grotesque than Sara's overly-magnified nose hairs or black heads, and new ones I've not seen: private junctions of hair and skin, glossy reaches of inner cheek and ear. You might even say, if you didn't know what you were looking at, that it looks natural, interesting, compelling.

The longer I look, the more I feel strangely protective of the rough-trod skin. I want to cover it, layer it in salves and put gauze and bandages on it, though it is no longer a series of open wounds. I want to protect it. I step down off the dais. As my tight right leg refuses to bend with ease and I stumble, a dozen hands reach out to help me, but I shrug them off and move toward Marly.

When I'm standing next to her, poised at last to see the show as it is meant to be seen—each image almost a holograph floating out of the darkness—I feel sick to my stomach.

"I'll give it to him," Marly says, "He's got talent."

I bend forward, my head swimmy, little bright particles floating across my eyes.

"Grace!" Marly realizes I'm not okay. She reaches out, grasps my arm, leans me into her. I'm vaguely aware that everyone in the crowd is looking at me, at us. Here I am, appearing to faint at the sight of my own face. This is not what they came for.

"I'm fine." I stand up straight, taking a deep breath. "Drink just went to my head, not enough food."

Marly turns and eyes Gus as though this is somehow his fault.

"You don't have to stay," she says.

"Yes, I do," I cringe in anticipation. "I said I'd do a healing as part of the show."

Marly's eyes blaze white in the eerie dim light. "Really?" Her tone is tight.

"Yes," I say. "Look, he's really sick—Gus is—Sara thinks he might not...that he might be dying, even."

Marly starts to laugh, shaking her head. "I know I shouldn't be surprised, Grace, but *I* ask you to do something to help sick children, and you run out of the hospital. *He* asks you to be Queen of the Show and you leap to it. She shakes her head. "I'm beat, I've gotta go rest," she says, but then, as though rethinking her words, turns back to me. "I'm happy for you, Grace."

She moves so fast there's no chance of catching her in the swarm of people.

Gus takes Marly's exit as a sign. The lights do their magic flipping routine again and then he puts out an arm in my direction, beckoning me back.

ൟ

It's only supposed to be one. That's all I agreed to. But the woman who approaches with an inflamed gall bladder and constant digestive pain is a breeze; it feels like I'm flipping marbles out of a soft purse; my serpent rises to the occasion and leaves me feeling strangely energized, and I hear myself saying "next?" with such conviction that Gus looks at me with surprise.

I don't know what is giving me such strength, but I work my way through a woman with skin cancer, a bad case of gout, and, the shy fellow whispers into my ear, a terrible case of hemorrhoids that require surgery. I feel like Hera on Mt. Olympus, up on my throne, the wounded laid out before me, the way the crowd's eyes seem to glow with anticipation and reverence in the blue light of the warehouse. Behind me, my face leaps out in the dark like a vision in a scrying bowl. I feel I could part seas and command the mists. My body runs hotter, sweat trickling down between my breasts, behind my knees, even gathering at my low back, but I don't care. It feels like the good, hard sweat of exertion.

After the sixth or eighth or maybe even tenth person to lie upon the table and sit up feeling better, while the crowd "ahh"s, the night steadily stretching into morning—I hone in on Gus, who's sitting on the floor, back against a column, underneath the dark and fuzzy innards of Sara's nose.

"How about you, Gus?" I call out. "Want to be my last?"

Even amidst the florid show of his tattoos, his smile looks weary. "You can't heal what ails me, Grace," he says softly.

"I'm not talking about your heart," I say, thinking that I should have a great carved wooden staff with a serpent head, and a headpiece.

He glances at Sara, the whites of his eyes the only part I can make out moving. He looks as though he's going to say something, but then he rises, claps his hands together. "Bravo!" he shouts. "To Grace, the eighth great wonder of the world," and the crowd follows suit.

Something is off with him, but there's too much flurry of people tossing their cards and their words of praise at me to walk over and talk to Gus. Plus I expect the exhaustion to hit me at any moment. Sara is my designated driver home, and there are even two beefy guys Gus hired in case I need to be carried, unconscious, to the car and up to Marly's apartment.

But the blackout does not come. I feel high. Euphoric, buzzing. Like I could sprint for miles, or swim a lake.

Gus strides by on his way to chat with someone, and I reach out to talk to him, thank him, offer him something. As I do so, my hand shakes so badly it looks as though I'm waving frantically. Gus responds by waving back. My teeth bounce off one another, and suddenly the shaking is so fierce it's like I've been submerged in ice water. Sara is the first to notice it; I'm sure I look odd in the dark room, the blue light, like I'm doing a strange dance rather than being unable to control any muscle in my body.

When she reaches me my jaw feels like two castanets being whipped together, and the room is so blurry I have to clamp my eyes shut to keep from throwing up.

I feel arms guiding me to the very table I just performed my work upon, voices speaking in low, worried whispers, as though I'm not right there, fingers cool and jarring on my searing body. I'm waiting for the blissful blackout sleep to come, the relief of it, but it won't—just wave after waves of these spasms, seizure-like and constant, my muscles bunching and shaking painfully.

"Call a doctor," Sara calls out firmly. This ignites a sudden, brief interlude of strength in me that allows me to shout, "No!"

No hospitals. Never again will I lie, unable to control my own body, at the hands of strangers gazing down at me under lights so bright they burn.

Gus is there then. "Pppplease..." I manage. "Sash...."

"Sasheen," he confirms.

"It's 4:00 a.m.," Sara insists in a tone I imagine her using with her psychotic patients—kind, but firm, ready to take you into hand.

Gus's voice is even firmer, "Call her."

As my body shakes it seems to disgorge images, pieces of the people I touched tonight. Adrift in a centrifuge of sensations—electric impulses up my legs, cords of heat undulating through my arms—a cowering child, a woman screaming as loud as she can, a fist smacking a cheek, and then soft, steady warm hands stroking mine.

The shaking doesn't cease all at once, but it lessens the moment Sasheen appears and holds my hands in hers. As she begins her usual work, it feels like nothing more than a massage—working each of my fingers through her thick palms, even my warped, enlarged thumbs—she is not shy, and her touch causes first pain as the tissue resists and then gives and then seems to spring open more deeply, releasing both tension and pain. The shaking subsides in slow passes.

As she works I feel like one of the caged birds back at the Wildlife Center in Drake's Bay, flexing her wings for the first time outside of captivity, terrified of the freedom before her, and yet knowing she has to go.

When I can finally open my eyes without the world blurring, she *tsks* at me. "You need rest." I'm looking at her upside down, her strong chin and high cheekbones making her face into a commanding, scary mask. "What did I say, Grace? You can't heal the world of all its problems. You're not God. If you don't listen, it's gonna get worse."

I'm a shamed child, an obedient dog. I nod and limp quietly with Sarah to her car, held up on either side by two silent brawny men. All the way home I wait for it to hit, the sleep of all sleep that is sure to follow.

It doesn't come.

I don't sleep all night, though I am no longer tired after Sasheen's restoration. I feel as though time has stopped, as though I'm stuck in a waking dream, mild and pleasant.

Marly doesn't come out of her room until it's time for work, and then she's off, toast in her hand, hair in a ponytail, a blur who won't even stop to say goodbye.

And though I know I should heed Sasheen's words, my body feels amazingly good and I wonder if perhaps I'm starting to reap the benefits of my own healings.

And that is why I do not cancel the healing scheduled the next day.

Chapter Twenty-Four

My hands bob to the surface of my client's hip rather than staying in the depths where healing takes place. My focus keeps drifting back to the look of hurt and resentment in Marly's eyes as she realized I had agreed to do a healing at Gus's show but not taken on her cause of healing all the world's children. I wrench myself to the present.

"Name's Ellie," the woman had said when she stepped into my little office at Drew's, the scent of freesias and lilacs blowing in from the open window. She is somewhere between old and elderly; she looks like the rich wife on *Gilligan's Island*, her fine pale blue cotton dress expensive and crisp, like it can only be dry-cleaned.

She gestures at her hip. "It's like lightning in my leg. Keeps me up at night and I can barely get around by day." Yet she'd slid into the chaise lounge with barely a hitch.

While I can feel the brittle corrosion of some arthritis in Ellie's joint, it doesn't feel capable of causing the level of pain she claims to have.

My sigh is irritated; I hope she doesn't notice. Though I've grown used to Vegas heat, it feels especially scorching today. Beads of sweat perch on my upper lip and behind my ears of all places. My knuckles ache. Ellie lets out a moan meant to simulate relief—dramatic and showy. She does this, however, right as I move my hand *away* from the locus of her pain. I fight back the next sigh; clearly I have a faker on my hands. My fingers now began to itch, and I badly want to pull them off her and scratch them.

I never promise my guests a healing duration; some are short and swift and some I can hardly touch, offering little more than pain relief. I am about to proclaim us done when my serpent catches a scent it has been leading me to on the sly more often. My hands move to a spot between her breasts. I feel the strum of her heartbeat, muffled beneath the tomb of her ribs, as though her chest is a sarcophagus and her heart is buried alive.

The top of my head is so hot that I take my eyes off her, looking for Marly. Before our fight, she would have been at the ready with a bottle of water, suggesting a break. But of course she isn't here.

Ellie doesn't open her eyes and the tomblike heart calls me back to her.

My serpent moves through a gallery of images: blurry at first and then painfully clear. A towering woman holds a switch made of sharp wood; a cowering toddler sits in a puddle of her own urine; a shivering girl lies in a thin nightgown, tied to her bed.

"I'm so sorry for your pain," I whisper. Her eyes lock on mine and I want to offer her more. I can see the echo of the images in her hazel eyes and know she felt me touch it.

"You don't know my pain," she says in a teeth-clenched whisper so full of hostility my hands ache with the energy. Before I think better of it, something defensive passes between my hands and her skin, something like an electric shock that makes a snapping sound and causes her to sit bolt upright. I smell—hallucinate?—smoke.

"Ow!" she cries, pushing my hands off of her. It feels as though she's wrenched the cord out of the socket, breaking the electrical connection, leaving me gasping and burning. Sweat boils in all my remaining pores. Her movement is so fast I'm not sure I really saw what I think I did: a hole, roughly fingertip sized, burned into her perfect skirt.

"You hurt me," she says, so softly that I'm not sure I heard her. "Fraud!" she shouts, struggling to stand.

I try to help her up but she shakes me off. My limbs feel wrapped in wool and drenched in hot water, my spine, sharp, as though the vertebrae are knife-edged.

"I told you the pain was in my hip but you tried to touch my breast! I don't know what kind of operation you think you're running but you don't have me fooled!"

Lights dance up behind my eyes. My lips feel melded together, my tongue gluey. I sway in place, so hot that I am sure, at any moment, I will burst into flame.

☙❧

Ma leans over me with a cool washcloth, humming Vivaldi. The room is so dim I can't make out anything but her bright eyes and the sound of her voice. "Ma, why can't I heal myself?"

"Shhh," she whispers. "Don't talk. Save your strength."

"Please, let me—"

She presses a finger to my lips, but it feels tiny, thin, not like Ma's fleshy digit at all. My body jolts awake. I was dreaming. It's Marly's face looming over me. Marly's finger on my lips. "You suffered serious heat stroke, Grace. Don't work up a lather."

"I thought you were Ma," I whisper, my voice weak and crackly sounding.

"Ha, yeah, well the resemblance is uncanny." She grins big.

When I smile, pain spikes across my bottom lip.

"You've split your lip." She presses the cold cloth there, which comes up blotted with blood. "Let me go get some Neosporin for that."

She hurries back with the sticky salve and applies it. "It's all my fault—I've been horrible to you, Grace. Let's just be friends again. Forget everything we've said. Start over. That lady was a nut. I know her kind."

"How could you have known," I croak.

"I *need* to apologize, Grace. I've been acting like a fucking child. I've been, well, let's just say that I don't understand why you're still here. I understand if you're staying just for her." She pats her belly.

I struggle up to sitting: the euphoria is gone, the sense that I can do anything, stay up all night, heal the world...all gone. I feel like a lump of clay—left to dry and crack. "I haven't felt this bad since I was in the hospital. Like I've been microwaved."

Marly's face has finally started to swell with the weight of pregnancy, making her look plump and hale. Backlit by the small lamp she looks like a medieval nun come to tend me back to health. "Grace." Her voice sounds thick. "I've been thinking about how to say this. I've tried so many times that I'm just going to say it while you can't run away."

"Don't, let's not apologize for anything," I say.

She shakes her head. "I have to. The night of the fire. I...I still have a nightmare. I've hit the bottom of the tree house, the smoke is curling in my lungs, and the whole thing is blazing. The longer I stand there, the longer you burn. I'm just stuck to the spot. Then I run, I run and run and run. Like by running I can wrench time back on its axis.'"

And just like that, I know she isn't talking about a dream. I remember with visceral clarity a summer day at the beach with my father. He always let me play in the waves close to shore, the ones that barely reached my shoulders and sent me soaring on a jetty of water. But this day, I'd gone out further than usual, and by the time I realized that the wave was bigger and faster than I could handle, its foaming head had descended upon me. I was pounded into the gritty ocean floor, saltwater and sand forced into my throat and nasal passages so that I could not breathe or find my sense of direction until I emerged, gasping at last. I feel this same way now.

"Nightmare?" I ask, trying to steady the emotion

shaking my voice. "Or memory?"

Marly bites her lip and puts her face in her hands for a second. I feel as though all sound has been absorbed into a vacuum.

"I hated you for not showing up," I say. "I thought for sure you'd be there at my bedside the next day in the hospital. But you couldn't face me, because you'd already abandoned me. That's what you're saying, right? You left me to burn?"

My words sound so logical, clean, but all of a sudden the thrum of my heartbeat pounding returns to me, loud, as though it can drown out the truth of what I'm saying.

Her face is crimped, as though she's suppressing a pang of nausea. "Oh Grace. I didn't know what to do. I know I should have stayed, waited until the paramedics got there, told you it would be okay. Honestly, I was sure you knew how I ran away, that you remembered, and that's why you didn't seek me out. And since we've come back together, I've been waiting for this perfect time to tell you—as if there is such a thing. I was going to when you came to my gram's house back in Drake's Bay, but then, it felt so good to have a real friend again. I don't deserve your friendship."

I reach for words that might comfort one of us, but find none. Finally I ask her to take the note out of my wallet—one written in Marly's gram's impeccably neat and tiny handwriting that I've kept for thirteen years.

Grace, I know how important girlhood friend-ships are. Before I married, my best friend Annie was the world to me. We taught each other a great deal. I love my granddaughter, fierce, Grace, and I think you do, too. She'll be staying at my house for just one night. It's all her parents will allow. This Saturday. If you can get away, it might be the last time you see each other for awhile.

  —Oona D.

Marly's face is stone, ice, everything suspended, and then the leak starts in her eyes, crumbling her features as the tears drip off her cheeks. She lifts her head high. "Always thought better of me than anyone else, my gram," she says at last. "If only she knew me better."

I know she's thinking of the night she took a fireplace poker to that guy's knee—perhaps the night that sealed our fates, forbidden as we were from seeing each other until her grandmother sent me that note.

The night of the fire Marly and I both squealed the moment I poked my head through the door of the tree house.

We hugged tightly, and I pretended not to notice the band-aids still stuck to her wrists. It had been nearly a month since we'd stood in each other's company, a physical ache in my bones relieved the moment I set eyes on her. The normally bare tree house room was decorated in candles, a wild illumination of flickering light that made her look like some fairytale princess come to life in a white beaded dress with flapper fringe. She had dayglo pink leggings on beneath it and her black Converse sneakers.

"Um, what are you wearing?" I asked, then regretted it in the sinking of her eyes.

"I thought this final act deserved a kind of ritual. Rituals require costumes."

I didn't like the way she said "final act," even though I knew that her parents were threatening to send her to boarding school, that Bryce was most likely taking a new job in Seattle, and that she had something important to tell me.

"I just thought we should, you know, like, make this moment significant." She parted her dark-blonde hair like drapes to either side of her shoulders, and plopped down on the faux-Persian carpet. "Now you pick something," she said.

In a pile behind her were a bunch of vintage dresses and beaded sweaters, but I felt silly putting them on. I selected an old yellow boa, a fringe of feathers that ringed my throat over my frayed tapered jeans and dark blue Esprit sweatshirt.

"Aren't you going to sit down?" There was something odd in her wide-eyed stare, her eager grin. She plunked several more fat candles down before her. Then she tipped an already lit candle in, and lit each one, white wax dripping in little puddles onto the floorboards.

"I hate Seattle. I hate rain. I hate men," Marly said. She ripped several hairs from her head and dropped them into the large candle flame where they curled into oblivion and puffed off a sulfurous odor. "What do you want out of your life?" she asked.

I wanted the fire to perform alchemy, to slide me free of the strictures of being Grace and into Marly's skin, to be bold and lush, intense and unafraid like she was. "I, um...I don't know," I mumbled.

"Grace, you're mistress of your destiny." She gave me a fierce gaze, eyes narrowed. "Come on! Tell the flame."

I cleared my throat. "I want to not be embarrassed to bring people over. I want to be..." Like you.

"What else?" Marly urged, leaning forward slightly on her knees.

"I want to look forward to the future, find my talent, make something of myself." What I couldn't say was: Take me away from this crowded life. As if she had any control.

"Hell yeah," she said. Her blue eyes were almost green in the yellow glare of the candles.

"Think of this as a ritual to shed our skins, Grace. We can still be anyone we want even though others want to control our destinies. Isn't that fucking exciting?"

"Yeah," I said, though a strange feeling was gathering behind my throat.

Marly shook her fingers at me. "Grace, stay with me. I want to tell you something, okay? We have to always be honest with each other."

"Of course."

"I'm not a virgin. My first time was with...I didn't know how to tell you before, but now—Grace. I didn't plan it. I didn't even want it."

She snapped a seal open on a precious vault inside me. How could she have kept this from me? Did she think I wasn't worthy of her trust? That night in the guys' apartment I already felt as though she was giving something of herself away, something I could never get back. She was my best friend; we were for each other. The words tasted like bile as I spoke them, "If you don't *want people calling you a slut, you shouldn't act like one."*

Marly drew back as though I'd physically pushed her. She took a deep breath and for several beats I thought she was going to storm out of the tree house. "I'm not a slut," she said evenly, though her hand shook when she straightened the row of candles between us. "No more than you're a prude."

We stared at each other. Her expression changed every few seconds in the shadows of the candles. Now her eyes narrowed, her cheeks softened. "Let's kiss on it," she said. "You know, to seal the deal. Oh wait, that's right—you're afraid I might, what, turn you? That you'll like it? Or worse—that you'll taste the nastiness in my soul?"

I was not going to let her get away with that. "I'm not scared," I said, and I leaned forward across the small city of candles she'd built.

It happened so fast.

The feather-like tufts of the boa drifted into a candle flame. My face was scorched by a necklace of fire. Marly reached for me but flame forced her to recoil. My hair, slick with hairspray, followed my face into petals of fire. Within seconds, fire was everywhere, springing up the polyester curtains, eating the plywood floor, and I was trapped within it.

"I never knew how to tell you. I was so mad," present-day Marly says, her voice little more than a rasp. "I tried to tell you about him. Then that thing you said, anger just gripped me, and then it spread so fast—"

"Stop," I say.

I don't tell her "Stop, it isn't true" because a little trap door has appeared in my memory, revealing a thing I have kept locked away for thirteen years: with a flick of her hand, Marly *tilted* the candle in at my chest level. Her eyes hooked mine, and before I could pull back or ask her what the hell she was doing, the first petals of the boa kissed the flame below me. "Oh!" Marly had said, a surprised sound, I'd always thought, but now I realize it was a sound of regret a moment too late.

I envy Marly's tears now; they look so cleansing, purifying. The act of confession sweeps away corrosion. Her wounds and minor scars are gone, healed at my hands. She's unraveled her darkness. Does it enter into me? I press my head back into the pillow that now feels too soft, and wish I was back in Drake's Bay, drenched in ocean mist, cloaked by the coastal fog.

"I need to be alone," I say to her imploring face. Marly nods, breath hitching over a sob that she suppresses. She tries to stand up, but has to press her palms into her thighs to do so. It is strange to see her struggle with a body that has always been effortless in its movements.

Chapter Twenty-Five

For the first time since I've come to Vegas—six months now—I feel its desolation in the sun-washed buildings we pass as the cab takes me to my little cottage. *Vegas*, the shiny, electric, holographic world that lives on The Strip like some form of alien life left to run amuck, is only a wild distraction from what would otherwise be just one, big, ugly desert town—a watering hole on the way to the lovelier parts of the southwest. I feel a yearning for the lushness of my hometown: nestled in soft yellow hills and their dark evergreen berets of oaks and redwoods.

The driver, Ali, tries to make conversation with me. "You live here or visit?"

Visit would suggest I came here to play, for pleasure. But didn't I? When did it get so serious? "Visit," I say.

"You go home?" It's a question but in his accent it

comes out almost like a command, like I'm being dismissed, and it makes me feel defensive. "I don't know," I snap. "There, the one with the little bridge over the pond." We've reached Drew's house, the side gate cracked as though someone has just come or gone.

"This town, bad for girls," he says simply. "You go home."

And you shut up, I'm thinking. *Learn some tact.* I lean across to give him his money and as he reaches for the twenty dollar bill, our fingers brush and there is popping sound and a singed smell.

"What the hell?" he says, rubbing his hand, glaring at me through the rearview mirror.

I pull back, alarmed, my own finger still tingling, and then I am sliding out of the cab, faster than usual, as if I could get away from my own hands. The cab driver peels away, leaving me in a cloud of dust, and, I realize too late, still clutching the bill I meant to give to him.

I can't quell the shaking, heated feeling in my muscles, like I've just finished an intense run and a cup of coffee at the same time and it takes me a moment to calm myself enough to walk through the side gate.

Drew bursts out of his side door, smiling. "Grace, you've surprised me."

"And you, me," I said. "I thought you'd be at work already." It's then I note that he's wearing blue plaid pajamas, slippers on his feet.

He runs a hand over his short blond hair. "Took a mental health day."

He glances back over his shoulder and suddenly I feel hot with embarrassment. "Oh god, is someone here?" I ask. *Marly?*

He frowns, fiddles with a button on the top of his pajamas. "No, I thought I heard the phone. You expecting a client?"

I shake my head. "Just needed a place to go and clear my head."

"Let me get you some coffee." He ushers me into the house and pours me a cup of coffee so strong it strips the coating on my tongue, but it gives me energy I sorely need.

The furniture in his living room is all so stiff, I'm afraid to sit on anything. I finally opt for an edge of his grey suede couch, which has the feel of a hairless cat under my palms. I pull back quickly, with the fear that I'll char the fabric. But that's absurd.

"Is something wrong?" Drew asks. He crosses one leg over the other and jitters the foot, as if impatient.

I press my fingertips together. What I want to say is stuck inside me, like smoke in a jar. I don't want to influence Drew's attitude about Marly. She's going to need somebody's help to take care of that baby when it arrives, and right now, I'm pretty sure it isn't going to be me. "I had a bad healing," I say instead.

"Marly told me." I twist in surprise to look at him and he says, "Oh, was I not supposed to know?"

Know? Does he know the other truth—what Marly did? I feel gypped of the chance to tell my own story, and suddenly defensive that she might have told Drew before she did me. "No, I mean, it's fine. But what if it's a temporary thing, this healing? What if it's even gone?"

Drew seems to gauge his words carefully. "You

mean because you had one client who didn't believe you could heal her?"

There's something to his tone that makes me feel edgy. I realize we've never really been alone together, never had a conversation where Marly wasn't there to referee.

"I don't think it had anything to do with whether she believed it. I felt what I felt; she didn't want me to see into a hurt place inside her. She pushed me away with her energy. The thing is, ever since then I feel like it's...going bad."

"I read a study about the placebo effect," he says, in a superior sort of way. "It said that healing is most profound when the practitioner and person seeking the healing both believe in the work being done. The results are quantifiably higher."

My spine stiffens. "So you think it's just mind over matter?"

"Wounds disappear before your eyes, Grace. Tumors shrink. I'd say that's real. I just question how much is coming from only you."

"But you were one of the people who pushed me into this." My anger is uncorked and ready to flow.

He holds up his hands defensively, as though he is but the messenger of these doubtful statements. "Like I said—I think you have a gift, Grace, a real gift of helping people toward their own ability to heal. If you're asking do I think you're a magician, using some magic force to heal people without their will, no, I don't think so. Everyone you've healed knew they were being healed."

"Except Marly," I counter him. "I didn't set out to heal her. It just happened."

"Yeah," he says, almost to himself. "But you and Marly have that thing..."

"Thing?" My voice is strained and high. *A thing, as in some chimera monster formed of desire, jealousy and broken loyalties.*

"That old childhood caretaker thing. You took care of her, she held on by the skin of her teeth to sanity so long as she had you. So even though you didn't stand up and say, 'Now, I heal thee!' I think it's clear that the dynamic between you was still in effect." His strained tone, delivered through tight lips makes me think he's angry, but not at me.

"What if I tell you it's changed?" I decide to trust him. "Turned into something dark. What would you say if I told you I have the power to harm people as well?"

He shakes his head. "That woman rattled you, clearly. I'm not bashing what you do, Grace. I think you really do have a talent. I'm just saying, maybe you give it too much power, maybe you could ease up a little on yourself."

He's backpedaling now, and I can't decide if it's because he thinks I am capable of harm, or because he just wants to end this conversation. I laser in on his bouncing leg. "You seem anxious," I say.

"Sorry. I was expecting Marly to call." His shoulders sag and he leans back into his chair, his limbs so long they all but hang over its edges. "I shouldn't blame her."

"Blame her for what?"

He stands up suddenly, as if his feelings are too big to be held down by gravity. "For being undecided about me, about that fucking ex."

"She's undecided about a guy who *beat* her?" I want to stand now too.

Drew straightens a stack of books that is already straight. "I'm afraid he's working very hard to convince her that he can change, that he has a genetic right to be in his child's life, seeing as she has no proof of that beating." When he looks at me, I read accusation in his eyes.

"You're afraid as in you know it, or you fear it?" I ask, heart pumping.

"There's very little I know for sure when it comes to Marly," he says. And with that cryptic finale he claps his hands together. "If you don't mind, I'm going to get a shower now." He moves a step toward me, as though he intends to come give me a hug, but then stops, eyeing me the way you might a suspicious salesman who appears on your door late at night. "I smell terrible," he says, and I know a lie when I hear one. If he didn't sound so convincing a few minutes ago, I'd say he was afraid I might hurt him.

ஓஇ

I refuse his offer to get me a cab and walk serenely, as unruffled as possible, out of his house though my fingers twitch with the urge to toss knick-knacks off shelves, pry paintings from his walls.

I have every intention to call myself a cab but it feels good to walk. I feel like if you could see me from a distance I would be giving off wisps of smoke, clouds forming over my head warning onlookers not to touch me, not to come near me. Sadly, even my scars are not enough to keep others safe from this slow-building reaction inside me: one part betrayal, one part fear; I can taste its copper tang on my tongue. I'm lethal.

I don't want to go back to the apartment just yet either, so I find myself in the mini-mart at a Chevron station, the cab driver's twenty still clutched in my hand. I'm not hungry or thirsty but maybe a cool drink will drench this heat that seems impossible to cool. A forty-ish man in khaki shorts and loafers stands contemplating beer on my way to the non-alcoholic cooler. Almost any other time in my life I would wait, hiding in the corner for him to move, but not today. "Excuse me," I say, tilting my chin up. This is my face, may it frighten or inspire, but I don't feel much like waiting. He turns toward me with a start and then freezes, emotions turning his pale cheeks red. I feel bad making him sputter and stumble to get out of my way for only a second—but then I shove past him, my arm brushing his arm, and there it is again, the spark, the jolt, this time not even from my hands, but as though my entire body is an electric fence. It feels almost good, the way an I.V.'s quick plunge used to bring a kind of release of adrenaline, almost a relief.

"Hey!" he says and scans my hands as though I'm holding some kind of weapon. I just shrug, like I've got no idea what his problem is. His eyes light on my bulky thumbs and he shakes his head slightly and bolts away without even picking out a beer. A feeling is growing inside of me, not unlike the way the air becomes charged before a thunderstorm, like I am becoming bigger, more fierce, more potent. Like nothing could hurt me.

I pull out a Gatorade and go to pay for it at the counter, letting my hand touch the tiny female cashier, who politely avoids looking at me too closely. When our hands make contact there is an audible snap, and she gasps, and I don't know why I do it, but I caress her fingers for a second and she moans like I've crushed bones.

It's then that fear takes hold. I mumble an apology and leave my money and my drink on the counter, running out into the heat of the day as though I can escape whatever's building inside me.

The dark truth is finally freed, or rather, released, surly and starved, from its cage. The thing kept pressed down into a corner of my mind all these years so that I wouldn't have to feel the sear of it. My best friend sought to burn me to ash, to reduce me to something that she could manage. For a moment, no matter how brief, Marly wanted to hurt me.

ℰℰℰ

With each floor I pass on my way up to the apartment in the elevator, I feel as though I'm rising through layers of understanding. Truth walks off the elevator with me. Marly is a vault of secrets, each one worse than the last. I tick them off on my fingers, those she's unburdened herself of: the baby, the bracelet, the relationship with Drew, her marriage. The fire. *What more does she hold?*

A decision makes itself when I walk into my room and see the edge of my black suitcase poking out from under my bed just a notch, as though it moved of its own accord to point me homeward. *Ma is too proud to ask for my help, and I've been a fool. If there's anything left of my ability to heal, I've got to save it for my mother.*

I'm well-packed when Marly finally comes home. She's sweaty and smells of the metallic whip of wind. "Are you...leaving?" Her voice is a tight rope.

"I need to see Ma, to help her, if I still can."

Her eyes dart from the suitcase to me several times, an idea working its way round her brain. "I'm coming with you."

It takes a painful effort to act civil with her. "No, don't be silly. You were right—it's not necessary for you to come." I look out at the hazy sky through her window. On her balcony, her pots of bright geraniums are folded in on themselves, a day's heat away from death.

She sets her mouth in a hard line. "I want to."

I want to reassure her that I'm not going home forever, that I've built something here, something that belongs to me. I have a purpose, even friends. Going home is just to make sure I have nothing to regret when it comes to my mother, but I can't say the words. I don't owe her anything. "I need to go alone."

"Fine," she says, in that tight way I remember from girlhood arguments. "But Grace. You've got a client tomorrow. You're not going to leave someone hanging, right?"

That is exactly what I'm going to do, if my electric hands are indicative of anything.

"Marly," I say. "Something's happening to me, maybe to the healing. It's changing. I hurt some people today, in the mini-mart, just by touching them. And these were light, tiny, nothing touches." I find her eyes, try to gaze in as accusing a way as I'm capable.

She tilts her head back, gives me a wary eye. "What am I supposed to say, Grace? Don't give in to the dark side? I don't even know how or why it works in you at all."

It's all because of you! I want to shout. The miraculous and the mundane, the healing and the darkness.

"It's like I was a live wire, and everyone who came into contact with me felt it, ok, and those were minor kinds of contact... If there's anything left, it's for Ma."

Marly folds her hands over her belly, and the gesture makes her look so self-righteous I want to slap her. "Your client is Gus." She still can't keep her contempt for him out of her voice, even now, even when he's nearly a saint in comparison.

Truth sinks in further. "You'd like it if I hurt him, then, wouldn't you? You've never liked him."

Her lips roll back as though she's going to swear at me, but she gets them under control, shakes her head. "You act like I'm some kind of monster." I try to ignore the look of hurt on her face. Then, softer: "I would take it back if I could."

My body feels suddenly heavy. I want so badly to lie down somewhere cool. I'm not going to let her work out her conscience now, not yet. *Why now, Gus?* "Well then. I'll talk to Gus, tell him why I can't help him. Then I go home to my mother. I'll take a cab."

She shakes her head so slightly it looks like a tic. "I'll drive. You shouldn't do another healing alone."

Chapter Twenty-Six

It's funny how you can stop viewing something, or someone, as strange after a long enough time. How the sight of Gus's face is no weirder than looking at Ma's. Having him here, alone with me in my healing space, feels even more intimate than it did in his odd desert house.

I've asked Marly to wait inside Drew's house or in the yard.

"That was really something, you at the show," he says. "I wish you could have seen yourself the way I saw you."

I'm not feeling up for another discussion about how I should be more accepting of myself, and the way I feel today, that empowered version of me is almost a dream. I rub my palms together, consider their pale slender length, except for the thumbs and a tiny reddish scar on the inside of each index finger.

"So what ails you? Hepatitis?"

He snorts. "I've lived with hepatitis C since I was a teenager, but my liver never could hold up to all the shit I poured into my body. It's just about worn out. And they won't let me onto a donor list, though I've been sober a long time. There are good people out there who never did anything to their bodies who need organs."

"You're a good person," I'm quick to point out.

Gus snorts. "I don't allow myself those kind of platitudes, Grace."

"Do you know that the liver is the only organ in the body that can regenerate itself?" I ask. "Doctor trivia. Picked that up working for one."

"I didn't know that," he touches the spot atop his shirt where his liver resides. "Why do you think it does that?"

I shrug. "I bet we'll figure out in some hundred years or so that pieces of the liver can be transplanted onto other organs and make them grow, too. Who knows."

"Or maybe God speaks in metaphors," Gus says, patting his liver as though it's a great book he's holding close.

"How do you mean?"

"I don't know. Seems interesting that the organ meant to filter all the toxic crap we take in should also be the only one that regenerates. You only get one heart, one brain, one stomach, but your crap filter, it's renewable!" He barks a phlegmy laugh. "I never asked you about your life back home, it just occurred to me," he says. "It's like you sprang fully formed from Zeus's head or something."

"Funny you should mention my home." A heavy sigh escapes me. "I'm going home tomorrow. My mother's sick."

"Oh, I'm sorry. Going for good?"

"I don't know."

Gus looks down at the floor. "I'm not here so you'll magically fix me," he says. You know how you said you see visions of people's pain when you touch them? Little movies in your mind?"

All too well.

"I was hoping you might be able to help me wake up a few more memories of Maya—really bring 'em into full relief. She's slipping away. Some days I can't even picture her face. It's a pain I want to feel."

I have the same reflexive urge to shout "no!" as I did with those parents in the intensive care unit. "Can I ask why? Is it to punish yourself more? Because I'm not going to help you—"

"I don't mean to be rude, Grace, but if you haven't had a child, you don't know what it's like to love someone so much more than yourself. Not in the way that commercials try to sell you. It's like..."

I've never allowed myself to imagine having a child.

He tilts his head up to the ceiling, "You love with your cells and organs. You love in a way that has teeth. It's not just big, it's an animal thing. So when you lose that child, that animal is forever gnashing those teeth and howling at the moon and starved of the love it felt."

His voice is thick. I can feel grief collecting inside and around him like static electricity.

"So, if we could wake up a memory of her, that animal in me is going to hurt, probably badly, for awhile. But it's a worthy hurt."

The only person I've ever let myself love so fully was Marly, when we were girls, and maybe Adam.

"I came here today, Gus, only to tell you that I don't know if I can even try. Something's...going on, with the healing. It feels wonky."

"Define wonky?"

"I mean, the last few people I touched recoiled like I was delivering an electric charge."

"Oh yeah?" He grins."Touch my hand now."

"No," I clutch my hands to myself.

"Come on, Grace. Do you think I'm afraid of a little shock?"

"But what if it's worse?" I ask.

Gus's grin stretches to an "I dare you" smile. In his presence I don't feel the weight of Marly's confession, just a sense of lightness that even in my scarred up state, I am enough.

"Try me, Grace." He claps his hands together like we're about to arm wrestle. "Try me. I am not afraid of pain."

Very slowly, I lower my hands onto his outstretched palms, like that game Marly and I played as girls, where you had to move fast to avoid getting your hands slapped. The penalty for getting hand-slapped was worse; you got a cheek slap, too, and sometimes one of her cheap rings would graze the skin, leave a tiny flesh wound.

As my hands close in on his there's a ticklish sensation in my palms, one short shock and a crackling sound and then suddenly Gus is laughing and the air smells sharp like just after a rain.

And then I'm laughing, though it's ridiculous that I should be able to do so after all that's happened, but it's something about Gus—the freedom in him releases something in me.

"You can't hurt me, Grace. Or no more than sliding down a slide at the local playground."

He kicks off his shoes and climbs up onto the table, his weight sinking grooves into the soft pleather.

I touch the tips of my fingers together. No further sparks emit. I take a deep breath. When I close my eyes to let my serpent take over, I find my head full, a cluttered drawer like something in Ma's bathroom, spilling out caked cosmetics, old and crumbling. *Flame warping wood. Flame seeking skin. Marly tilting her candle in.* My hands are so hot I'm afraid to touch him again. I shake my head as though it will settle the debris, and hold in my mind an image of cool, flowing water.

I stay behind his head, place my hands on his chest, one over each lung. It's important not to go too directly in sometimes.

"Hell, your hands are on fire," he says.

I almost wrench them off, thinking he means it literally, when, without its usual meandering preamble, the serpent yanks me around his body, traveling a red highway of blood cells gone bad. "It's not from drugs," I say softly to myself. It's not the hepatitis, either. What's making him sick feels like hot, carbonated water, burbling and rumbling through the veins, aggravating the heart, lying in wait. It hides and lurks. I feel it beneath the veins, in the bones, gathering strength, ready to spread. The word *leukemia* presents itself to me.

It's more than I can heal—not all at once, at least. There are no dark tumors to scoop out, no sticky patches of cancer vines to clear away; it's a molten force that burns through every part of him.

My serpent backs away, but I force myself forward, trying to find the teeth of his memories of Maya. There are ripples of her face—a vague outline, dark curls, small lips, small fingers curling around the tail of a stuffed cat. Small feet in tiny white shoes stumbling over a dirt path: a face with big brown eyes. I go searching for more, past half-carved images of color and light until we land. I see her only for a split second, squatting, and she's holding a big old camera, barely able to hold it, photographing the ground, ants marching there. Sunlight filtered through trees.

"Yes," he says, takes a big, deep breath and squeezes my hand so tightly I squeal, afraid my fingers will break. *Then I'm reeling backwards and away from him, and it's Harlan's face I see, my father—kids around town called him Han Solo, he looked so much like the young Harrison Ford. His dark brown bangs slip over his eyes as he nods at me, "Yes, just like that, darlin'." I'm standing on a big rock, perched in front of a duck pond, smiling big enough to reveal my latest lost tooth, an enormous gap in the front of my face.*

My mother is standing just to the right of him, shading her eyes against the sun and staring off in the distance. She is so beautiful. They love me so much...

Gus gasps, coughs, reaches toward me as though a part of him is caught in my arms, and then makes an alarming dog-like whine. All Gus's images are blown away like smoke in a fan. I'm being drawn into his body by an incredible vacuum, as though the void of his daughter needs to be filled. I pull my hand out of his, causing a charge of pain to surge through my arms. His body convulses twice, and he heaves as though trying to cough again. He stands up, a sleepwalker barely awakened, and eyes wide, he begins to tilt toward me, but there's no way I can hold him, and so I stumble out of the way, watching in horror as he hits the floor with a thundering boom, and then goes completely still.

I instantly check for a pulse, but it's so weak it's like listening for a miner at the bottom of a shaft; I can't be sure I feel it at all. I shout for Marly, "Call 911!" at the same moment that she's thrusting open the door saying, "What the hell was that?"

"Oh my god," she says at the sight of Gus toppled on the floor.

"It was me; I should never have done this one!" I moan, pacing the room. "I knew something was going bad in me, I knew it."

"Grace, no, you can't do this to yourself—"

I rear back, away from her touch. "I wasn't ready. I needed time first. Time. What if it's gone? My mother needs me, and now what?"

Marly, swollen and heavy, stands staring at me as though she's looking for a rope to throw and drag me out of a thrashing sea. Gus's body is so still I'm afraid to look again for his pulse, afraid to touch him for fear that this force turning dark inside me will finish him off.

"This is all your fault!" I shout. And I realize I mean

everything: The tree house, the fire, bringing me to Vegas, pushing me to heal, betraying my illusion of us, of our perfect bond, a second time.

Marly shakes her head, her eyes wet with tears as she dials 911 on her cell phone.

We are still standing there when the paramedics arrive. I move back to the corner of the room as the men work. A foamy puddle of drool has wet the carpet beneath his mouth. His face is dark purple. CPR is done, then they pull out the awful paddles, and I cringe away, tucking myself almost into the ficus tree, away from the charge of electricity, as though I am a lightning rod and it is another form of fire come to finish me off.

They shout "clear" and the paddles strike, and before long they're wagging their heads sadly and wheeling in a stretcher.

I have the terrifying feeling that I won't be able to take another breath, and I'm nearly hugging the wall to hold myself upright.

When the outcome is clear, the short, stocky bald paramedic comes back to take a report. "What happened here?" he asks Marly.

"It was just a massage," Marly says, chin up, as though defying him to ask why he was clothed, why there is no massage lotion or sheet to cover him with. "He must have a heart condition." I suddenly see her in the same stance talking with Officer Markson, thirteen years earlier. Bottle of peach schnapps tossed behind her in the tall grass at the side of the road, breasts thrust in his direction. *"We were just taking a walk, officer. I didn't throw anything, officer."*

The paramedic looks from me, with my bad thumbs and birdlike frame, to Marly, gravid with pregnancy. He taps a pen against his top teeth, eyes narrowed, as though trying to reconcile the likelihood of either of us giving a massage to the tattooed man now cold in the van. "We've called the police, so stick around."

I hold back sobs as Marly speaks for me. As the ambulance shuts its doors and eats gravel on its way out, suddenly Drew is standing in the doorway to my little studio, panting as though he ran here. I have an empty feeling that this might be the last time the three of us stand here together.

I think of Sara, how I will have to tell her.

"What happened?" he asks. His brow softens a tiny bit at the sight of Marly, standing, not in any kind of obvious labor.

"I think." My voice halts in my throat. "I think I just killed my friend."

∾⃝

Every second I sit answering the officer's questions out in Drew's yard, is a worse agony than the last. I all but feel my mother's life draining away, my healing gift reducing to a faint trickle. My eyes keep trying to fold in on themselves, and I close my eyes and try to look grieved rather than near passing out. I keep my arms folded across my chest, my hands tucked beneath my armpits. My clothes are stuck to me with sweat.

Marly stands off to the side of me, talking to an officer, a woman with acne-scarred skin who sizes Marly up. The officer is frowning at her like she's one of those high school girls who made school a living hell for the not-pretty. In a way, I think, she did. I can't help myself, even now as I look at the officer's acne scars and I think: what a shame; I could heal those.

I don't see the point in lying, so I tell officer Bailey, the one who is droning on at me, as simply as I can that I do a form of natural healing that is like massage.

"No, I'm not certified in the state of Nevada," I answer truthfully. "I'm not certified anywhere."

His questions are banal, run of the mill, how I knew Gus, if he paid me money, if sexual favors were exchanged. I try not to laugh, sound caustic, but I'm near ready to come apart with exhaustion.

The officers finish near the same time, say they'll be in touch, and then Marly strides toward me, as though we're going to share some kind of post-mortem. But I turn away. I turn away from the hope in her eyes that everything can ever go back to how it was.

Running away. You're running away. The accusation is in my head, and I'm already defending myself. Yes, I'm running away, toward the one person I should never have left. My mother.

༂ⓞⓖ༂

The cab pulls up to the blue two-story house with the red brick walkway, and I see with dismay that the shrubs have shot up and sprouted unruly feelers that grope anyone daring to walk past. The red geraniums spill out in unchecked profusion, choking out once sprightly little marigolds.

I debated calling first, but that felt too much like asking permission.

As I stand on the sidewalk, clutching my travel bag, the front door opens and a tall blonde woman dressed in a pink jogging suit emerges. She jumps when she sees me and clutches the gold cross at her neck as though to ward off a demon. "You startled me," she says. "I didn't see anyone there."

"Sorry," I say, sure that it's more than my simple presence that startled her; I've left off a wig or scarf today.

"You're Grace," she says matter-of-factly.

So my reputation precedes me. How Ma must tell people about me: *Grace, my burned child. Don't jump when you see her, she can't help how she looks.*

"Doreen." She points at herself. "She's sleeping now," she says, pointing at the window that is Ma's bedroom.

"That's okay, I won't bother her." Although I have every intention of doing just that.

She wiggles her fingers at me in a semblance of a wave and hurries off to her car. It's only as she squeals away that I see the magnetic Hospice sign on her passenger side door and suddenly every footstep feels heavier.

The screen door squeaks in pain when I open it. It was my job to apply the WD-40 to all the hinges in the household, getting up on a chair for those I can't reach otherwise because Ma's weight has ruined her knees. I enter the foyer and recoil from a distinctly musty stench. It's cloyingly hot inside; the fans scattered in different rooms are all turned off. Bags of garbage not cinched tight are piled from kitchen to living room, disgorging food particles and paper, flies buzzing in obsessive circles. Those that are closed—and I can only guess the Hospice folks are responsible for those—have been gnawed open by the opportunistic cats. One of them darts in front of my foot and without much thought I try to kick it but I miss. There is suddenly nothing cute about these fuzzy little scavengers. I suspect they'd gnaw on one of our corpses if hungry enough.

The veil that covers the mirror in the entryway is hanging down, suspended by only one tack. I skip past it, refusing to look.

The walls of the house feel like big wet lungs around me and smells like something much worse. *Did I really spend my life here?*

Magazines litter the dining room table; what looks like the entire contents of Ma's old art supplies closet are clustered on the couch; dishes are stacked in the sink, crusted with half-eaten soups and buzzing with flies. Tears climb up my eyes but stick, gathering in my head, making it pound.

I walk as quietly down the hall as I can, not so that she can sleep, but to keep my presence a secret. But it's impossible to do this quietly. The Diet Coke cans are all over the hallway, kicked aside, many of them crushed, as though by people who had to get to Ma in a hurry, with no care for what looks like random garbage.

Her bedroom door is slightly ajar, and the telltale flicker of television draws bizarre shadows in the crease. I'm afraid to look in.

"I see your shadow." Ma's voice rents the stillness. I inhale and push the door open. Past the piles of boxes and brown paper, and several taller hills of clothing, she lies in bed with the covers pulled up to her chin, looking unnervingly small beneath her mounded covers. Sweat trickles down my brow. It must be eighty degrees in here.

I make my own path, skirting as much as possible, careful not to step on anything, and sit at the edge of the bed, taking in her features. Her cheeks are sunken. Her color is hard to assess in the dim room, but it looks ashy.

"You lied to me about getting better, didn't you?"

She sighs, looks up at the ceiling. "I didn't want you to come rushing home like this, Gracie. The doctors don't really know how much time I have left, but I knew I wasn't going to waste it on pointless chemotherapy and surgery, or make you give up any more happiness." She reaches her hand up to my face, a gesture she hasn't made since I was a girl, and strokes my rough cheek. "You look different," she says.

I laugh.

"It's not in your features," she says with a snort of impatience. "Come hug me."

"I can't," I say. "I can't even touch you. I'm a danger, it's all gone dark..."

"Hush." My mother holds out her arms to me. "You can't hurt me."

That's what Gus said, what I believed, but she's frail, so close to death. Her belly is swollen with the common bloating of her illness—though I can tell by the slack hang of flesh on her legs and arms that she's lost too much weight too quickly to be good.

"I'm going to get a cool washcloth," I say, though I'm not sure for whom, and move toward her bathroom.

"No, Gracie, please...don't," she calls after me. I don't hear the true desperation in her voice until I've walked straight into the center of it. I never, ever went into her bathroom—the only off limits room in the whole house.

From the ceiling hang dozens of little mesh baskets bleeding lipsticks and eyeliners, like bulging tumors. The edges of the room are piled high with crumpled tissues and toilet paper, dark with yellowish-orange discharge, rising in such height, that if I could actually reach the window to open it, they would spill out like moths into the yard. The toilet bowl is stained a disturbing reddish brown, and caked in layers of grime I don't want to linger on. The shower holds nothing but bottles and random trash, so that it can't be opened without danger.

The only clean things in the room are a stack of baby wipes. I pull several from the box and pour cold water on them, the tears building to a staccato throb in my head. The once white sink is trashed, and iridescent gold and blue eye shadow glimmers from a hundred tiny cracks, like a vein of crystal.

I left her to this. This reality is a punch to my diaphragm, bringing me to my knees. I left her alone to drown in her own refuse. *What kind of daughter does that?*

When I emerge, stifling the tears, she's staring at me with wide eyes, mouth drawn, sorrow etching what's left of her once plump cheeks. *How have we spent all these years behaving as if this is normal?*

"I'm serious, Gracie, come over here and sit with me." She holds out her arms and the child in me can't resist; I walk there slowly, making my way around detritus on the floor, sit beside her, suddenly aware of the sweet-rot unwashed scent of her, the reality of how rarely she has left this bed since I've been gone. I want to say so much. She takes my hand, and the burning center inside me that has been throbbing since I left Gus's lifeless body suddenly stills. My serpent is at once awake, however, and begins to move through her. Within seconds I travel the sorrows of my mother's body. I fold into pockets of flesh and feel, beneath them, the cutting remarks my grandfather used to carve her down to bone, until she was so empty and hollow that the only thing to fill her up again was food. I slide through the lesser scars of appendix removal and a broken humerus. Through the runnels of the two kidney stones she passed, and through the memory of a baby that came very close to term—the older sibling I might have had—I am tossed into memories of my own, surfacing like sea monsters in dark water.

The time I slammed my hand in the car door, palm and back of hand the color of wine grapes for several weeks; the time the rope swing at the lake had cut so deeply into my shin that I needed stitches; a case of pneumonia so bad they had had to put me in an oxygen tent. But as my own memories flash through me, I realize I'm feeling them *through* Ma. They are *her* memories of my pain, seared deep into her very cells. I press on, determined to make it to where her illness hunkers.

There's a momentary resistance, like passing through a thin, permeable membrane before I reach the cancer, a dark vortex at the center of her.

I feel the cancerous pebbles, tendrils of sticky sludge holding them down, the perfect manifestation of dark feelings turned inward—self-loathing, disappointment, hatred, fear, disbelief that a loving God could have let such a thing happen to her beautiful child. In the dying walls of her womb, I have a vision of... myself: a shriveled, wounded child, fighting for breath, tortured by pain. I am seared with small hot pins to the heart, an emotional pain that's worse than anything I have ever experienced bodily.

I try to pull away from that feeling, but it dogs me, makes me feel weak and tired. I try to begin the work of removing the cancer stones, but the energy rebounds and I am catapulted backwards, my hands repulsed from Ma's body as though I've been pushed.

"My ability is gone," I moan aloud. "I can't heal anymore."

"No, honey, it's not gone, it's forged in you. You can't heal me for the same reason you can't heal yourself," Ma whispers. "It's like asking water to make itself wet." She looks at me with uncommon tenderness. "You're part of me and I'm part of you. I know you felt that."

Or is it as Drew said: that Ma does not believe, and so I am, essentially, powerless? A fraud, as that woman Ellie shouted on the day of my heatstroke?

I am shivering with an emotional echo of what Ma experienced after I burned, of the realization that she felt the presence of my serpent, even if it could do nothing for her.

"You lost a baby," I say.

Ma inclines her head back into the pillow, as if holding it up at all is too much effort. "Two, actually: one before you, one after. First one, a little girl we called Melody, lived ten days; heart abnormality, poor sweetheart. We took her home. I didn't tell Harlan about the miscarriage; it would have broken his heart."

Two died. One burned. My body heaves with painful understanding and I recall the image I saw when I last touched Ma, a baby in a bassinet...not me after all. "I can't heal you," I say, for confirmation to myself.

"I don't think so," she says. "But you can live your life now however you see fit."

"No I can't." Gus's strange and familiar face rises into my mind. I don't want to believe he's gone, or worse, that my hands had something to do with his death, but I know it must be true. "Something has happened, and I don't know how to fix it."

She eases herself gingerly up to sitting. "Tell me."

I am too exhausted to resist. And in some way, I feel joined with Ma at the edge of death, though mine isn't literal; when I picture my future, I see a horizon cloaked in ash. So I tell her everything about Marly's revelation, saving the details of Gus's death, though they burn a hole inside my throat.

Ma's tone is heavy, but not angry. "I knew she was responsible for the fire, Gracie, one way or another."

"What? How did you know?"

Ma coughs, points to a box on the end table, which I

hand to her. She pulls out a pale pink tissue, spits into it. "I knew instantly that the fire was no accident. Why do you think I worked so hard to keep you girls apart? After that incident with the young men, coming to pick up my baby girl at the police station, well I knew it would be something, Grace. She'd get you to jump out of a moving vehicle, or play with fire...I forgave Marly a long time ago for what she did to you," Ma says, "once I realized what a damaged little girl she was."

Why didn't we didn't talk about any of this sooner? "So why did you give me, and her, such a hard time when she came back to town?"

Ma grabs my hands gently and pulls me down into her chest with surprising strength. It feels good to be folded into her bosom. "I didn't want to take away your good memories. Marly was your best friend, no matter what I thought of her. I wanted you to remember her that way. Of course, I didn't think you'd ever see her again, so when she came looking for you, well...I had a feeling she'd give in to the need to unburden herself. I was afraid of what it would do to you."

She pulls me tighter to her, but not so that she hurts me. "Forgiveness has to come on its own—it can't be forced."

Chapter Twenty-Seven

The air in my mother's room smells of bad coffee and onions. I rise and pull open one of her curtains, which looks out onto a tiny, tangled backyard made even tinier by wildflowers and grass growing together as if in collusion to choke out the apple tree. "I should weed all that," I say. "Plant you a little vegetable garden."

Ma shuts off Judge Judy. "No way on God's green earth."

I turn back around. Ma squints in the afternoon sunlight like a cat awakened abruptly.

"It's no big deal. It would be meditative. I do stuff like this at the Wildlife Center all the time."

"Did. You *did* stuff like that. You're not staying here. "You have a life...in Las Vegas. Not where I pictured you ending up, but it's like your Aunt Mo would say—

wherever you go, there you are. You're there, and you're doing something that's important to you. Keep doing it. Don't come back here."

"Ma, you need help."

Ma scoffs, and sits up higher in her bed. "I'm a fighter, Grace. Aren't you proof of that? Aren't I? And you know what?" She pats her belly. "I finally found a way all this flesh is a good thing—there's too much of me for cancer to take all at once."

Her words are soft and sharp, both, but I don't find myself arguing with her. Something else has just occurred to me. "Ma, I'm going to ask you something, and please, I just want you to tell me yes, or no. No lecture."

She falls into a coughing fit, and I wonder if she's faking it. At last she says, "Okay, Grace."

"Do you have Dad's most recent address?" Maybe he can come and help out. Maybe there's a spark of concern, or a sinewy cord of guilt I can yank on.

The air feels charged between us. "Has he gotten in touch with you?" she asks at last.

"No, of course not. When does he ever bother? Just, look, either you do or you don't, and it's fine if you don't—"

"I do."

I'm not sure I heard her right. "You do?"

"And his phone number." And then she rattles off a phone and address by memory.

"Have you and Dad been in touch?" Shock pushes me up straighter.

"Nothing like that, Grace. I suspect you can ask him the rest."

༄༅༄

I walk through the neighborhood before I do what I need to do next.

The bus drops me off not far from Adam's office, set inside an old, blue Victorian with white scrollwork, something I loved immediately about working for him. No sterile white hallways or patient rooms. Adam's office is like an extension of his own home.

Standing on the sidewalk, behind a thick magnolia tree, I can see the front office through the wide-open bay window. And there he is; the sight of him is like an electric charge to my solar plexus. He's leaned forward over the front desk. But it isn't Miranda, the head receptionist, sitting there, it's Helen: the nurse who cringed away from me at every turn, the one who always stands too close to him, entering his personal space as if she's earned it. And Adam is laughing with her, an open-mouthed, face-full-of-pleasure kind of laugh.

My breath has claws as it climbs up my throat. *An animal thing.*

I turn, quickly, before he has a chance to see me and walk as fast as I am able back toward the bus stop. What's the point in trying to cultivate a relationship with a man in Drake's Bay, if I am going to leave? *And who already has a more attractive woman in his life.* I swallow cement.

My next stop is the Wildlife Center. Tucked away in a grove of pines on the outskirts of town, it's the last place the bus stops before the long valley stretch out to the coast. A haven.

The peeling red gate still squeaks when I enter. There's the gnarled old central building, a "portable" that once served as a school for children with mental disabilities. The "CAUTION, BROKEN STAIR" sign is still affixed, dangling by one nail at an angle.

There are two, big bird enclosures covered by netting, each containing a slightly stagnant pool of water and buckets of dead fish. The smell is like a fish kill at low tide. Inside the main building are all the small mammals: raccoons, rabbits, rodents. Then there are the last two big outside pens: one called "The Grotto," which houses Brownie, the bear; the other is for wounded mountain lions, or the occasional deer.

A squeal that is distinctly human comes from the main building. Natalie, my supervisor, a tiny woman with a massive head of curly black hair, comes running my way. "Grace!" She stops shy of hugging me, but her smile is as wide as an embrace. "We've missed you. I hear you're living in Las Vegas now?" She sounds impressed.

"Yeah, strange, huh?"

"Not strange if it makes you happy."

"I hope my leaving hasn't left you all in the lurch here. I feel terrible. But I wanted to come say 'hi.' Especially to Brownie. I actually dreamt about him while I was gone. I miss the big old guy."

To my surprise, Natalie tears up. "Oh Grace," her face takes on soft lines. "Brownie died. About a month ago. I thought you knew. It got written up in the *Drake's Bay Gazette.* Figured your mom would tell you, or Adam."

I have a sudden feeling of being upside down. "Oh

no," I manage to say before tears come. Natalie is shaking her head, mumbling "I'm so sorry" over and over, and then she's guiding me away, out of the center, my feet not registering the contact of the earth beneath them. She floats me on an eddy of my own grief to a bench.

"It's just a stupid bear," I cry, picturing the slightly oily, spiky pelt of the great beast, who once took a fish right out of my hand and then licked my arm, a rasp surprisingly strong and sharp—a tongue for gouging honey out of bees nests and deboning a salmon.

"It's not stupid," Natalie says. "You've got amazing empathy, Grace. It's what made you so natural with the animals, and why I loved having you around—and that is not guilt, okay? If it makes you feel better, I still cry, too, every time I walk past his grotto."

Natalie and I have never touched before. She treated me with the same cautious respect as the wounded animals we tended. When I lean into her, she is, at first, tentative. And at the end of it all, in the hollow of the last sob I can squeeze out of me, my serpent becomes aware of two heartbeats, one big, one tiny, beating in such close harmony they could be mistaken for one.

"You're pregnant," I say without thinking.

Natalie pulls back sharply. "How'd you...?"

I look up at her, eyes wide, shaking my head. There is no way to explain.

Natalie smiles, takes my hand. "I always knew there was something special about you, Grace."

Chapter Twenty-Eight

The town car pulls onto a private road that runs about a mile and leads up to a large ranch-style home with salmon-colored stucco exterior. I paid the driver at the outset, and so he leaves as soon as I close the door behind me, dropped here, a traveler in a familiar land.

A white fountain gurgles in a little landscaped courtyard surrounded by tall juniper shrubs shaped into tapered tips and laid down with red bark. These are what Marly might call "seriously nice digs." In contrast, the untamed yard of our house in Drake's Bay comes to mind.

"Oh shit," I say, as a lovely auburn-haired woman in an empire style yellow sundress emerges from the front door, porting a toddler on one hip. She can't be more than thirty-five. As the woman squints into the sun, I see a man come out and put a hand on her shoulder. I stare at the vaguely familiar outline of my father. I can barely believe it. It's him.

And the child. Even at this distance I see the work of his genes. You could have held up a picture of me at age three and said with certainty that the tiny girl on the woman's hip and my young self were sisters.

He walks toward me, neither rushing, nor dawdling. When he reaches me my hand is trembling. His hair is grayer up close and lines are now carved deep and furrowed, mapping out the years on his face.

"Grace? I...Is everything okay? Are you okay?"

I effort up some politeness. "I'm sorry to show up like this. I didn't mean to barge in."

He clears his throat roughly. "No, are you kidding? It's not barging! Celine and I—you're welcome anytime, you know that. I'm just mighty surprised, is all."

I stare at his nose, because it's easier than looking into his eyes. "Celine?" I point to the doorstep where the woman holds her hand, visor-like, over her eyes and sways the toddler. She's thin in a way that would corrode Ma with jealousy, with upswept blondish hair, dark at the roots. She's pretty in a bland sort of way—like a canvas awaiting paint.

"And little Melody," he says with a straight face. *Melody—the name of the child he and Ma lost?* I want to throttle him right there at the callousness.

"Come on inside and I'll get you something to drink," he says. "Celine, can you believe it? It's Grace!" Harlan calls. A stranger would see this as kindness, but I know it's guilt-driven politeness. I know what he's capable of: walking away from his own blood.

We walk a flagstone path lined with lavender and rosemary and a bush that sprouts tiny white flowers, like little peace flags. I have the urge to step on them. "Hello!" Celine greets me in a customer service, falsely friendly tone when we reach the door.

We enter a living room that could easily star in *House Beautiful*. The entire room, save one wall, is windows, and the ceilings are high and open-beamed. The tile floors are so pristine I am afraid to walk on them. In a far corner is an immaculate gray marble-front fireplace. But the eye-catching detail of the room is an enormous painting of a trio of nude women, one old, one middle-aged, one barely a teen, over the couch. The colors are bold jewel-tones, attention getting, yet the forms soft, subtle, suggesting melding or union somewhere between maternal and sexual.

"Celine's an artist," My father says in an awkward attempt at breaking the silence.

She puts a hand on his shoulder. "Your father and I met when his photo show debuted. I know he'd hoped you would come to see it."

Come to see it? How on earth has Harlan kept his lack of contact with me a secret from his own wife?

"Well," my father clears his throat, as if afraid to go down that road. "Are you thirsty? Hungry?"

I am thirsty, but feel an ache of pride on Ma's behalf. At home we drink out of Snoopy drinking glasses she found for twenty-five cents each at a garage sale. Celine's glasses are probably hand-blown in Italy. I feel as though to eat or drink anything provided by her would be a betrayal of Ma. Does Harlan not see the hypocrisy of having left my mother to a life where she had to work twice as hard to support us to pay for my medical bills?

Celine clears her throat. I'm rooted in place, silently shaking my head. "I'd love something to drink," I say, to save myself from saying worse.

Celine hands the little girl—I have trouble thinking of her as my sister—to Harlan wordlessly, and then disappears around a towering fern into what I presume is the kitchen. I envision an enormous island in the center of a gleaming expanse crowned by copper cooking pots and a spotless stainless steel fridge. Harlan deposits the child in a gated play nook.

"Please, sit down," he offers, tense and fidgety, the picture of unease. I am wondering what I can or should tell him. I finally ease into a red leather recliner.

Celine returns with a serving tray of iced teas in elegant, pink glasses and delicate cake-like pastries frosted white. She sets them down on the mahogany coffee table.

"Grace," she says softly, as if tasting my name.

"Yes?" I ask when nothing else follows. Her green eyes travel frankly over my face, boldly assessing what she sees. I decide I will meet her gaze rather than flinch away from it.

"Grace was one of my choices for a girl's name before I met your father. Then of course, I learned it was already taken, so we went with Melody."

"Was it easy for you to move on?" I ask Harlan in a tight voice. "Have a new family without any tragedy in it?"

He clears his throat and looks to Celine, mouth open.

"No, Grace, it's not like that..." Celine says.

"Grace, why don't you tell me why you're here," Harlan cuts in. His face looks pinched, as though my presence causes him pain. "It seems unlikely of you to come for no reason when I never hear from you."

My ears begin to ring and then I'm talking without any care for how I sound or their feelings. "You left us after the fire, and all I got from you was a stupid Christmas card every year." I'm shaking. "I come here and find out about your new family by accident!"

Harlan's eyes are wide. "Honey...what? I sent you lots of letters. Your Ma never—?" My father shakes his head. "Now, for the record, I'm not saying I'm a saint, but your Ma wanted me gone. After the accident we said things to each other I'll forever regret. We blamed each other. And I drank too much—I'm not pretending here. But when you didn't want to talk to me, I felt hamstrung. I called for two years until I finally gave up."

"You never called—" But even as I say it I can picture Ma holding her hand over the phone receiver while ushering me out of earshot. Ma was my gatekeeper—keeping out the world, and I let her, because I was afraid.

My father looks directly at me, then drags his thick fingers down his cheeks. "I had no idea you didn't know...oh God. I should have tried harder. I should have come to see you. But that house, it was painful for me to see your Ma falling into that way of life."

"Well maybe if you'd stuck around you could have helped her out of it!" The part of me that has spent twelve years believing he abandoned us isn't ready to let go of that story entirely.

Harlan puts his face in his hands momentarily. "Grace, marriage is complicated. You can't just make someone change."

"It is what it is," Celine says softly. "You're together now. Grace, tell us what you need."

Just spit it out. "Ma is sick. Cancer, and she won't get the medical help she needs." Death suddenly feels like bad weather, my own personal storm. Gus's face looms large, fills me with pain. I take a deep breath. "I honestly came here to ask...well, it seems stupid now that I know what I know."

"You wanted him to help care for her, didn't you?" Celine asks. "Of course you did."

It bothers me that she's so understanding; but I finish telling them everything, and when I stop talking my father puts his hands on his knees and sighs. "In whatever way we can, we'll help your mom, I want you to know that. She's proud, though, so I have to say it's unlikely she will accept much. I guess we'll figure something out."

I get up, stretch my aching leg, look around their spacious lovely house, so free of junk and clutter. *Can I blame my father for feeling pushed out?* I approach a series of framed photographs on the far wall: rows of photos comprised solely of me, me and him, and even a family portrait I've never seen. In it, the three of us are seated on a bench against the backdrop of a lush green picnic area, complete with duck pond and one lone duck in its waters. I am perhaps nine in the photo, with a small red balloon tied to my wrist and a joyous, gap-toothed smile. Ma looks thin in a vertically striped green and white summer dress, and Dad, hair to his shoulders, wears a blue Hawaiian button up. I can't remember Ma ever looking that happy or thin. And then it hits me: *this is the memory I had on the day of Gus's death.*

I gaze closely at my young face. "I was a pretty child." The kind that many mothers would have thrust into acting or commercials that sold things wistful and pure.

"You were," says my father, and I hear him leave the room.

The photographs are in chronological order, and stop with me at fifteen—before the face I once found plain, but now see as gorgeous, was erased. In the photo I sit staring at the camera as though I want to punch whoever is holding it. Considering how unpleasant my expression is, I find it odd that he displays this image.

"Grace, please don't hold it against him that there are no recent photos of you," Celine frowns. "I took the most recent one down." She turns to face me, her gaze unflinching. "I couldn't stand how sad he became looking at you after your accident. I was angry for him. We didn't know your mother was interfering with his letters and cards. The checks were cashed so we knew they were reaching you. We thought you'd made the choice to cut him off."

"I didn't even know there were any photos of me *after*," I say. "I can't remember letting anyone take a photo of me then."

"You were in your hospital bed the day of your release. With a young doctor."

Adam, I think, his powdery scent suddenly rich in my nose, his absence an added ache.

I stand there, staring at the happy portrait of a family I barely remember, and Harlan shuffles back in, carrying Melody. She's such a calm child. He hands their daughter off to Celine and sidles up to me. I'm still reflexively bent on seeing him as the bad guy; it takes several deep breaths to realize that he was also a victim of lies.

"I need to tell you something, Grace. Something I've never had the courage to tell."

Oh great, I think. *More confessions.*

He looks at me full on. It's been a long time since he's had to look at my scarred face. I dare him to look away, to break eye contact first, to prove that he can't handle it, but he doesn't.

"The night of the fire, Marly was just back from the psych ward. Your ma didn't want you going over there. She was tweaked with fury about it and threatened she'd leave me if I let you go. She had a pretty strong mother's intuition..."

I want to tell him to stop, that there's really no point to unburdening himself now, when the damage has been done.

"I should have listened. But you were just so damn sad, not having seen her for so long—after that stupid incident with the cops. I wanted to be the good guy, the sympathetic dad. I never wanted you to look back and say...well..." He makes a choking sound, before saying, "I let you go even though your ma forbade it."

Celine is watching us, her face ringed with sadness.

How nice, I think with cynicism, for him to have her to worry about his every feeling.

"Neither of us ever forgave me for that, Grace."

Pieces of it come back to me. How I'd stared at Oona Donovan's letter letting me know I could see Marly at her house. How I'd torn all the clothes off the hangers in my closet in a fury after Ma said no. And then, Harlan's soft, tentative knock on the door. "You came up to my room, whispered to me that I should go while Ma was watching her show." I can almost remember the swell of elation at his words.

"I'm so sorry, Grace," he says, and I know he means it.

III

Chapter Twenty-Nine

It's only as I'm leaving my father's house that I realize I am going back to Las Vegas. There are too many threads unfinished.

From the airport I go straight to Marly's work, since I don't know if I can stand the emptiness of her apartment. Only one mermaid is swimming in the cool aquamarine tank when I arrive. Marly told me they never leave it empty; the illusion must never be broken, even if there are no customers. I stand for a moment regarding the lone woman who swims with the strength of an athlete, dragging her sequin-studded tail, clutching the seaweed ropes to thrust herself through the tank. There's no sign of Marly, so she must be up in the office buried in paperwork, staying off her ankles, which swell with the heat.

Sabrina, however, is tending bar. She sees me and waves, but something dark gathers in her eyes. "Grace, oh it's good you're here. Marly was worried you weren't coming back. And frankly, I was a little worried, too."

"Why? Is it her health? Early contractions?" My pulse picks up.

Sabrina sets down a beer stein. "Despite how tough she can seem, she's kind of...easy to influence. I think especially when it comes to guys." She looks away from me, as though checking who might be listening. "You should talk to her. She's running payroll upstairs."

I make my way past the bathrooms, through a seashell curtain and up the back stairs to the office. The door is shut and I experience a *déjà-vu* of the moment I came to find her at her grandmother's funeral months ago. A spiky anxiety climbs my spine as I knock.

"C'm in," she calls out, exhaling a harried sigh.

I push inside. She's sitting on the floor, with a big pillow propped up behind her, papers in a pile between her outstretched knees. She's partially in her seaweed green uniform—tight tank top stretched over her big belly, shimmery net shawl around her shoulders, though she's wearing black sweat pants and flip-flops. Her hair is greasy, however, lank and piled in a mess at the top of her head, strands falling out in all directions. Dark circles rim her eyes, and though she quickly tries to hide it under her shawl, there are four fingertip shaped bruises up her left arm.

"What happened to you?" *I was only gone four days!*

I'm expecting defense, denial, protestations, but instead, Marly pushes herself off the ground, papers fluttering off her lap and lunges into a hug. I'm caught off guard, and stumble backwards into the door, bruising my back.

"Sorry," she cries when I squeal my discomfort. "I really missed you. I was afraid I'd really lost you forever this time."

"Okay, okay. Just sit down. It's okay."

Marly shakes her head. "No, it's not okay. It's not." She clutches her arms and rocks backwards on her feet and I have to fight the urge to do the same thing. "I really thought you wouldn't come back." Her voice is so small and childlike I want to lay her head in my lap.

"Honey," I hear myself soothing. Oh these old familiar words. "What happened? Tell me."She looks down at her feet, and wiggles her swollen toes. "Loser wants to fight for custody of the baby when she's born. He won't give me a divorce if I don't agree to that. I just wanted to talk to him."

"Marly, you went to him by yourself?"

She unconsciously strokes her bruises. "It was a public location. I thought he'd want to talk. I told him I never had any intention of pressing charges for the incident in the garage."

"Why'd you tell him that? Don't give him anything!" I understand it's too late, that she's already done the things she's talking about, but scolding her is only thing that keeps me from feeling the scrape of guilt for leaving.

"He knows about Drew. I think he's been following me."

"I think the word for that is 'stalking.'" I may have no personal experience with relationships, but I've watched enough episodes of *Oprah* over Ma's shoulder. "So, what did he do to you?"

She bites her bottom lip and hugs herself. "He just has this way of talking, you know, coercive and, and I feel like I have to listen. So he wanted to walk, and at first I wouldn't so he grabbed my arm, and squeezed, and I just, I didn't want to make a scene. That's what Sonya taught me so well: don't make a fucking scene." She's breathing too fast. "So I walked with him, and the next thing I know he's found some alley and he backs me up against the wall and he starts jabbing his finger into my chest, right over my heart, really hard, yelling, and calling me a whore, and telling me that he will do whatever it takes to get the baby from me if I don't work with him. He has friends all over Vegas, he says, who will do whatever he needs them to do."

She's hiccupping and crying now.

A tar-like energy is slithering through my veins, twisting out my limbs. I want to do this man harm. My fingers feel hot. She's panting and I'm afraid if I don't calm her down she'll go into early labor.

"Grace, you know what? I need to breathe. I can't breathe in this office with its...choking walls!" She leans past me, shoves the door open. "Come with me for a drive, please?"

ᏇᎾᏇ

"Are you okay to drive?" I ask once we're outside, though she's already breathing slower. We climb into her car, and soon enough the desert unspools like a bride's train behind us. Though I know it's absurd, I think of mob movies I've seen where long drives lead to a desolate location, and a bullet in the back of the head.

Marly is wedged tightly into her seat, belly almost pressed into the steering wheel, seatbelt cutting a painful-looking path between her breasts.

"You must think me weak, an idiot, just like that broken, fucked up girl you had to rescue all the time, Grace. I don't know why you came back." She's driving a little fast, and now I'm wondering if I've made a mistake. "Listen to me, I didn't even ask about your mother," she says, voice almost sing-song.

"I couldn't heal her. It didn't work." *What if I've used up my healing potential? What if all I'm capable of now is harm?*

Marly stares at the windshield as though it is her duty not to turn away from it, though I know she is afraid to look at me. "It's my fault. I stressed you out." Then her hand smacks my cheek so fast it's as though I imagined it. "I'm sorry, Grace. I don't know what's wrong with me lately." She swerves around something in the road I can't see, and am not entirely sure is even there.

My pulse is hammering in the joints of my jaw, clenched shut. "Pull over."

"What?"

"You need to stop driving. You're freaking me out. Pull over. Let's just stop."

"I'm fine. Driving is cathartic."

Marly reaches out and touches my hand. "Sorry I slapped you," she says.

The layers of all that has happened slam into me. I've lived so long without my father, the idea that he might be back in my life now is as overwhelming as the potential loss of Ma. Confusing waves of pain ache and sting, leaving my chest with the hollow, empty feeling I used to get once I was released from my pressure garments for a little while.

"Just slow a little, okay?" Marly takes the speed down a notch, just enough to stop my pulse from hammering. A thought I've long held but never asked is out of my mouth before I can think better of it. "How did you lose your father?"

She wipes sweat off her brow. "Aneurism," she says "Thirty-two years old, handsome, strong, in perfect health. And blammo—dead in minutes."

"Oh no. That's awful."

"He was pushing me in a jogging stroller. He'd gotten on some healthy jag after my mother nagged him about his weight." She barks a laugh. "He'd gone off the beaten path—out in the Cascades, where there are all these man-trampled trails that aren't officially trails. It took hours for another jogger to find him and by then I'd worked my way free of the stroller straps. I was just slumped on top of him, wailing."

"Oh Marly." *I can't even imagine.*

"Bryce manipulated me with that info. Told me if I didn't listen to him, didn't do what he said, I'd die just like my father." She pushes in the cigarette lighter as though she's going to have one. "I've spent pretty much every day of my life waiting for the same thing to happen to me."

I snap a look at her. "You have? You never told me any of this."

"You never asked. There are a lot of things you never asked, Grace." Marly pulls herself upright, as though I've said something offensive. "That night in the tree house, do you know that I was trying to talk to you about something important?"

It feels as if all the air of the desert has gone unnaturally still.

"I knew that you kissed him." Her voice is a needle.

Nausea instantly overtakes me. *That kiss. What was that kiss?* I'd always thought it was confirmation that I was desirable, that I was like Marly.

She clutches her belly with one arm. "I waited for you to tell me about it. I'd seen him do it when I was coming up the stairs, and I was ready to punch him, tear him off you. But you never said a word to me. You didn't say anything, and so I knew."

"Knew what?" I manage.

Marly turns her head slowly and when she looks at me, her eyes are glassy and sharp. "I knew that you liked it."

"I was fifteen," I whisper, as if it is an apology.

"I was ten," she says. "When he started."

Understanding emerges with a sickening lurch, as though I've always known: his leering smiles, the way he was always close enough to touch an exposed body part, so quick it could hardly be suspect—hands brushing thighs, shoulders, butt. That kiss—I thought of it as a moment of desirability but it was an expression of perversion. I thought she hated him because he wasn't her dad, because he was too young for her mother. "Oh god," is all I can manage to say. Then, "I'm so sorry,

Marly. Did you tell anyone?" *Why not me?*

"My mother. Big mistake." Marly looks away and the dropped eye contact comes as a relief. "I was sent to Langley Porter, the mental hospital, Grace, less than a week after you were burned." Her voice is unnervingly calm. "She thought I was acting out, and she's always accused me of punishing her for my father's death."

"I had no idea," I say. *I should have asked more questions. Maybe I didn't want to know.*

"Everything is Bryce's fault. If not for him, we wouldn't have been in that fucking tree house with all those goddamn candles, and none of the rest would have happened. I hoped that's what my mom was coming to tell me when she was here, that he was dead. That it was something awful, too, like he got painfully crushed in a car accident or was accidentally dismembered by chainsaw."

A lone bird wheels in the sky for just a second outside the window of the car—something fierce and proud, like an eagle, though too far away too tell. I squint away from the ball of sun that sears my retina. When I look back at Marly she's a black outline against the bright desert day. A weighty grief pins me to my seat, mine and Marly's mingling indistinguishably, as though we exchanged pieces of each other in the fire.

"I'm sorry, Marly. I wasn't there for you. I could have told Ma and she would have personally strangled him with her bare hands."

We're both able to laugh then, suddenly.

Marly shrugs and takes a deep, startled breath, pressing two fingers into her belly button. "Woo, this little girl is kick-boxer." She rolls down her window, letting in the whoosh of cars driving past on the road, dust spinning up in little vortexes.

"Do you think I killed Gus?" I am in need of some reassurance.

Marly bites her lip. "I don't know, Grace. Your power is the first thing in years that's really made me feel hope again. But I don't know. Everything good in my life has always been tinged. I'll never get free of Loser unless I pack up and move to the other side of the world in the middle of the night."

"Let me see the other bruise, on your chest," I say.

She looks warily at me, at my hands.

"Don't worry, I won't touch it. I just want to see."

Marly yanks down the tank to reveal more bruises, livid and dark. "He dragged you to an alley, and poked you?"

"Yes, people came walking by, and I sort of snapped out of it. I started walking away from him."

"I thought he had you backed up against a wall?"

"Grace, fuck, do you think I'm making this up? Holy shit." She starts to cry again, big gulping sobs.

"No, no, I'm sorry. I'm not doubting you, I'm trying to figure out what he wants, where he's coming from. What does he want with a baby anyway?"

"He doesn't. I don't think he gives a shit about her. He wants me. Or the idea of me. He hates rejection. Don't all men?"

I remember suddenly Marly saying about Bryce when we were girls, *"He acts like he's my slave-owner, not my stepdad."*

"I don't know what the fuck I'm going to do," Marly says in a whisper. Her shirt is still pulled down, revealing the dark bruises, her eyes dark. *Grace, I hate him.* "I'm seven and a half months pregnant and Loser's got money. He's resourceful, he grew up here, and he knows this town like he built it."

I think of the tall, dark man from the wedding Polaroid, the air of possession in his arms as they encircled Marly's waist like a shackle. "You could go back to Drake's Bay for awhile."

"Fuck no," she says. "Besides, he knows my gram's address."

"What about Drew's?"

"He followed me there. Drew's sleeping with a baseball bat by his bedside."

Marly looks at me as though we are soldiers heading off to war. She plants a hand on my shoulder and I am rocked into a memory. *Strong shoulders flexing beneath a white shirt—the hard taste of vodka and juice still stinging my mouth. Duran Duran playing "Rio."*

"Gotta let yourself go," Bryce saying. "You're not little girls anymore."

Marly stepping between me and him. "Go home, Grace. He's had too much to drink."

My vision blurs at the edges. I may not have protected her then, but now, I finally can.

Chapter Thirty

I feel swimmy, high, adrenaline on full tilt, though I haven't consumed a drop of alcohol. "We need to subdue him first," I hear myself say. "Can't just slap a hand on his face and hope it knocks him out."

Marly nods, though she is too encumbered to move quickly, and me—there's no guarantee of what I can do.

"I have pepper spray," she fidgets with her purse as though she's about to withdraw it. "And it's not like we have to break in, Grace. He'll let us in when he sees it's me. He'll think I'm coming to talk."

"Okay, then," I say, before I lose my nerve. And we get in her car and drive.

We park and walk four residential blocks. The streets are lit by yellow halogen lamps, but there's also a nearly-full moon. Its bold light makes me feel bolstered, sanctioned. Marly points to his condo, one square box among many in a beige world of homogenous residences.

"This could have been my life," Marly whispers, her face a portrait of disgust. "I should be in that kitchen right now making dinner, then go spread my legs for him. I can't *believe* he thought he could get away with what he did to me."

The guilt surges through me again. If only I hadn't healed away the evidence. But we didn't know. Nobody could have known.

"Let's do it soon, before I chicken out." My palms have begun to ache with heat.

"Damn straight," she agrees, and the toss of her hair is so familiar it's like we're fifteen again.

Simultaneously, we take a deep breath.

Marly repeats her lines, "I'll say we're here to talk— that I brought you as my friend and witness. That will put him on best behavior. And you?"

I choke a little on my own saliva, cough, and answer, "I'll ask for a glass of water, say I got too much sun today. He'll take one look at me and have a hard time refusing, right?"

Marly pats her purse. "Let's go." She's always one step ahead of me.

I catch up to her, walk beside her until we're on his porch and she jams her finger into the doorbell. There's the glow of a TV behind blinds, signs of life. Marly folds her hands over her belly. She looks like a Jehovah's Witness come to warn Loser of his ultimate doom.

"Hey, what's his real name?" it occurs to me to ask.

But the door is already opening a crack, then wider

when the person doing so sees who is there, and Marly is moving forward, all business. "Alan," she says simply.

My brain goes on tilt for a second. *Alan* is a professor's name, a man of letters, a kind man. It doesn't register with this controlling man of violent temper.

"Marly, what are you doing here this late?"

"I came to talk. This is Grace." She says my name with an emphasis that tells me it's not the first time I've been mentioned.

The man who peers out of the door to look at me with wide, concerned eyes is a tired, rumpled-looking version of Mr. Tall, Dark and Handsome from the wedding picture. He's in a gray tee-shirt and plaid pajama pants. Even at this distance I can smell the yeast-tang of beer, and see its pull in the tilt of his eyelids. My heart is thrusting itself at my rib cage painfully and I am sure that at any minute my hands will begin to steam or smoke.

But then Marly makes a wincing expression and grips her low belly. "I'm either going to piss on your doorstep," she says through a deep breath, "Or you're letting us in."

Alan steps back, shaking his head and motions for us to come in with a resigned grimace that says he feels forced to do so.

How do you like it? I think.

Inside it is a guy's apartment in every way. Bulky black furniture, no pictures or decorations, except a poster of football star Peyton Manning and a mysterious red tulip in a vase on one end table near the TV. Cast off work clothes, big yellow boots, dark green, and soiled cargo pants sit in piles at the base of a staircase, as if he undresses there and then goes to bed naked.

Marly does make a beeline for the bathroom, leaving me standing in the living room of the guy who once knocked me down to the hard cement floor of a parking garage and then beat the shit out of my best friend. Should I thank him for waking up my talents, or curse him for all that followed? If he recognizes me from the garage, he doesn't show it—but then again, it was dark; I could have been anyone.

You have some fucking nerve, I think. But what I say is, "Can I please have a glass of water?"

His face is unshaven, and the circles around his eyes are immensely dark, like he hasn't slept in weeks. He looks at me like he hasn't heard me right, like this whole moment is too strange for words, before finally nodding and heading off to the kitchen.

My hands are so hot they're beading up with sweat. As I watch Alan move with masculine grace through his kitchen, fetching me water, it hits me: this is all on me. I have to do this by myself. It's only fair. Marly's purse is on the edge of the couch. I slide my hand in, relieved to feel the tiny canister of pepper spray easily among lipsticks, wallet and keys. I clutch it in my hand and then lean into the couch, so he can't see that hand.

He walks back toward me, glass out, as Marly emerges from the bathroom, red-eyed and grim. And that is when time enters a distorted vortex. My hand rises and hits the spray nozzle. The glass of water in his hand catapults up into the air, lands on the entryway tile and shatters as he shouts, "What the fuck!" Stumbling backwards, he cuts himself on glass shards, hopping on one foot as he grabs at it with his hands.

Marly takes this chance to shove him down to the hard floor of his entryway, his head thudding painfully against the tiles. "How do you like it now, Fucker?" She straddles him, a move that looks obscene as he bucks beneath her. But she's got thirty pounds of baby weight on her and she keeps him pinned.

I run around behind his head, slap my hot hands down onto his chest thinking how much I want to make him feel what he caused Marly, how much he needs to pay. He is now the entire locus of all the evil perpetuated on both of us, a stand-in for Bryce who deserves this all on his own.

"What the fuck are you doing, you crazy fucking bitch?" he screams. And I don't know if he means me or Marly.

"Payback, you asshole. You're signing the divorce papers tonight, and this custody agreement that says you get jack shit where rights to this baby is concerned."

My serpent is a dragon filled with fury. It runs amuck, streaking through Alan's strong body, sniffing out hurts. Everywhere it finds one: old broken bones in his elbow and rib, an ulcer in his stomach, something much deeper inflicted by someone much bigger and older on him. It magnifies the pain, and ripples of this travel backwards and through my body, waking up pain in me, too. *The harsh rip of fire over new flesh. Skin stripped away, oozing fluid. Stitches and incisions that burn and itch. The quick burn of a finger into my most private skin. Marly's eyes wide and scared, candle in her*

hand. "No, oh no, Grace," she's saying. "You were supposed to take me, too."

The three of us complete a circuit I can't break. I
want to pull away, but I am locked in place. Alan is
screaming his agony, Marly is yelling words I can't make
out at him, then punching her fists into his stomach.
Pain is enlarging in me—big waves like nothing I've ever
felt before, gripping, deeply gouging. "I never touched
you in that garage. I never beat you," he's crying.

"I saw you." Her whole body is shaking. "*I saw you!*"

"It wasn't me!" he says. "It wasn't me. Ah fuck, did
you just piss on me?" Dark fluid is spreading through
the fabric of Alan's pants, beneath Marly.

The waves of pain aren't stopping, but Marly has
stopped her limb-flailing frenzy and now I understand
what these waves are, what I'm feeling as it travels
through Alan like a conduit from her to me. Worse, I feel
the truth in his words, beneath my hands. The pain is
receding and in its ebb I'm left with the knowledge that
we have made a terrible mistake. He's telling the truth.

I wrench my hands off him and sink back onto my
knees, vaguely aware of a sharp gnaw of pain, most likely a shard of the broken glass.

"Oh no, oh fuck," Marly cries. She scrambles backwards off Alan, who sits up, rubbing his chest, cau-
tiously touching his right eye, which is now completely
swollen shut.

"What is she talking about being attacked?" he says.
"You tell me right now or I call the fucking police!"

Marly clutches her belly, groaning.

"We were attacked in her parking garage, six months

ago. Marly was beaten badly." I sit there, my hands stinging and hot. If Alan didn't attack Marly, then who the
hell was it? A rape averted? A mugging gone bad?

Marly's moaning mounts; Alan heaves himself to
his feet, stumbles, looking dizzy. I'm expecting him to
come after me, reach for my throat. Instead he hobbles
off to the kitchen, pulls an ice pack from the freezer.
Marly has begun to whine and cry, and bloody fluid is
leaking from between her legs onto Alan's beige carpet.
"The baby...I think she's...oh God!"

Alan drops his ice pack and looks at me.

"Call the paramedics." I don't know how I manage
to be clear-headed all of a sudden, but I am. "This baby
is not ready yet."

"No...hospital!" Marly shrieks.

"Do it!" I command, despite all the explaining we'll
have to do when they get here.

He nods, turns to find his phone, then back to me,
"Help her!" he says, soft but urgent.

I come up close to Marly but my hands are still
achy-hot in a way that scares me. Another contraction
and she groans like an opera singer warming up. "Can't
you just take away the pain?" she begs.

Can't I? Can I? "I don't want to hurt the baby. I'm
afraid!"

Marly tosses her head back, eyes clenched tight. "She
wants out of me. She knows I'm evil," she cries, tears
coursing down her bright red cheeks. "And so do you."

"No, it's not true. You're not responsible for everything that happened."

"Grace, please, Grace," Marly begs. "It hurts!"

I move so I'm facing between Marly's legs, but I'm not about to reach in and pull off her underpants, daring any contact that could injure her. *Where are the fucking paramedics?*

Marly arches and wails through another contraction that lasts minutes. To my surprise, Alan comes over to Marly, drops to her side, tries to smooth her hair out of her face, but she wrenches her head away. "I swear to you," he says anyway, "I did not mean to hurt you the other day. I'm sorry I grabbed your arm. I'm sorry if I got pissed, but I would never beat you. I am not that kind of guy. And we both know this is my goddamn kid—"

"Grace, damn it," Marly howls. "Hands on me. Please, this pain, I'm not...it's going to kill me." Her panting is perilously near to hyperventilating.

"I thought labor was supposed to happen, you know, slow," Alan says, running his hands through his hair.

I thought so too. What if Marly's right—the baby wouldn't tolerate what we were doing, inflicting pain. What have we done?

Marly suddenly sits bolt upright, turns onto all fours. Her sudden silence terrifies me. "She's coming," she says in a gulp, and then begins to pant and moan again. "Grace, please!"

"Help her," Alan says, his voice small and choked. I feel suddenly the enormity of this for him, that he does feel some responsibility for this baby.

I flip up the soft grey folds of her dress, pull down the flimsy black fabric of her underwear with a terrible feeling of taboo, of looking into the most intimate part of Marly, the source of so many of her wounds, a place that should always have been private, given only by her permission.

"Grace, please!" Marly cries, and this time, her voice is so plaintive I lean toward her but as my hands reach for her a surge of heat and pain so immense causes me to cry out. "I can't!"

"You're punishing me, aren't you?" she shrieks. "Because I set...you...on fire!" She grasps my hand, an electric shock passing between us. I wait and when nothing more happens, I set both of my hands gingerly atop her low back. The pain in my hands rumbles down to a soft simmer and then dissipates, and I feel as though I'm dipping them into warm honey, though I become aware of her agony, which is a burning, squeezing sensation, ever tighter. And that's when I understand: the baby has the cord wrapped around her neck.

"Marly, you can't take any breaks. You can't rest now. She needs to come out *right now*. She's very close—I can see her."

Alan cranes in behind me, peering over my shoulder, his breath hot on my neck. He inhales sharply when he sees the top of the baby's head, her dark hair.

Marly obeys and makes a determined warrior cry, half shout, half groan. I draw up my courage and move my hands into catching position, as the top of the baby's head becomes her tiny scrunched face, and then a shoulder, and with a last effort, Marly births the entire baby in a gush of fluid into my arms.

"Is she okay?" Marly cries.

Even looking at the baby, I don't know. Her color is purplish, she makes no sound.

"Is she?" Marly cranes toward her but she's too weak to move.

And then the child makes a bleating wail that floods me with an emotion I cannot name, tears and giddiness overtaking me. I turn to Alan, whose expression, even with the swollen eyes, is of a man who has just found God, or been saved at sea. "Take her," I say, handing him the baby, "but don't move from where you are. Marly still has to deliver the placenta. Hold the baby close to your chest until then. Keep telling her to push."

He doesn't even flinch as I pass the slick baby into his arms.

"Come here, Grace," Marly says. Her voice is a hoarse whisper, scraped of all energy. Its weakness alarms me. I come up close to her face. "I need to tell you the truth," she says.

"She's bleeding a lot," Alan says, sounding scared. "Is it normal?"

Marly grips my hands and pulls them to her face. She feels cool. My serpent is too spent to do anything useful now. She pulls down her shirt, revealing the bruise on her clavicle she claimed Alan made in the alley. "I did this to myself. I had that old urge to hurt myself again, like when I used to cut." She exhales a soppy sounding breath. "It was no accident. The fire."

"You didn't plan it Marly, let's not dwell on it now."

She shakes her head. Hair is plastered to her white face. "I did! That was the whole point of the meeting,

Grace! I did plan it. After I saw you kiss Bryce, when what was evil to me was something exciting to you, I hated you." She's panting between words and I'm afraid she'll hyperventilate. "I thought if I gave you a real experience with guys our age, it would even us out somehow. But then we nearly got arrested, and your mom said we couldn't see each other—and I slit my wrists. The minute I came home from the hospital, I made plans. I wanted us to go together. I had every intention, Grace. We would both burn up in that fucking tree house. I fucked it up. I couldn't even die the way I wanted to."

There's a loud pound on the door. Marly closes her eyes and goes very still. I leap away from her as if she is death itself.

Chapter Thirty-One

I've forgotten that I have Marly's cell phone in my pocket until it vibrates insistently. I see that it's Drew. No one has told him about the baby, nor can he know yet about the events of last night. I really don't want to be the one to tell him about Alan, about how wrong we were.

"Drew, it's Grace."

He makes no pretension that he wants to talk to me. "Is everything ok?"

Can I really leave him hanging? Pretend I know nothing?

"Drew, don't freak out, okay, but Marly went into early labor late last night. The baby was born. Marly's having a little surgery, a blood transfusion, and the baby's in the NICU." Alan is parked there, the only one allowed with the baby, who is nestled into an incubator, too small.

Drew gasps, then it almost sounds like he's crying. "Why didn't you call me?" I don't have to answer for him. "He's there, isn't he. She let that asshole come, but didn't call me?"

"It's not that simple, Drew. But I need to let her tell you the rest. I'll have her call you when she's out of surgery."

Drew is silent a long moment. I think we've lost the call when he suddenly speaks again, "Actually, Grace, I need to talk to you. Can you get away for an hour? I'll pick you up, we can go get coffee."

"I'd really rather not leave if I don't have to."

"Well that's just it, Grace. The cops have contacted me, too, about that guy who died in my cottage, since it's on my property. I think that you and I should get our details straight, so it doesn't seem like there was anything out of the ordinary going on."

"My friend," I want to correct. Not "that guy." *And there was so very much out of the ordinary going on.* I look at the clock. 5:00 a.m. Marly surely won't miss me for several more hours.

"I'll meet you out front in twenty."

When we hang up, I think more on his words. The cops want to talk with him, too. Which suggests that they also want to talk with me. Which would make sense, except I haven't heard a word from them. Marly is the keeper of all messages. Clients call her phone and she passes on the information to me. Or does she? Would she keep a thing like the cops calling me to herself?

It's only as I'm making my way out, toward the elevators, that the fact of being in a hospital hits me like a cold hand on the back. The obliterating smell of antiseptic, the monotonous beep-beeping of monitors, nurses and doctors in scrubs of all colors. In my memory everything was gray and cold, stinging or burning, a world of torture.

And yet.

As I step out onto the street, desert's morning air already promising a heat that will make my sweater superfluous, my very cells are buzzing with a realization. I am alive. I'm *alive!*

The sun is a hint at the dark line of the horizon when Drew pulls up. He pops the lock. I slide into his car. He's already showered and smelling of a slightly-too-sweet cologne that makes my nostrils twitch. Hair is gelled back on his head, skin freshly shaved. He's dressed in a button-up shirt and khakis. Me, on the other hand: my soft cotton pants, thankfully black, are still crusted with dried fluid and blood. "So they're okay, baby's going to make it?" His voice rises an octave.

"That's what they say. She'll need to stay in NICU awhile, to make sure her lungs are working, but otherwise okay."

The world past the car is a blur of lights, making my sleep-deprived brain feel dizzy.

Drew bites down on his lip, the vein in his right temple popping out. "I can't believe she let that fucker come to the birth," he mutters to himself, as though I'm not in the car at all. Then he slams the flat of his hand against the steering wheel. "Fuck!" The car swerves and suddenly, I'm wide awake.

"Hey, take it easy," I aim to sound soothing. "Don't worry—there's no big reunion on the horizon, ok? I shouldn't be speaking for her, though."

"I've spent five years trying to have a relationship with Marly. I have given her ALL of me, made myself available, taken care of her when she's falling apart and off her meds and thinking a little too hard about razor blades and bottles of pills. I have put up with more than you can ever know, and for what?" He flings a hand in the air like he's slapping a phantom cheek. "She marries another guy, gets pregnant, and keeps me dangling on a chain for whenever he doesn't play nice. Fuck that!"

We could easily play a trump game here. I know *exactly* what it feels like to help Marly stay off the edge, to suffer betrayal at the realization that I was not the only one for her. "I think you're forgetting who you're talking to." I hug myself against the cool air. It's then I realize we are driving out of town, away from any coffee shops or restaurants that I know of. I start talking fast. "Drew, I think a lot is going to change now that the baby's here. Marly's ready to get things figured out in her life." *She's unburdened herself of all her dark secrets; wreaked revenge, even if on the wrong guy.*

"Oh yeah, she's going to have so much time for me now that she's a mother."

I'm struck by the petulance in Drew's voice. Certainty docks in my mind. My hands, so cold for the past few hours, begin to feel hot again. The sun starts to edge up from the lip of the desert, paint splashed across a canvas. "I was really looking forward to that cup of coffee," I say softly.

Drew says nothing, keeps driving as though I haven't spoken.

My adrenaline is throbbing, tingles of an almost

electrical nature sparking in my muscles. *Can I jump out of the car?* But there's nothing around, and this is the desert. *Can I overtake him at the wheel?* "It was you in the parking garage, wasn't it?" I want to slap him. But there's the more pressing realization that I've got to get out of this car.

"Drew, listen to me, I won't say a thing. Just turn around and take me back to the hospital, okay?"

Drew makes a low moan, which I realize is actually a sob. "I didn't mean to hurt her. I wasn't going to. Just wanted to scare her. Wanted her to give him up. But then there was you—I didn't know what to do about you."

I want to soothe him just long enough to get out of the car, but I'm afraid of what will happen if I touch him. I don't know if I can reign in the storm of rage building in me.

"I just loved her so much."

His sudden use of the past tense alarms me. "She loves you, too! Don't worry. She doesn't have to know, ok? I won't tell. You can start over! It's going to be ok. Just pull over."

He's crying, and as he tries to shake his head and wipe tears from his eyes, he swerves into the other lane, a truck oncoming. With a scream, I grab the wheel and swerve it back, but I overcompensate and the car is going too fast, off the shoulder, and straight for an electrical pole.

I am smacked into a dream, my body gone from me, way down below. I am floating on a placid lake, smooth and content. What comes to me here in a shimmering, agonizing moment of clarity is this: *I wanted it. When*

Marly leaned in with her candle, tilted it toward me with intention, I wanted the purge of heat, the catharsis of undoing. My mother is suddenly next to me. "Come home to me, Grace. I'm waiting," she says. "But not for long." She reaches out for my hand. "Don't touch me, Ma!" I shout. "It's all gone dark."

ƱƆ

The face frowning at me is young, female, framed in crisp blonde hair pulled back into a tight bun. Something silver glitters at her chest. It takes me a minute to realize she's dressed in a highway patrol uniform, and that a cruiser is parked behind her, its lights flashing.

At first she is a silent movie speaking to me with concern on her face; I can't hear anything. Behind her appears another face, also female. That woman is holding instruments that she brings toward me, black, silver. Something is wrapped around my arm, tight, squeezing, and something cold is slid up against the heat of my chest. It's only then I become aware of the sound of my heart pumping as sure as ever.

The rest of the sounds follow: voices chattering, a radio fritzing with static and stern voices, cars whooshing past.

"Minor concussion," the paramedic says to the cop. "Think she's okay."

They frown in another direction. "He's gonna need surgery," they say, and I remember that they mean Drew. I remember that I have been a fool over and over again.

Chapter Thirty-Two

I wait only long enough to find out that Marly came through her surgery fine, and that Alan will stay with them, and then I go home. A path has been carved through the refuse downstairs—some of the stacks are gone, and most of the garbage emptied. This swath of emptiness terrifies me. Ma would never do this on her own. I rush down the hall to her room. The cans are all gone from the columns in the hallway. Worse, when I enter her room, the clothing stacks have been consolidated into a massive pile of neatly folded squares. She is sleeping, but her breathing is rattling, too fast.

"Oh no, Ma," I say, not sure if she can hear me. I climb up on the bed next to her and lay my head on her pillow, her hair tickling the baldness of my scalp. Her eyes open and light on me, mouth forms the briefest of smiles, but that is all. I can't say how long it is before awareness tiptoes into my brain that Ma's breathing is silent. I rest my hand upon her abdomen, I find it still.

She waited for me.

And now, when I am ready to need her, she's gone.

Grief crawls up to the top of my throat. I feel its weight like a chunk of ice at the back of my tongue. I curl against Ma's still form and press my face into her neck. She smells of a gardenia perfume that used to choke me with its rich-sweet musk. Now I don't mind its scent. Behind my eyes there's a light. The light expands around me, encircles me in ripples, like a...serpent. *My* serpent, only I don't feel as though I am controlling it. Its energy is soft and strong all at once, gentle and determined. It moves through me, as though I have become water and it's swimming my channels. As it passes, all my dark emotions rise and ripple, and begin to dissolve and drift away. *It was my time.* With Ma's words comes an immense relief. When the serpent passes into a place of pain—my bad right leg, my thumbs, I feel a momentary pop, a static electric charge, and then a cool, almost narcotic relief.

And then I swear Ma's arms encircle me, cradles me, swaying me as though I am an infant. I am water, I am earth, I am a pure and untouchable cluster of light, and for one timeless stretch—I can't call it a moment or an hour—that truth heals me, until it ebbs and drops me into a comfortable darkness so void it might be death.

When I wake again, my body is light, though my heart is still heavy. I hurry down the hall, noticing a smoothness in my stride. My right leg doesn't cramp; I have no limp. Soon I stand in the entryway before the antique oval mirror lined with gray silk. I rip the material down, looking into the age-veined silver surface with a feeling of hope so powerful it shames me. And there I am: left side as scarred as ever, right side's untrammeled inches mocking the rest of me. Though I know it's an exercise in futility, I lift my hands to find my thumbs as I have known them for thirteen years. So: I have been healed of all the glitchy pains inside, but I've been left exactly the same on the outside.

ᖡᥐᚷ

The men from the funeral home are young, efficient and soft spoken. I sign their form and point them to Ma's room. In death, all her extra weight seems to have fallen away, and they don't even break a sweat in lifting her onto the gurney. It's all I can do not to get into the van with them and follow Ma's body off to the mortuary where she will be cremated, as per her wishes.

An hour later, after I shove an uncharacteristically cuddly Beatrix off my lap, I let Adam into the house. His familiar face brings tears up. "I'm so glad you called me, Grace. I wasn't sure I'd hear from you again."

Before I can think where to start, he pulls me into his arms. Warmth and relief rush in over the chill that's stiffened my limbs. I don't want to cry, am afraid that if I start, I might never stop, but the insistent beating of his heart and his sturdy grip leave me no other option. "Yes," he whispers into my neck. "Yes."

Eventually I pull back, wipe my face, and look at him more closely than I've permitted myself in years. "I can't believe Ma is gone."

"What can I do?"

"I don't know. I have to tell you something, first. The reason I couldn't let you stay when you came to Vegas."

"It's okay, Grace, you don't—"

"I can heal people by laying my hands on them. The pain I felt all those years from touching people, I think I was picking up more...impressions...than I could handle and my body interpreted it as pain."

His eyes assess me as if I am a patient with an unusual complaint. "You can heal."

I can't read his tone. Is he disbelieving or merely repeating it himself to see if he really understood me? "I discovered it by accident. I think the fire awakened it in me, but I didn't know what it was. I couldn't tell you. I know what you think of that sort of thing."

Doubt weighs down his eyes. I need to give him evidence. "I felt her, you know, in your body, when we touched that first time in Vegas. Your sister. The one who drowned. You carry a lot of pain from that."

Adam's eyes can't get any wider. "And I'll bet that broken clavicle that never quite healed doesn't ache any more, does it? The one you got from a bicycle accident?"

His fingers move unconsciously to the long bone below his throat. "I haven't told anyone about what happened to my sister."

༂ⓖⓖ༂

345

A week passes, and my sense of home is entirely rear-ranged. My father stands on the doorstep of the house that he once shared with my mother, tugging at the bottom of his jacket, and scratching his neck. I know he's afraid to come in. "Hi Dad," I say, and tears finish the sentence.

Celine comes up the walk wearing a tasteful navy blue dress and heels, and greets me with a hug and kiss. She looks pale, with dark circles under her eyes. "Oh Grace, I'm so sorry about your mother. I hope you'll let us be your family."

I nod. I want to extend to Celine the same kindness she has to me. Perhaps I will visit them on holidays, impress my face on my young sister so that she doesn't grow up scared of me. I lead them inside. The carpets are stained and ruined, chewed up by cockroaches and imbued with a funk that will require ripping them out. The furniture is full of holes where cats cleaned their claws, the walls moldy, paint chipped and yellow, but it is empty. It is so, so empty. And being with my father only intensifies the sense of loss. I grab his outstretched hand, and his fingers run across mine as though to soothe an ache. "She's out of pain, Gracie."

"We're going to lose the house," I say, because it was his house too, once.

He shakes his head. "Not if I help, you won't."

I squeeze his hand. "I think I could make it really nice." This is the closest thing to "thank you" I can manage in the moment.

When Adam arrives, an electric feeling passes through me. I think the world must be able to feel it.

"Well!" Celine and Harlan say at the same moment.

"Dad, Celine," I say, "I want to introduce you to someone very special."

Epilogue

"**H**ow is she?" I ask. "Did they say when she can come out of the NICU?"

"She's breathing completely on her own," Marly says, sounding purely joyful. "But she's got jaundice so she has to be under this special lamp and they want to be sure she's pooping properly, though she's drinking the milk I'm pumping. Oh man, you should see the tiny bottles we feed her with—like she's a kitten."

Relief courses through me.

"So Alan is..."

"Not a monster," she says softly. Though not a saint either. He did turn my furniture upside down, and he was rough with me more than a few times. But most of it was..."

"Selective truth telling," I offer for her.

"I guess. Speaking of which, Drew confessed to me,"

she says softly. "I'm sorry he scared you, hurt you, too. I really thought that I was inviting you into a better life, Grace. I pressed charges, and even though there's no evidence, he confessed. He'll do some time, though I feel somewhat responsible."

"Will you stay in Vegas?"

"Gram left her house to me, did I tell you? I can live in it or sell it."

I try to picture the two of us living in this town again, in the emptied houses of the women who loved us best. Could it work?

"I'm naming my daughter after her. And you. Oona Grace." And then, before I can reply, "I should have told the truth about the fire, about so many things, sooner. You deserved to know it all."

In this week apart I asked Adam to help me piece together some of Marly's erratic behavior. "You're bipolar, aren't you?" I know it's true.

She sighs. "I hate the label—because, really, is it all the shitty life experiences that made the brain chemistry go nuts, or is it genetic? My mother always told me I was just like my grandmother, and I thought that meant I was artistic. I hate the meds, but I have to take them if I'm going to be a good mother. And I really want to be a good mother. Do you hate me, Grace?"

I almost laugh, except I don't want to hurt her feelings. "Marly, I don't hate you. No one was ever looking out for you. There's a lot I didn't want to know, or to remember. A lot I willingly chose not to see."

"Well that's not what I thought you'd say. I think you *should* hate me for a little while. Just try it on. Not just for the fire, but for all the ways I've lied to you. I think you might find hating me productive."

I can't help myself; I laugh. "How will hating you be productive?"

"I'll tell you how: I want you in our lives, mine and Oona's. And I don't want residual hate spilling out some time down the road when she's old enough to feel it, too. So please, I beg you, hate me now, good and hard. Blame me. Really soak in it. And when you're done, even if it takes years, you come back to us. You come back and be my best friend again, and Oona's auntie, and see that you did the right thing helping me get here."

I sit quietly for a long time. "How about I hate the things that happened to you, the lies we've both told. That's about all the hate I can muster."

"Gus," she says softly, his name a segue all its own. "I want to tell you, it was a heart attack, Grace. He had a weak heart from years of drug abuse on top of several other things. You didn't kill him. Frankly it's a miracle he was still alive."

I feel like I've just shed a heavy, wet coat. Tears, which are now all too easily at the ready since Ma's passing, slip out, and wet my cheeks. "How'd you find out?"

"I talked to Sara. I knew she'd want to know about his last moments, and though I wasn't in the room, I reconstructed them for her—let her know he wasn't in pain. I knew you weren't in any position to tell her."

"You did that?" I'm genuinely touched.

"I did that," she says.

"Well then," I say. "When do I get to hold that baby?"

"We're going to come back to Drake's Bay for a little while," she says. "I've got to deal with some last paperwork. I want to repaint, have a yard sale. And I'm cutting that damn tree down."

"I'll help. This time, I can even wield an axe. Ceremonially, I mean." And even though she can't see me, I lift my arms to show myself, if not her, that for the first time in thirteen years, thanks to this strange force that fire awakened in me, I can raise my arms over my head, can reach toward the future.

Acknowledgements

This labor of love needs a long list of thanks!

I'm indebted to Erika Mailman, who took an exhausted new mother's old scribblings and suggested they were worth pursuing; without her vote of confidence, I'm not sure this book would ever have been finished. To all of my readers, in all of this novel's incarnations, who also happen to be dear friends and champions: Elizabeth Beechwood, Eros-Alegra Clarke, Myfanwy Collins, Stephanie Garcia Cowan, Patry Francis, Amy Holly, Kemari Howell, Janneke Jobsis-Brown, Rebecca Lawton, Ellen Meister, Amy McElroy, Stephanie Naman, Julia Park Tracey, Robin Slick, Chelsea Starling, and Tomi Wiley James. And to the writers who championed me early on: Ellen Biechler, Susan Bono, Marlene Cullen, Christine Falcon, Claudia Larson, and Barbara Spicer.

To the Master Editrix, Allison McCabe, without whose wise counsel this version of the novel would not exist. And profound thanks to Casey Pagan, a courageous and talented girl who just happens to also be a burn survivor, for her insights into her experience. My sentences are especially grateful to my copy-editor, Susanna Rosen for a quality job (any remaining typos are purely my own).

To ALL the ladies of indie-visible.com for your courage and support! You are brave and bold.

To "the bitches," most of whom are mentioned above, but including other dearests: Klay Arsenault, Emily Brown, Suzi Sellers and Roslyn Weatherall, who allow me room to vent my "not fit" side in safety.

To my parents and grandparents: whose conviction that I would succeed as a writer, and steady flow of journals, typewriter ink, writing guides and encouragement made it possible.

Reader Discussion Guide

1. What is the source of Grace's healing gift and its relationship to her physical trauma? What does it represent to Grace, and to other characters?

2. Discuss empathy. At what point does empathy cross over into co-dependence? How does that apply to Grace and Marly's relationship? To relationships with minor characters?

3. What was it like to read this first person narrative, which plants you so deeply inside Grace's perspective? Did it make it harder or easier to understand what she has been through?

4. How did you feel about Grace's choice not to heal sick children? Why do you think she ultimately chose not to?

5. Did your feelings about Marly change from the beginning of the book to the end? Did you have more or less compassion for her at different points in the book?

6. What do you make of the varying uses of fire and water symbols in the book?

7. Discuss the theme of sexuality in the novel, and the ways that Marly and Grace use their sexuality for both healthy and unhealthy means.

8. Discuss the nature of the bond between Grace and Marly. What is their friendship really founded upon? What does each need to learn in order to become whole, healthy adults?

9. How are themes of internal and external beauty,

and self-perception, particularly in the form of photographs, used in this novel? Discuss "kinds of seeing"—with the eyes, and with the heart. What is seen and not seen?

10. What do you make of Grace's power turning "dark." What's happening? What is the author trying to convey?

11. Did you find the author's use of small flashbacks, most of them gleaned through Grace's contact with other people, effective at revealing the characters' back-story, or not?

12. What future do you envision or hope for the main characters after the book's end?

13. Discuss the character of Gus. What did he represent, both in the book, and to Grace? Why do you think the author chose the particular fate she did for him?

About the Author, Jordan E. Rosenfeld

Jordan E. Rosenfeld learned early on that people prefer a storyteller to a know-it-all. She channeled any Hermione-esque tendencies into a career as a writing coach, editor and freelance journalist, and saves the Tall Tales for her novels. She earned her MFA from the Bennington Writing Seminars and is the author of the books, *Make a Scene: Crafting a Powerful Story One Scene at a Time* (Writer's Digest Books)—which has sold over 20,000 copies, and co-author of *Write Free! Attracting the Creative Life* with Rebecca Lawton (BeijaFlor Books). Jordan's essays and articles have appeared in such publications as *AlterNet.org, Publisher's Weekly, the San Francisco Chronicle, the St. Petersburg Times, The Writer* and *Writer's Digest* magazine. Her book commentaries have appeared on *The California Report*, a news-magazine produced by NPR-affiliate KQED radio. She lives in Northern California with her superhero-obsessed son and Psychologist husband.

www.jordanrosenfeld.net.
She also blogs the column My Big Mouth at
www.indie-visible.com.

CPSIA information can be obtained
at www.ICGtesting.com
Printed in the USA
FSHW022017181020
74982FS